DIRTY KISS

RHYS FORD

Dreamspinner Press

Published by
Dreamspinner Press
4760 Preston Road
Suite 244-149
Frisco, TX 75034
http://www.dreamspinnerpress.com/

Dirty Kiss

Cover Art by Anne Cain   annecain.art@gmail.com
Cover Design by Mara McKennen

ISBN: 978-1-61581-958-4

Printed in the United States of America
First Edition
July 2011

eBook edition available
eBook ISBN: 978-1-61581-959-1

To the Five, Ree, and Ren.
Haato and Love.

ACKNOWLEDGMENTS

I OWE a world of gratitude and then some to the following people: Mom, without whom I'd still be unformed cells; the Five, Jenn, Tamm, Penn, and Lea, who have walked with me on this writing thing for a long, long time (don't do the math. It'll just hurt your head); Ren, Ree, and a lot of my LJ friends, who have coaxed and cheered as I've struggled to make some sense of the pictures in my head.

I have to thank the following people who have provided me comfort, anguish, and late nights with no sleep: Ilona Andrews, Lynn Flewelling, and Josh Lanyon. Thanks for the stories and for all of the mental cookies.

Many thanks and kudos to Elizabeth for sharing my taste in pretty Korean men; Lynn, who guided me into the fray; Ginnifer for being very patient with my flailing… and everyone else at Dreamspinner who helped me get from there to here. And, of course, Anne Cain, who just fricking rocks.

And lastly, I want to thank Harrison Ford. Because I can. And let's face it, he shaped as much of my world and imagination as anyone else I can think of. I owe him a hell of a lot.

CHAPTER ONE

WHEN I was growing up, I innocently believed that grandmothers were mostly round-faced, cheery women who supplied you with cookies and a bit of money when your parents weren't looking. Sadly, despite having reached manhood with most of my delusions shattered by reality, I seemed to have clung to that naïve myth of grandmothers and cookies.

Which was probably why I was now running down the length of an overly landscaped backyard with shotgun blasts going off behind me.

It was supposed to be an easy job. When Mr. Brinkerhoff, a pleasant-looking elderly man, came into my office to ask if I would take a case, I agreed to it, thinking it would be a piece of cake. Hell, I even cut my rates down because I thought it would be a simple matter of trailing his grandmotherly, churchgoing wife as she ran around town one evening. He suspected that she was cheating on him, but in his heart of hearts, he didn't believe it. Not his Adele.

Love makes a man do stupid things. I certainly wasn't doing this for love. And the money definitely wasn't enough to risk my life for. Mr. Brinkerhoff and I were going to have a serious talk when I got back to the office. Provided, of course, I even made it back to the office.

Branches tore at my sleeve as I pounded past a topiary. A leafy-green elephant reached up to the stars with its elegant trunk. Or at least it did before the blast of shot tore its head right off. Debris flew, and the scent of evergreen overpowered me when the tree's resin struck my face. My cheek stung where the bush's remains struck me, and I almost slipped before I made it to the relative safety of a large Grecian-style vase. The grass was wet from the rain, a passing deluge that had left the ground too soft to run on, and I'd gained far less distance than I wanted.

Despite what they say, it does rain in Southern California, usually when I'm trying to run away from someone shooting at me.

An ache developed in my chest, more from the twinges of panic than overexertion. Taking what cover I could from the maze of evergreens and hedges scattered about the tiered garden, I plotted my way through seemingly random brick paths, hoping I could find where I'd left my Range Rover. The scenery turned familiar as I scanned my surroundings. An overgrown morning glory nearly choked the rim of a fountain. I'd spotted that first when I'd come through the back gate to spy on Mrs. Brinkerhoff's evening pleasures. The back gate would be nearby, and unlike when I'd arrived, I wouldn't have to pick the lock to get in.

The high, wooden-slat fence separated me from my car. Standing nearly eight feet tall, the fence was a residential requirement to hide pools away from roaming packs of hot children looking for a watering hole to play in during the summer. I'd parked in one of the many back alleys that cut through Los Angeles's streets. Here in the more upper-class neighborhoods, they served as a way to hide servants' and gardeners' cars from the street. Perfect place to park my old Rover.

Lights were starting to come on in the enormous houses around the one I'd found Mrs. Brinkerhoff in. In a few minutes, I would be enjoying the company of LA's finest unless I got my ass in gear. Hearing the distinct click of a shotgun being reloaded gave me my incentive to scale the fence. Damn the gate, I needed to get out of there as quickly as possible before the cops were standing over my cooling body, making off-color jokes about how I got my kicks.

The wood dug splinters into my hands as I grabbed the top of the fence. My sneakers found a little purchase on the rough surface, and I pulled myself up, hooking a foot over the top. The fence edge slid against the inside of my thigh, and a shock hit me when my sac met the unforgiving wooden slats. I wanted to take a moment to breathe and get myself under some sort of control, but Mrs. Brinkerhoff had other ideas.

From my higher vantage point on the fence, it was easy to spot her white, coiffed helmet, a frosty cap of fine hair artfully arranged around her rosy cheeks and pert bow mouth. She'd been cute when she was younger. The kind of girl that men flirted with casually and dreamed about taking home to Mother. Her body was rounded into a pleasant, huggable shape that children would find a comfortable lap to sit on. It just wasn't a body made for the leather bra and panties set, glinting with diamond studs, she wore as she hunted me across the mansion's landscaped back lawn.

I was going to have to splash a bucket of bleach into my eyes to get rid of the sight of Mrs. Brinkerhoff and her lover frolicking around a red-velvet-curtained bed. I didn't find women sexually attractive, so unlike most men, two women getting it on means that there's twice as much stuff going on that I'm not interested in, but there was just something wrong about seeing mounds of infirm, pillowy flesh undulating over crimson sheets, or the sight of Mrs. Brinkerhoff's mouth on another woman's privates. The leather getups were an added bonus, and after taking pictures of what happened on that bed, I wasn't going to switch to women anytime soon.

The woman moved carefully around the topiary corpse, silent on her bare feet. If I hadn't been the one she was stalking, I'd have to give it to the old lady. She was definitely not someone to mess with. The shotgun barrel was kept pointed down, her hands gripped expertly on the stock and at the ready to pull it up if she spotted me. Any other time, I'd have applauded her hunting skills, but right now, I just wanted out of there before she filled me full of holes.

"Great," I mumbled, watching Mrs. Brinkerhoff's head bob up and down among the sculpted trees. "She's on fricking safari and I'm the goddamned antelope."

The ground seemed to be a lot farther away on the other side, built on a gentle slope that would take excess runoff and channel it toward grates set in the middle of the tight alley. Calculating the distance down, I wondered if I would break my leg when I dropped on the mold-slick cement below.

Mrs. Brinkerhoff's head jerked up when I slid to get a better angle to fall from, and I couldn't stop a small moan escaping between my clenched teeth as the fence dug deeper into the crux of my thighs. Her hair gleamed, a white poof of silvery cotton that made my spine tingle when I saw it. In the dim light from the floods along the side of the house, I saw her eyes squint and the pinprick of a murderous gleam form when she spotted me straddling the fence. Shadows winked away when the shotgun turned to fix on me, the watery orange of the streetlights catching on its dull metal surface.

I did what any sane man would do when a pixie-faced grandmother lined him up in her sights: I jumped.

Hitting cement is never pleasant, especially after an eight-foot drop. The top of the fence exploded, going the way of Mr. Elephant's head. It was raining wood on my head, and off in the distance, amid the echo of the shotgun blast reverberating in my ears, I heard sirens approaching. Definitely time to get into my car and speed away.

Patting at my chest, I heaved a sigh of relief. I still had the slim camera in my jacket pocket, captured evidence of Mrs. Brinkerhoff's indiscretions and probably the source of my therapy bills for years to come. No sense nearly getting my head blown off if I wasn't going to get paid for it. My keys were there too, even better luck since breaking into my own car wasn't on my things-to-do-tonight list.

The Rover started up with a roar, matching the bark of Mrs. Brinkerhoff's weapon. I gunned the engine and barreled down the alley just in time to see her pale, plump shape poke out of a gate near the end of the fence. She brought the shotgun up, nestling the barrel against her soft shoulder, and aimed. I caught sight of her in my rearview mirror, standing bare to the cold wind coming down the alley.

Take away the leather bikini get-up and shotgun, replace it with a flowered housecoat and some potholders, and I'd have that warm, sweet grandmother I'd imagined she was. Or at least that was what I was thinking when the shotgun went off again, shattering the Rover's back window. Pebbled glass flew forward, hitting my shoulders and the back of my head.

"Shit." The blast tore at my hearing, leaving me with a throbbing headache and a ringing that resembled the church bells from my old Catholic school. The Rover hit the street hard, its back tire jumping off the curb. Squealing to the right side of the street, I pressed the pedal down and peeled away, leaving Mrs. Brinkerhoff and her equally doughy lover behind me.

I PULLED the Rover up to the old building I'd bought when I'd first decided to become a private investigator. It was in what was once a rundown part of Los Angeles, one of those neighborhoods that showed its belly to people looking for someplace cheap and hip to live. There were now at least five coffee shops within walking distance of my front door and more sushi bars than I could even count. If I liked sushi, it would be great. I was consoled by the presence of an Irish pub a block down. The quasi-ghetto turned into a thriving community while I slaved away to restore a building that most people thought was a lost cause. It was a nice place to live, an even nicer place to work.

Seeing the building still gave me a sense of pride when I drove up to it, its weathered gold brick exterior lit up from the outside with small floodlights hidden amid the bushes. Its restoration took me two years, each day spent with cursing, sweat, and more than a few drops of my blood. The building had no intention of making it easy for me, and I'd earned every damned inch of its resurrection.

When the building was new, it was a law office or someplace where tiger oak paneling and high, arched windows were a requirement for doing business. I'd given the place the once-over, sizing up how long it would take me to strip off the paint from the wood and repair the abuse to the interior walls, and fallen in love. I'd seen the potential in its abandoned squalor, and I certainly had the time and money to spend on turning the rooms into someplace I could live and work.

Besides, the hard labor of stripping varnish and sanding down endless yards of wood kept my mind off of Rick. At that time, that was what I needed the most. I'm not sure I've stopped needing it, but I've run out of wood to sand down.

I'd divided up the building into two spaces, the front part of the first floor serving as an office for my investigation work. A separate entrance off of the front porch gleamed with a brass plaque announcing to a client that they'd found Cole McGinnis, Private Investigator. A covered side porch protected the entrance to my home, a living room and a kitchen downstairs and a pair of rooms above it. I'd knocked down walls to create a large bedroom away from the street, leaving the shotgun-style room in the front as a library of sorts. The space was large enough for a family, if I'd had one, but I didn't. It echoed around me. Living there suited me. I felt about as empty as the house, most of the time.

I backed the Rover into the carport. There was nothing in the car to steal, but with its rear window missing, I wasn't going to borrow trouble. There was a light on in the back half of the first floor. The last thing I wanted right now was company, but there'd be no avoiding him. I'd spotted my brother's car when I'd driven up, and Mike wasn't someone I could dodge for long, especially when he was stalking me in my own living room.

Slouched on one of the red couches, Mike didn't look dangerous. I knew better. I'd grown up with him. The bump on my nose was testament to the hardness of his fists. The only thing that saved me was he'd stopped growing at five-nine while I'd kept going for a few more inches. It didn't make me more intimidating. My height just meant I had longer legs to run away with.

Mike took after our Japanese mother. His face was broad, and his thick black hair was cut into a bristled hedgehog he ran his hand over when he was thinking something out. I got more of our father's Irish coloring and build, light brown eyes and hair, but we definitely shared our mother's face. She existed for me in flat paper squares, photographs taken when my father first met her in Tokyo up until when she died. I had a picture of her holding a baby, her eyes nearly closed with her smile. The baby was Mike. She hadn't lived long enough to hold me.

"You're coming home very late, little brother," Mike said, glancing up from a stack of papers. Even while stalking, his mind was on his security business. There was a half-empty beer bottle on the coffee table, a coaster advertising a brand of tequila I'd never bought soaking up the condensation. "And you've got branches in your hair. Another jealous-husband case?"

I handed him the camera as a response, telling him to go through the pictures while I got myself a beer. His lurching snorts were audible from the kitchen, and by the time I returned to the living room, his face had turned a bright, beet red. I wasn't certain if there was an actual chortle, but he came close to choking on his own laughter as he ran through the images.

"This is disgusting," he said, waving the camera at me. "Someone paid you to take these?"

"Her husband," I replied, leaning over my brother's shoulders and tapping a close-up of Mrs. Brinkerhoff's cherubic face. "Apparently he suspected that she was cheating on him. He could have told me she can shoot the balls off a fly. Her girlfriend saw me in the window and screamed. Next thing I know, there's a shotgun pointed at my face and bits of a tree elephant in my hair."

"You should come work for me. No one shoots at us, and you definitely don't have to deal with this kind of emotional scarring." Mike leaned over, picking the last of the leaves out of my hair. Tugging at the long strands near my jaw, he shook his head. "You'll have to cut this first. No one wants their bodyguard looking like he dropped off a romance cover."

"Cute," I said, poking him with my bare foot. "And thanks, but no. I suffered enough growing up with you. I sure as hell ain't going to work for you."

"You're just jealous because teachers knew you lacked my brilliance." Mike shot me a sly grin, poking at a long-healed-over scab. Older than me by three years, he spent high school being the smart, intelligent McGinnis. It made life hell for me following him, always being compared to what he'd done before. Struggling with being gay at the time didn't help either.

"Any reason you're here?" The beer was cold, soothing in my throat. "It's late, and somehow I don't think Mad Dog sent you over here with leftover casserole to pawn off on your younger brother."

"Don't call her that. Her name's Madeline."

"You married her. She should be committed just for that," I replied, shrugging.

"Wait till you get a new boyfriend," he threatened. "There's going to be hell to pay on that."

"Don't hold your breath. Look how my last relationship turned out."

Rick hung between us, a crucified sacrifice to my choices in life. Mike's eyes fell, his wide-open smile fading as the memories of what had happened flooded both of us. I didn't want to revisit those events. I certainly never wanted to relive that night, but it came back to me when I slept, sometimes even creeping up on me during the day when I least expected it. I knew Mike had his own guilt he carried around. Neither of us was going to rake that night open and spread its entrails out in front of us to look for good fortune. Nothing good ever came of talking about it, and we weren't about to start now.

"And you're wrong." Mike broke the silence. "I did bring some casserole. Tamale pie, even. You don't eat well, Cole. How many times a week can you eat steak?"

"Seven," I answered with a shaky grin. "Sometimes I even go out and get someone to cook it for me. But thanks for the food. I promise I'll eat it."

"I came over because I've got a job for you."

"If it includes taking pictures of septuagenarian lesbians, I'm going to have to pass."

"Nice use of a big word there, little brother. And if it did, then I wouldn't tell you, just so I could see your face when you found out," Mike snorted. "One of my clients' son committed suicide. They swear he wouldn't do that to the family and want someone to take a look at what happened."

"People do that kind of thing to their families all the time." Shrugging, I took another sip of my beer, leaning back into the softness of the couch. "It's kind of what suicide does."

"His father insists his son never would have done it." Shaking his head, my brother sighed. "Look, I think he killed himself, but the father's a big client. They use our security details all the time, and I can't just tell him he's full of shit because he doesn't want to believe his son did himself."

"So what do you want me to do?"

"Just look into it." Mike slid a thick manila envelope out of his pile of papers and passed it over to me. Flicking open the tab, I saw the number of zeros on the check fastened to the top of a paper-clipped report. "Take some time, maybe a couple of weeks, and poke around what he was doing. There's probably nothing there, but I want the family to feel like at least someone took a second look."

"But the kid definitely killed himself?" The package held photos of a smiling young Korean, some by himself while others showed him with groups of people or with a thin-faced Caucasian woman. "This is his girlfriend?"

"Wife." Mike dug through the photos and pulled out one of the young man holding a bowlegged toddler. "Not a kid, really. Late twenties, married, and already with a son. Good Korean boy by all accounts. Pride of the family and all that."

"Kim Hyun-Shik? Am I pronouncing that right? Kim's the last name, yes?" It was hard to roll the syllables off my tongue. I studied the young man's face. He was good-looking, a pretty mouth set into a strong face. His black hair was shaped into a conservative brush much like my brother's, and his eyes were dark and sparkling. There was love in those eyes for the young boy he held up for the camera, pride beaming out from his face.

I was jealous of that pride and love. It had been a long time since I'd seen that look in my father's eyes.

"When did he die?" There were reports in the envelope: an autopsy report and lists of places that Hyun-Shik frequented. I recognized a few restaurants, and then a familiar name jumped out at me. "I know this place, Dirty Kiss. It's... a guest bar."

"Just a couple of weeks ago. And a guest bar, my ass. It's a gay whorehouse," Mike interjected. "Call it what it is, Cole."

"Whorehouse just seemed a bit rough." I shuffled the reports, looking for cause of death. "Most customers don't even make it to the sex rooms. Female impersonators perform shows on the main floor. You have to be a member to get into the upper area."

"Yeah, well, our boy made it to the upper rooms." The label on Mike's beer was taking a beating from his fingernails, its edge peeled back into strips. He was trying to act nonchalant, skirting around a question he wanted to ask but couldn't. "You go there? For company, I mean? Not that it's bad. You should get some, once in a while."

"Mike, it was one of the places I ended up looking into when I was a cop." The thought of paying someone to dance naked in front of me would have seemed like a good time a few years ago. Times definitely had changed. "I worked Vice, remember? There's a lot of vice in places like that. The family knows he was a member?"

"I don't know. He was found there, overdosed on a handful of pills. They didn't get much when they pumped out his stomach." He drained the rest of his beer, wincing at its warmth. "His father insists that Hyun-Shik wouldn't kill himself but won't talk about his son being gay."

"A lot of fathers refuse to believe their sons are gay. Look at ours." Mike shifted uncomfortably, and his face took on a very familiar twisted look.

"Yeah, about Dad," he said, rubbing at the back of his neck. "He and Mom are coming for a visit in a couple of weeks. Maddy wants to know if you'd like to come to dinner. Maybe bring a guest."

"Come on, Mike, don't pull that kind of shit on me." The beer was tasteless in my mouth, but I drank it anyway, anything to wash out the sawdust clogging my throat. "The old man doesn't want to see me."

"It's been, what… twelve years, Cole?" His eyes were dark, almost moist in the lamplight. "When are the two of you going to stop being stubborn and at least meet halfway?"

Mike hated the schism in our family, hated being the bridge between me and my father. Our Irish Catholic upbringing was good at feeding the guilt that plagued both of us. Mike blamed himself for not being there that night when I told my dad about loving men, and I blamed myself for not being what my family wanted. I'd gotten over mine, but Mike was still working on his.

"Halfway to what?"

I could still hear the slam of the door behind me. The last face I'd seen before it shut was Barbara's, my father's second wife and the woman I'd called Mom all of my life. She still wore the look of horror she'd had on since I'd told them my biggest secret, hoping that no matter what, they loved me enough to still call me son. I'd been wrong. "You want me to hide who I am because Dad's got a problem with it?"

"This isn't about Dad. This is about you," Mike said softly. "Tasha's coming with them. She's a sophomore now. She wants to see you."

Our youngest sister had been three when I'd left the family. Other than pictures, I'd not seen her or our other two sisters in years. Mike was a master at playing me. No one else could coax me into doing things I didn't want to do like he could.

"I'll think about it." I eyed my brother, looking for any sign of triumph in his face. "You smile and I'll punch you."

"I'm not smiling," he said, fighting a shit-eating grin. "I'd bring her here if I thought Dad would go for it. Just come over for dinner and be pleasant. Maddy was serious about bringing someone. She thinks it's about time you date."

"Tell Mad Dog McGinnis that I'm fine being single." Mike's wife meant well, but she'd been on the outskirts of my spiral downward. Mike knew better. Other than not-so-subtle hints that I should get laid, he wasn't going to push me into anything. "Besides, you think I'd want to inflict Dad on anyone I was interested in? Look how much shit he gave Maddy, and you're the favorite son."

"I've got to get going." Glancing at his watch, he winced at the late hour. "Do yourself a favor and take a shower before you go to bed. You smell like one of those pine tree air fresheners you hang in the car."

"Yeah, right." I was tired all of a sudden, too many ghosts and relationships flying through my head. "I'll lock the door behind you."

"You going to take the job?" Mike gathered up his paperwork, shuffling the pages into their proper order. "I like the guy, Cole. He doesn't expect you to find anything, really, but he's got to do something. The kid was his only son."

"Yeah, I'll take a look around. I kind of knew one of the performers at the club there. She might be able to give me something." I snagged the bottles and stood, stretching my body up until I felt my spine crack. A throb started along my ribcage, working outward in a steady, numbing circle. Dropping the glass into the recycling bin, I leaned against the archway and rubbed at the spot.

"Does it hurt?" Mike spotted me working at the spot with the tips of my fingers, worry creasing his heavy eyebrows. "When was the last time you saw the doctor?"

"It's scar tissue, dude." The keloid eased its grip on my tangled nerve bundles, and the muscles around the scar slowly began to relax. "Nothing to do about it. I just have to deal with it."

He didn't look convinced. Mike was a worrier. He'd been my de facto mother for years. I didn't see that changing. It got worse after Dad turned his back on me. If anything else happened to me, I was pretty sure he would move me into a spare bedroom of his house so he could keep a closer eye on me.

"Go home to your wife, Mike," I said, pushing him toward the door. He might be stockier than me, but I had longer arms, and his halfhearted swing at me swished by my shoulder.

"Stop in on the Kim family before you go to that club." He stopped on the stoop, holding the security screen open. "The father's up in San Francisco, but his mother's down here with the rest of the family. Mr. Kim said his wife's taking it hard since the cops called to tell them about Hyun-Shik."

"She knows someone's looking into her son's death?" The last thing I wanted was to show up on a grieving mother's doorstep asking questions she wasn't ready to answer.

"Yeah, I got the feeling Mr. Kim's doing this for her. He didn't say it, but that's what I got when I spoke with him." Mike was almost down the steps when I called out to him to stop. The porch light cast shadows over my brother's face, his prominent cheekbones stark under the glare.

"What if I find something?" I asked. "What then?"

"Then, little brother." He cracked a smile, back to being the superior sibling I'd known and loved all my life. "I expect you to chase it down and find out the truth. Put that pigheadedness of yours to good use. I don't expect you to do anything less."

THE water felt good on my body. What felt even better was washing out the last of the bark from my hair. I leaned against the tile, one hand holding my weight as I watched the dirty water swirl down the drain. The shower spray beat against my neck, and I worked the fingers of my other hand over my scalp, making sure there were no remnants of the night's activities left. A minute leaf, newly formed and spring green, fell and bobbed on the current. I worked it down the drain with the edge of my toe. The color reminded me too much of Rick's eyes. They were never that green, but he'd often worn contacts to pop their intensity, liking the startling effect against his tanned skin.

He'd been wearing them that night. Bright greens mocked me at times. The leaf was no exception.

Turning off the water, I grabbed a towel and scrubbed the water from my legs. A bruise was forming along the inside of my thigh, a long line of purple from the thick edge of the wooden fence. The mark ended at the edge of the gunshot scar on my leg, the smallest of my wounds. The bullet had torn through the muscle, passing straight through and embedding into the brick wall behind us.

It was the last shot taken, and I didn't remember getting hit there.

I passed the towel over my chest and down over my stomach. If I woke up early enough, I could head down to the gym and get a few rounds in before I started work. Working out helped keep the scar tissue on my ribs limber, or so I kept telling myself. At the very least, it helped keep me in shape so I could outrun rabid old women with shotguns.

The nodule of tissue on my ribs was still florid, darker than the one on my chest, and prominent. Rubbing the reducing salve over the circular scars, I let my mind wander, thinking about the young man and his suicide.

There'd been a note of sorts amid the papers, a copy of a paper scrap scrawled with a few bits of Korean. The hand was masculine and strong, confidently marching the letters across the page. If Hyun-Shik was doubting himself, it certainly hadn't shown in his handwriting.

I recognized the language with the circles and dashes from seeing restaurant signs more than from any knowledge on my part. I could speak English and passable Spanish, but Korean was far outside of my comfort zone. I might have had a Japanese mother, but other than knowing the difference between noodles and rice, I was about as Asian as a bowl of cornflakes.

"Need someone to translate that," I mumbled to the empty bedroom as I hunted for a pair of boxers. My dresser was sadly lacking in clean clothes. I added laundry to my list of things to do in the morning. Something didn't seem right about the note. It nagged at me as I turned off the light and lay back on the bed. "What's there that made them sure it was a suicide? And why would you write your suicide note on a torn piece of paper?" But then that made as much sense as swallowing a bunch of pills at a karaoke sex club in Garden Grove.

Sighing, I closed my eyes, letting my fatigue finally take me. The last image I had in my mind as I fell asleep was of Hyun-Shik's face as he held his son. The happiness there was at odds with the desperation of a man driven to suicide. But then, I told myself, everyone has demons they keep hidden. It's when those demons fight free that we find out the truth of things.

CHAPTER TWO

I COULDN'T blink away the clouds in my eyes. No matter how hard I tried, they wouldn't clear. I tried to turn my head, but I was much too tired. The sheets were rough under my cheek, starched hard and fixed tight against the mattress. The room was fuzzy, but I knew where I was. The smell of antiseptic and bleach overwhelmed me. Despite the acrid stench, I could still smell vomit and urine under it.

There was another odor, metallic and bitter. I knew that smell too. It was blood. And there was a lot of it.

Machines beeped around me, a steady burp of noises and burbles, marking each of my breaths and heartbeats. There was a rhythm to it, my life counted off as each second passed. There were shapes around me, dark and light blobs that grew more solid as I blinked.

It hurt to breathe. Something was catching on my lungs, and there was a hard cylinder in my throat. I almost laughed at the irony of finally being able to swallow something that deep. I had a gag reflex that couldn't stop once it started. It kicked in now, and I choked against the tube that kept my lungs clear of fluids. My body fought the foreign intrusions, but there was no hope for it. I was paralyzed, trapped in the cocoon of my immoveable body.

The room came into view, slowly becoming solid around me. A powder-blue paint covered the walls, and flickering lights reflected back at me from the chrome of the hospital bed next to mine. The faint, steady sound I heard under the blips grew louder, and I watched in horror as the linens on the next bed slowly turned crimson, the excess blood splattering to the floor as it dripped. Something lay on the bed, a familiar something, and I tried to speak, but no words could come out around the white plastic in my throat.

I knew those eyes because their brilliance haunted me. I watched, helpless and immobile, as Rick reached for me, his hand gnarled and shaking when he tried to span the distance between us.

An echoing boom took off Rick's face, leaving only one of those spring green eyes staring back at me. His body twitched, trying to come to grips with its own death, and I screamed silently as his brains splattered into my mouth and onto my face. Blood spurted over me, tasting of Rick's life as it drained away from him. Then the pain hit me, and everything went black.

The sentient part of my mind—the part that knew I was in a dream—screamed to get out. It knew Rick never made it to the hospital. I'd never seen him on a bed or hooked up to monitors. None of those things ever happened, but my subconscious didn't care.

The chirrup of the machines continued, cold and uncaring, as Rick died all over again in my nightmares. Again. Always dying, and I'm always helpless to stop it.

THE ringing of my house phone was what woke me, an incessant tug of sound on my ears. I stank of sweat, and for a moment, the foul, cloying scent of blood filled my nose, but it dissipated as I struggled to clear the dream from my head.

Reaching for the receiver, I blearily looked at my alarm clock, wondering where the night had gone. It seemed like seconds since I'd lain down, but here it was, nine in the morning, and more than likely, Claudia was calling me from downstairs.

"Hello?" I know I sounded rough. My throat was raw, as if the tube had been real. Phantom memories, left over from the days after they took me off the hospital machines. The scar on my ribs hurt, twisting nerves sending little shockwaves through my belly. And if that wasn't bad enough, I had to pee very badly.

"Honey, are you coming in to work today?" Claudia's accent was a thick molasses in my ears. She swore she'd never lived anywhere but California, but there was more than a hint of Southern in her voice. "Because if you're not, then I'm going to bust your head open for making me come in."

Ah yes, dear, sweet Claudia, who could probably bench press me with one hand behind her back. I hired her because she was friendly and wouldn't scare off any fidgety clients that might walk through the door. She'd raised eight sons in the depths of Long Beach and gotten each one into college. There was steel under that soft exterior. I had no doubt in my mind that she could crack my head open with a flick of her fingers.

"I just need to wake up. Must have slept through the alarm." I mumbled an apology to my sole employee. "I'll be down in a bit."

I wasn't an idiot. Claudia kept me on the straight and narrow, as it were. She'd finally stopped trying to fix me up with her son, Marcus, having decided I probably wasn't good enough for him, but she still treated me like I was one of her boys. I'd tried growing a mustache once, and it lasted all of half an hour. She'd come in, taken one look at me, and sniffed that I looked like trash. I went upstairs and took it off without even arguing. I would damn my father to hell with my last breath, but I'd be damned if I disappointed Claudia.

"Take your time. I've got coffee on and some apple pie down here," she replied. "I'm going to be watching some of the morning shows. They've got some dancing dog on right now. Tell me, who the hell needs a dancing dog? You want to impress me? Get the damned thing to do dishes."

I hung up after mumbling a goodbye. It's best to cut Claudia off before she gets on a tear, especially when there was coffee and pie waiting for me. She might be bossy, but she kept my books in order and was as dependable as the sun. The morning she walked into my office to answer the ad I'd placed in the paper was the best day of my life.

There were some reservations on my part when a large woman, wearing her Sunday best, arrived on my doorstep. I couldn't guess her age, but there was a steady wisdom about her, and there was no denying she was a force of nature. Our interview was short and sweet: I told her I was gay and had some issues, she told me she was black and had high blood pressure.

At the time, she knew next to nothing about computers, and I let her spend the day either knitting or watching her stories on the television I'd bought her, but she kept my schedule tight, my bills paid, and if I needed feeding, she took care of that too. Claudia worked because she didn't want her brain to get rusty after retiring from the school district. I worked because I didn't want to turn into a couch slug, no matter how much money I'd gotten from the department. It was a winning scenario all around.

Except that she and Mike often conspired against me. God help me if they both decided at the same time that I needed to date. There'd be no saving me.

I did a quick shower to get the night sweats off of me. I debated dressing with a bit more care than I usually did. A visit to the Kim household probably would require more professionalism than I normally sported. Most of my clients were more interested in seeing what their spouses were doing or digging up dirt on employees who were claiming debilitating injuries. A pair of jeans wasn't going to cut it.

Dark khakis won out. My closet was limited in choices. It was either the khakis or black denim. I must have skipped fashion sense when I stood in line for my gay genes, because Mike was of the opinion that I couldn't dress myself. A cream polo was about as risky as I was going to get with the pants.

And apparently I'd guessed wrong when I went downstairs to the office and greeted Claudia with a cheery hello.

She took one look at me and held up her index finger, turning it around in the air and pointing up, silently telling me to go back and try again. There was a pinch to her brows when she did it, her face screwed up into either pain or displeasure.

"What? These go together!" I stared down at the pants and shirt. They both were kind of brownish.

"It is no wonder why you can't get a date." She went back to her crossword puzzle, reaching for her cup and taking a sip. "Your pants are green, and your shirt is the color of my coffee. Go change something before you blind someone."

I came back down after changing into the black jeans, my only other choice for the day. I got a grunt of semi-approval from my office manager. Grabbing at the paper plate with a slice of apple pie on it, I shoved a large bite in my mouth, drifting off into a cinnamon-laced fruit heaven. As I chewed, Claudia stood, shuffling over to the coffee machine, and filled a travel mug, handing it to me as she went back to her desk.

"Shut up, I got you coffee because I felt sorry for your ass. Don't think it's going to happen that often." She cut me off before I could protest. "Your brother called. He said that he spoke to some girl named Kim and that you can go see her any time today. Here's the address. Is this a case? Should I be making a new file?"

"Yeah, it's a new case," I said, handing her the check and the rest of the contents of the envelope. I copied the suicide note using the small all-in-one machine I'd gotten from an office supply store, satisfied that the resolution held up despite being a second generation image, and passed that over to Claudia as well. She pursed her lips when she saw the amount on the check, raising her painted-on eyebrows in surprise.

"And Kim's the family's last name. It's not a girl."

"What kind of name is that?" An expanding red-rope folder appeared from the cavernous depths of her wide desk, and she pasted a white label on the front flap, carefully lettering a string of numbers underneath the family's name. There was no censure in her tone, merely curiosity.

"It's Korean." I knew better than to say anything other than that. I loved Claudia, but there were times when she was going to have an opinion about something, and that was it.

"I like that hot cabbage stuff they make. That's good." She nodded emphatically. "Marcel's got an Asian girl. You can't show up at their doorstep without taking something. It's bad manners. Be sure to stop at the store and get something."

"What kind of something?"

"Cookies, usually," she said, touching at the corner of her mouth with the tip of her finger, wiping away a dot of bright red lipstick. "Just something nice. Maybe flowers?"

"I'll see what I can grab down the street. If you could deposit that, that'll be great." Other than Marcus, I couldn't keep any details of Claudia's huge family in my head, so I wasn't going to comment on Marcel's girlfriend or her ethnicity. "It's one of Mike's jobs, so at least we know the check's good."

"You doing okay?" There was a mother hen look on her face, a searching pierce for information.

"Yeah, I'm fine. Just a hard night," I reassured her. Bending over to kiss her cheek, I couldn't dodge the stinging swat she gave my butt when I stepped back. "If you want to leave early, go ahead. It's a Friday. No sense in keeping the place open past one."

"I'll call Martin and have him swing by then." She nodded. The suspicion in her face hadn't subsided, and I smiled to alleviate her worries. "Eat something, Cole. And I saw your back window when I came in this morning. You and I are going to have a little talk sometime about what you're doing at night."

"Yeah, thanks for reminding me. I have to give you the camera to get images off of it. Mr. Brinkerhoff's wife was doing nasty things with a friend of hers. I'll have to give him a call later and tell him the bad news." I thought about it for a moment, then shrugged. "Or good news, depending on how he wants to take it."

"You just keep that kind of stuff to yourself." Waving a pen at me, Claudia tsked her disapproval. "And I had a man come to fix that car window, since you slept in so late. I took money out of petty cash to pay him. He even vacuumed up the broken glass. I gave him a good tip, seeing as he'll probably be out here again."

THE Rover and I weren't much on technology, so I used my trusty book of maps to locate the Kims' residence. I could have mapped it out on the computer before I left, but that would have meant taking a bit more of Claudia's abuse, and I was still too wrung out by the nightmare I'd had. Smiling and faking it could only last so long. Eventually, I caved in and showed how I truly felt. Claudia would have been on me in a moment, pulling at every last bit of emotion she could press out.

Los Angeles traffic was problematic at best and chaos at its worst. The only way to really escape the brunt of it was to head out to the 405 and hug the coast. On a map, it looked like a roundabout way of doing things, but the reality of life was, it was really the only way to get from point A to point B in under five hours.

I headed south after stopping off at a florist and grabbing a blooming orchid from the display. After shoving the receipt into a plastic folder Claudia gave me to keep track of my business expenses, I worked the Rover through the streams of midday traffic.

The Kim house was tucked into the cleft of a canyon, surrounded by a perimeter of ice plant and high stone walls. I parked the Rover behind a battered white Explorer. Both vehicles stood out among the low-slung sports cars and high-priced imports cluttering the neighborhood's driveways. I didn't even want to imagine what cars were deemed good enough to actually sit in the garage.

It was a long walk to the front door. I realized when my feet hit the pavement that I really didn't have any idea what to say to a woman who had lost her son to suicide. When I was a cop, I never dealt with informing families about a loved one being murdered, and after making detective, I worked Vice, so any death I came across immediately went over to the guys in Homicide.

I summoned up some of the rote empathy words I'd learned and knocked on the door, hoping I could go in, ask a few questions, and head on out.

Unfortunately for me, as soon as the door opened, I lost all control of my brain.

I'd never been into Asian men, maybe because they reminded me of Mike, but the young man answering the door took my breath away.

If there was any evidence of a God, it was standing right in front of me, I was sure of it. His large, almond-shaped eyes were tawny, a bronze, golden-brown surrounded by long, black lashes. Black hair swept down onto his pale skin, falling artfully over his face and his neck, and his high cheekbones were slightly flushed from the warmth outside. But it was his mouth that drew me in, full and tinged pink, a faint ring of teeth marks dimpling his lower lip.

It took me a moment to realize he was staring at me nearly eye to eye, standing just an inch or two under my six-two. I chanced a glance down his lean, tight body, drinking in the sight of long legs in beat-up jeans and the fit of a worn T-shirt hugging his torso. Swallowing, I tried to find something intelligent to say but he spoke first.

"Can I help you?" There was a fluidity to his speech, accented with an Eastern tint.

"Uh, yeah." Juggling the orchid plant, I dug a business card out from the leather portfolio I took with me on interviews, using the notebook inside to jot down information. "I'm Cole McGinnis. My brother Mike said he called ahead. It's about Kim Hyun-Shik. Are you a relative?"

"I'm… his cousin." He obviously struggled with what to say. The death was too new to shove Hyun-Shik into the past tense. "Please.

Come in. Grace spoke to Mr. McGinnis this morning. I don't know if she's told Auntie that you were coming."

"This is for the family. I'm really sorry for your loss." Unsure of what to do with the plant, I solved my problem by handing it to Hyun's cousin. I flicked open the portfolio, starting to outline the family dynamics. At the very least, it would help me diagram who I spoke to. "Grace is…?"

"Henry's older sister." He placed the bobbing purple-bloomed stalk on an ornate wood credenza in the hall entrance, motioning for me to enter. "Sorry, Hyun-Shik is Henry's Korean name. He used Henry for school and work."

I entered the house and brushed past him. Damn, he even smelled good, a citrus, masculine scent with tea under notes. "Does Grace have a Korean name too?"

"We all do." His smile was tight, a tinge of bitter or sadness to it, but I couldn't determine which. "Grace doesn't use it. She's just Grace Kim."

The house was quiet, the solemn quiet of a home mourning a loved one. I followed him down the hall to an elegant living room, trying to keep my eyes up off the seat of his jeans. Fixing my gaze onto the center of his back didn't help much, but it was better than letting my mind wander.

Four well-dressed Korean women were in the room, one of them sitting in a loveseat while a younger woman patted her thigh, murmuring something I couldn't understand. The woman at the center of their attention glanced up at the young man with me, and her face changed from sorrow to anger, her swollen eyes bulging as she started to scream.

I didn't know Korean, but whatever was said made his face tighten, and his mouth twisted as he struggled not to respond to the vitriol being flung at him. There was ugliness in those words, and she used them like knives, plunging them over and over into his heart until he bled out in front of her.

The younger woman stood, grabbing at Hyun-Shik's cousin, but he eluded her, twisting away and walking out of the room. She turned to me, glancing back at the now subdued older woman, the others surrounding her and calming her down. "I'm sorry, but this is a bad time for my mother. I didn't tell her that you were coming. I'd hoped to have more time, but then Jae-Min showed up, and I've had to deal with that too."

"He's Jae-Min? Your cousin? The one who let me in?"

"'Cousin' is a loose term. Our grandfathers were first cousins," she said. Fatigue made her face a bit puffy, but there was a porcelain prettiness to her features, and I could see a resemblance to the man who'd let me in. "Umma's having a hard time dealing with Henry being gone. Seeing Jae-Min here instead of my brother makes her mad. I'm sorry you came out here for nothing, but I don't think my mother can speak to you right now."

"No problem." There was something not being said to me, and I wanted to dig it out. It didn't make sense for Mrs. Kim to be pissed off about Hyun-Shik's cousin, but then I wasn't that up on Korean culture. "Maybe I'll just talk to your cousin. Did he know Henry well? He might have something to add."

"Talk to Jae all you want. He's probably in the kitchen." Her smile held a smirk, lurking beyond the pleasantness. I was now sure there was something else going on. "It's down that hall and to the right. Tell him I'll be in to refill the tea in a bit, if he can have it ready."

It was easy to find the kitchen. It was larger than my office and gleaming with yards of stainless steel and granite. There was also no sign of Jae-Min and then I spotted him standing outside of a set of French doors, smoking a kretek on the veranda. His back was to me, his shoulder blades jutting out to poke his T-shirt up as he leaned on the railing, exhaling blue-grey smoke into spirals around his head. It looked like a familiar position for him to be in, as if he'd stood there many times before.

I found a chrome teapot on the stove and filled it with water from the filtered dispenser on the sink. I'd leave the tea selection to Grace if she came back in, but I turned the gas stove on until bright blue flames licked at the bottom of the pot. He'd glanced back when he'd heard the water turn on, catching me staring at his shoulders. Jae-Min's face was closed, his emotions shuttered behind a pretty mask.

The teapot had started to babble over the flame by the time he finished his clove cigarette. I watched him stamp out the end in a pot of sand, picking up the stub and throwing it into a trash can outside. The door squeaked when Jae-Min opened it and stepped into the kitchen.

He moved around the kitchen with a practiced ease, pulling out an ornamental service set from a sideboard. A bag of loose-leaf tea emerged from another cabinet, and he measured out a portion into a strainer, setting it into the silver server.

"Did you need something else?" His voice was soft, edged with a trembling pain.

"I just wanted to ask you a few questions about Hyun-Shik," I replied, resting against the counter where he arranged sugar cubes in the service's bowl. "Were you close?"

He looked up at me, measuring me with a long stare. A keen intelligence gleamed in his golden-brown eyes, but something wilder lurked there as well. With that look, I realized what he reminded me of.

Growing up as a Marine Corp brat, I moved around a lot until my father retired when I was thirteen. One of the places we lived was a small town in Hawai'i where a feral cat colony lived next to the base. The cats and people seemed to come to a détente of sorts: the cats kept the rat population down, and every once in a while, the people would poach a particularly cute kitten from the roaming prides that scattered when a human approached. I'd spent a month coaxing a young cat out, hoping to convince my parents into letting me keep it if I could tame it. The cat would come close enough to get his ears scratched and take the food I offered, but any move to go past his shoulders sent him back into the tall grasses.

Jae-Min reminded me of that cat.

There was a feral quality to him. Someone had coaxed him into the house and fed him, but he probably would flee or scratch if held too tightly. He seemed out of place with the tightly wound perfection of the home we were in, but he definitely knew where everything was and was even willing to help make tea for a woman who seemed to hate him.

Life had all sorts of surprises for me. This one was something I wanted to figure out.

He must have decided it was okay to talk to me, because he gave me a half nod. The sugar cubes also were extremely interesting, because he took his time stacking them after turning the stove off, letting the boiling water settle.

"Uncle, Hyun-Shik's father, arranged for me to go to high school down here." I stayed silent, waiting for more. "My family lives in Sacramento. My mother thought it would be better if I was here. Hyun-Shik is… was four years older than me."

"So he was like a brother?"

His expression barely changed, but the mask cracked, a bit of irony seeping out. "No, I never thought of hyung as my brother."

How many nicknames did this guy have? I was trying to play catch-up on my notes when Grace scurried into the kitchen, her bare feet nearly sliding out from under her as she hit the slick wood floor. Shit. Looking down, I winced, finding my shoes were still firmly on my own feet.

"Good." She grabbed at the sugar bowl, placing it on the tray. "There's some sliced lemon in the fridge. Jae, grab some for me and put it on that dish. Umma has other guests coming. Are you staying?"

"If you need me to," he replied. The coldness was back, placid as a glacier moving through still waters.

"Yes." Grace stopped arranging dainty teacups on the tray, taking the plate of lemons from his hand. "Just stay out of sight. I'll come in here when I need something. Can you see if we have something to serve people? Maybe nine or so?"

"I'll look around." Jae-Min stood as she bustled around him. She left the kitchen in a whirl of skirt and chatter, a wave of fragrant tea marking her exit. He caught the look on my face, quirking his mouth at me. "What?"

"I'm guessing that what Mrs. Kim said to you wasn't all that pleasant, but you're offering to make tea and finger sandwiches for her and her friends. Why?"

"Is this a part of your investigation in Hyun-Shik's death?"

"It'll help give me some idea of how this family works. Let's just say that some things aren't adding up for me. I'm being paid a lot of money to poke around, so I'm going to poke."

"My family owes a lot to Uncle's family. I'm here because…." He bit his lower lip with his teeth. It was obviously a habit he had when thinking. As habits go, it was better than my brother's hedgehog hair brushing. "It's an obligation. It would be… wrong to leave when Uncle's family needed help."

"A family thing," I said, stepping in to take vegetables from his hands as he unloaded the refrigerator.

"Yes, a family thing. A Korean thing." He risked another look at me, looking more than ever like the feral cat I'd tried to get to come home with me. "You don't need to help. I can do this."

"The most help I can give you is chopping things up and putting on water to boil. After that, you're on your own. And I can probably open a can or two. It'll give me something to do while we talk."

"There's not much to talk about. Hyun-ah lived with his wife. I didn't socialize with him unless it was for a holiday or a funeral."

"His wife, Victoria." I had to look in my papers to find her name. "How does she get along with the family?"

"She's hyung's wife." He said it like those three words explained everything. A small shrug when he turned, but other than that, nothing more.

"Was she supportive of him? Did he have problems with her?" Trying another angle, I dug a little deeper. "Was he unhappy with his marriage, or was he cheating on her with someone else?"

"Hyun-ah wasn't seeing anyone else."

"You say that like you know, but you said the two of you didn't socialize."

"We talked, sometimes." There was a tiny verbal step toward me, just enough to reach for something else. Jae placed a large pot in the sink, filling it halfway with water before putting it on the stove. The gas ignited under it, and he began to chop up stalky green vegetables that I couldn't identify if my life depended on it. "There was only Victoria and their son, Will."

"Will?" That seemed out of place with the rest of the family's traditions, despite Grace's dismissal of her given name. "Odd choice."

"He has a Korean middle name. Chang-shik." He had to brush past me to get to a cabinet, and my body sang from the casual, warm contact. If I stayed around Jae-Min much longer, I was going to have to take a very cold shower when I got home. Or pray for a thunderstorm to hit me when I got outside. My notes were lying open, and he stopped, looking at my block lettering. Taking the pen from my hand, he crossed out something I'd written, correcting it underneath. "It's Jae-Min Kim, or just Jae. With an E. Not a Y."

"I promise I would have clarified spelling before I wrote my report."

"You're writing a report?" He frowned, returning to nibble on his lip. "Who for? Vicki?"

"No, Mr. Kim. Technically I'm working for my brother, Mike, but it's at your uncle's request. I file a report for every case. Sometimes even two or three, depending on how extensive of an investigation it is."

"This should be short then, right?" The greens waited while he added some brown flakes to the water and a fishy aroma filled the kitchen. It wasn't unpleasant, a whiff of sea and meat around the stove. "How much more is there to find out?"

"I don't know." Leaning my elbows against the counter, I watched his face, wondering why his eyes were dull and shut down as he stirred the broth. "What did Mrs. Kim say to you?" It was bold to ask, and I knew it. "What did she say that hurt you?"

"She said that I should be the one who died in that place. That Hyun-Shik should be here instead of me." The flatness in his voice never wavered. It was as if he were discussing something mildly unpleasant, like someone crossing the street against the light or finding a dead bug on his windshield. "Auntie thinks that I deserved that kind of death, not her son."

"Why would she say something like that?" I wanted to reach out to touch his stiff shoulders, but I'd been scratched before, by more feral things than a pretty-faced, young Korean man. "Yeah, Hyun-Shik made a choice, however fucked-up it might be. You had nothing to do with it. Did you?"

"No." His black hair gleamed under the soft lights in the kitchen, and he turned to grab handfuls of the chopped leaves, adding them slowly to the simmering liquid. "I had nothing to do with Hyun-Shik's death."

"Then why say something that hateful? Or is that a Korean thing too?"

"No, she'll either apologize or we'll pretend as if nothing was said. That's how we deal with uncomfortable things that happen." More vegetables were pulled from paper bags, and an onion lay in line for execution under his sharp knife. "She said that because Hyun-Shik shouldn't have died in a gay club. It's one thing to kill himself, but to shame the family that way is too much."

"And she thinks it would be okay for you to die there?" My opinion of Mrs. Kim was falling lower and lower as Jae minced a clove of garlic on the chopping board.

"Yes, because in her mind, my family has little to lose." The bits of garlic joined the vegetables in the pot. "She's one of the few family members that knows I like men. If someone in the family had to die there, it would have been better if it were me and not Hyun-Shik."

CHAPTER THREE

I'D NEVER been smooth with men. This wasn't any exception. I struggled with the possibilities of what to say. Eventually, my brain kicked out something brilliant.

"Wow. Um, okay." Not my best, but after the closed-mouth atmosphere in the household, I was struck speechless.

"Are you going to put that in your report?" Jae stopped fiddling with the soup and turned to face me. There was more than suspicion there. With his chin tilted up, there was a definite challenge in his stance. I might have outweighed him by forty pounds, but he wasn't going to go down without some kind of fight.

I was left to wonder: who was he fighting?

"No," I replied. "How long has your aunt known?"

The tautness was back around his eyes. Steam rose from the soup pot, a light, fragrant mist that made my stomach rumble. It'd been a long time since I'd had that piece of Claudia's pie, and my body was letting me know it. While the soup smelled good, I wasn't certain I wanted to eat anything in that house. The Kim family seemed like the type that regularly poisoned one another just for kicks.

"I don't know," Jae said, frowning slightly. "She blames me for what happened to Hyun-Shik."

"Why?" I stole a bit of a chopped vegetable and was about to put it in my mouth when Jae's long fingers closed over my wrist. "What? You can't eat this raw?"

"It's bitter melon. You won't like it." He went into the fridge and came out with something that looked halfway familiar. "Here, leftover bao. There's char siu inside."

"The red pork stuff? Yeah, I like that. I thought it was Chinese."

"It is. We also eat hamburgers and spaghetti."

"Cute. I was joking." I smiled as I bit into the cold, white-bread dumpling. Cold food and I have always had a loving relationship. "So, before you distracted me with food, why does your aunt blame you for Hyun-Shik's death?"

"She thinks I've been a bad influence on him." More guilt surfaced as he struggled again with the changing of tense. "Hyun-Shik made up his own mind on what he wanted to do or not do. He didn't need me to influence him to do anything."

I let that sink in. My picture of Hyun-Shik wasn't a clear one, far from it. On one hand, he'd taken a handful of pills and died in a gay escort club, hardly the picture of self-esteem. Jae-Min saw him differently, and it was at odds with the personality I'd formed in my head. Sure, people often didn't show their true selves to people around them, but the Kims were an opaque mess. I didn't know which Hyun-Shik to buy as the real one.

But I did know what I could ask Jae to help me with. Then again, I was going to have to trust he'd tell me the truth on that too. He was hard to read, other than flashes of anger under the surface. Pulling out the copy of the suicide note, I placed it on the counter for Jae to look at.

"Have you seen this yet?" I wanted to see Jae's gut reaction to his cousin's note. Surprise is usually an investigator's best weapon when asking questions. "Can you tell me what this says?"

His fingers trembled when he touched the paper. A softness warmed his mouth, giving me wicked thoughts I didn't need at the moment. "No, I haven't seen it. Is this…?"

Jae left the question unfinished. Another secret lurked around us. Now I was certain there was something more than a light acquaintance between the two. He was troubled, stricken at the sight of his cousin's handwriting on a copied piece of paper.

"Can you tell me what this says?" I asked again, hoping to jar him from his distress. "I have a translation in the file, but I don't know Korean and I wanted someone who knew Hyun-Shik to tell me what they thought."

"I guessed that. The not reading Korean part." Tracing the symbols with his fingers, Jae pursed his mouth, a look of confusion briefly flitting over his face. "This doesn't make sense."

"Suicide rarely makes sense." I'd heard that in the past. A couple of years ago, I'd found out how true that saying was. "Believe me; it always leaves more questions than answers."

Kim Jae-Min was more perceptive than I gave him credit for. His tawny gaze raked over me, a silent question in his eyes, but he left the matter alone and picked up the piece of paper to hold it in his hands. "I meant the note. It doesn't make sense."

"The report said it translated as he was sorry for doing this... the suicide." I came closer, looking over his shoulder. It wasn't an excuse to press against him. Actually, I wasn't even sure why I drew near since I wouldn't be able to read what he was pointing out to me. It seemed rude to suddenly jerk back, and the scent of him filled me, that tangy masculine smell sweetening the strain of the conversation.

"Hyun-Shik wrote, 'Mian, naneun igorseul haeya haeyo'." Jae looked up from the note. I turned, giving him some room. His shoulder brushed my arm, and he left it there, the barest of touches between us. He moved with an unconscious sensuality. Either that or it was so practiced that he didn't think about it anymore. "It would make more sense if the note said, 'Irokke hal su pakke obsor yukamida'."

"And the difference is?" I was going to have to learn Korean before the end of this case. The subtleties in the culture and language were going to kill me.

"It kind of means the same thing, but what he wrote has to do with an obligation. Not that he regretted causing pain to others." Jae struggled to find the right words to express his thoughts. "The other one is closer to, 'I regret I have to do this'. Hyung wrote, 'Sorry, I'm obliged to do this'."

"Maybe he was thinking of the family's honor?" I dismissed that as soon as I said it, and not just because Jae-Min rolled his eyes at me.

"We're Korean. We just avoid doing things to embarrass ourselves. We don't slice ourselves open like gutted fish because we've dishonored our family."

"Hey, I was thinking out loud," I protested. Jae's reproachful look was nearly as searing as Claudia's. "And I rethought it. He wouldn't have killed himself in a... um."

"You can say sex club." Jae went back to stirring the soup, checking the firmness of the vegetables, taking his warmth with him. "I know what Dorthi Ki Seu is."

"Okay," I replied. "So what was he obligated to do? And why did he kill himself at the club?"

"Isn't that what Uncle is paying you for? To find those things out?" There were sounds coming from the living area, a loud chatter of women's voices, and he glanced at the door as if expecting Grace to come flying back into the kitchen.

"The truth is, I'm being paid to sniff around a little bit and then go away." Diplomacy was never my specialty. I was more of a "club people over the head to get information" and apparently "running away from shotgun-toting elderly lesbians" kind of guy, but I wasn't going to share that with Jae-Min. Our relationship hadn't progressed to a point where humiliation was served up with a cup of tea and a smile. "But I've never liked following orders."

"Someone ordered you to walk away from hyung's death?" His hands stilled, holding a handful of mushrooms over the broth.

"No, not walk away. It's just assumed that Hyun-Shik killed himself, so there wouldn't be much to investigate." The soup now had mushrooms in it, the curled ears bobbing in the hot liquid.

"Is that what you think? That Hyun-Shik killed himself?" Jae's teeth returned to their nibbling, marking his lower lip. If he kept it up, he'd draw blood in a few minutes. "It looks like he did, but I knew him. Not like this. He wouldn't have done this to his family."

"People keep saying that. Your uncle included." Resting an elbow on the counter, I picked up one of the mushrooms he'd left on the chopping board, sniffing at its aromatic meatiness. "I guess the question really is, how are you going to feel if I find out he did kill himself? What then?"

My phone rang before he answered me, and I debated letting it go, but Jae-Min returned to his soup-making, leaving me with his back to talk to. Cursing under my breath, I checked the number and cursed again, louder and with more fire than the first spate. Jae spared me a flick of his attention, then ignored me as I answered it.

"Yes, Claudia?" I took a look at the clock on the wall, frowning at the time. "What are you still doing over there? I thought you were going home."

"I was planning on it, but those people who hired you are here. You know, that man with the wife." Claudia was good about keeping secrets, so I guessed that there was someone in the office with her. "They'd like to talk to you."

"They?"

"Yep, both of them. The husband and the wife." She paused, and I heard a murmur outside of my hearing range, then her speaking to someone else. "You go on down the street and get me something cold to drink. Here, get yourself something."

"What the hell?" There was silence, and then I winced. "Sorry. They're both there?"

"It's okay. I understand that it's probably been a long day for you, what with waking up so late and then driving down to Orange County." Her voice was light, but Claudia's sugar was laced with sarcasm. "And yes, both of them. They're outside getting some air. I wasn't sure if I should feel insulted or just glad they weren't in the office."

This coming from a woman I pay to watch television for most of the day, I thought. Not being stupid, I kept my mouth shut until the urge to speak those idiotic words passed. When my mind finally saw some sense, and I could trust my tongue, I said, "I'm about forty-five minutes out, if the traffic gods love me. Are they willing to wait?"

"I think so," she responded smoothly, as if all was forgiven between us. "Both of them came in here as sweet as honey, asking if they can see you. And that's not the type of woman you'd expect to be doing those things. Well, maybe doing, but not wearing that outfit."

I suppressed the laughter choking my chest. "You looked?"

"Of course I looked!" Claudia snorted. "I'm human. I get curious. And that's some sickness going on in that marriage."

"I could give you the 'everyone loves differently' speech you gave me," I reminded her.

"Yes, I know," she replied. "Are you coming back here, or should I send them off?"

"No, I'll be out there in a bit. Just give me some time. Ask them to wait. Thanks, Claudia." I hung up the phone and rested it against my forehead. My life was getting stranger by the day, too odd for even me to imagine. The Brinkerhoffs would have to be dealt with, and I wasn't even sure where to begin.

"Is Claudia your girlfriend?" Jae turned the flame off, covering the pot with a glass lid. It steamed up almost immediately.

"No, she's my office manager." I smiled at the idea of dating Claudia. Her being a woman aside, she was a hard taskmaster, and I imagined my life would be even more strictly run than what she dictated now. "She keeps my life in order."

"So she's your wife." He grinned. His smile burned away any sadness left lingering in his face. Tucking a thick piece of hair behind his ear, he laughed when I grimaced.

"Not a wife, but she bosses me around like one." I should have told him I was gay. Opening up would go a long way in cementing a camaraderie that I probably would need if I was going to go any further in Hyun-Shik's death. My throat closed up around the words. It was like standing in front of my father again, unwilling to crack open and be vulnerable. There was nothing to lose, except perhaps the job. Suddenly, I wasn't certain the Kims would appreciate a gay man looking into the death of their son. "You have my card, right?"

"Yeah." Patting his front pocket, the smile dimmed just a bit.

"Call me, please," I asked softly. The edge of my card was peeking out of the pocket, his thumb pressing down against the corner. "If you have anything to add or if you want to talk about your cousin."

"Sure." We both instinctively stiffened when the taps of high heels in the hallway alerted us to Grace's approach. "You'd best head out before Almira Gulch catches you here."

It wasn't until I was halfway to my office that I realized I'd laughed more in that short time in the kitchen than I had for the last two years. My ribs ached a bit, and I rubbed at the scar stretching over my abdomen. It hurt, as did the one on my leg, but that was from running away from Mrs. Brinkerhoff. The pain stabbed into my gut. A treacherous twist echoed in my chest as I thought of Rick for a fleeting moment. With any luck, I wouldn't hear from Jae-Min Kim again, and I'd be better off for it.

THERE was a section of a redwood tree standing on the front porch to my office. It wasn't a real tree, just one of Claudia's many offspring. In all of the time that I'd known Claudia and her brood, there was never a mention of Mr. Claudia, and I'd never worked up the guts to ask. For all I knew, he was alive and well, chained someplace in her house with a never-ending honey-do list, a fate worse than death in my book.

As I mounted the steps, I noticed the man on the porch was, at most, in his late teens, and if possible, even larger than my mind could comprehend. I was tall, but he stood nearly a foot taller than me and a solid six inches or so wider across the shoulders. He saw me look at him, and he straightened, distancing his head from mine even more.

"Hey, Mr. McGinnis." I tried not to flinch, hearing myself age about twenty years as he spoke.

"Hey." I nodded my chin at him. It might not have earned me cool points, but maybe I could gain back a decade or so of my youth. "Which one are you?"

"Mo. Martin's my dad." Dangling a set of keys from his fingers, he gave me a sly smile. "He said if I picked Nana up this afternoon, I could have the car tonight to go out with."

"Excellent deal." I saw movement in the office, shadows moving behind the black-screen security door. "Guess I better get in there before she comes out here and gets me."

"Yeah, you don't want that," he rumbled. "Nana told me to wait out here on account that you all had business. That okay?"

"Oh yeah, it's all good." Nodding again, I braced myself for the Brinkerhoffs. "I'll send her out. Sorry you had to wait."

"No problem." His grin was wide, creasing his strong face nearly in half. "I got out of mowing the lawn. Sissy had to do it instead."

There wasn't a gender line dividing tasks in the Clan of Claudia, and other than not being massive enough to form a sea wall to hold back a tsunami, the girls in the family were expected to do the same chores as the boys and vice versa. Self-sufficiency was a stern requirement in that genetic pool. Made me wonder what they did to the ones who failed to live up to their matriarch's expectations.

Dressed, Mrs. Brinkerhoff looked much more of the traditional grandmother I'd had in mind when I set out to stalk her the night before. There was not a shred of black studded leather in sight, her lush body covered by a floral-print dress. She sat primly in one of the comfortable wing chairs I'd reupholstered in a red faux suede, her trim legs crossed at the ankles and her dainty feet encased in a pair of sensible black pumps. If it wasn't for the knife-sharp glare she gave me when I came through the door, I'd have expected her to dab her index finger with grandma spit and wipe a spot clean off my face.

I wasn't planning on getting within less than five feet of her.

It went smoothly. Her husband spoke for the most part while Claudia stood behind me, providing me with at least visual backup. I wasn't above being thankful for it. I'd already learned that I'm not invincible to bullets, and Mrs. Brinkerhoff's purse was certainly large enough to hold a sawed-off shotgun. If things went against it, I planned on grabbing Mr. Brinkerhoff and using him as a shield while Claudia escaped out the front door.

The door had barely closed behind them when Claudia breathed a sigh of relief, fanning herself with a stack of papers. Her grandson's bulk cast a long shadow across the screen door, and she waved at him, telling him to go warm up the car and she'd follow along in a moment.

"Thanks, honey." I gave her a kiss on the cheek, pulling back before she smacked me again. "You're a sweetheart for staying, even though I'm sure I could have taken them."

"I just wanted to see if they were going to give you crap about the bill." Grabbing her purse, she hunted around in its depths until she came out with a pair of oversized sunglasses. Putting them on, she patted at her hair and headed to the door. "I charged them for repairing your car window and a little extra for replacing the clothes that you tore on that fence."

"I didn't tear...." I stopped, very familiar with Claudia's creative billing techniques. "Got it. Have a good night."

"You too." She stepped onto the porch, stopping to give me one last critical look. "You have a good weekend. Be sure to get some food in you."

"Look at me. Do I look like I'm starving?" I patted my stomach, straining to create a pot belly. "Promise. I'll eat."

Letting the door slam behind her, Claudia gave me a parting shot. "And something other than red meat. I swear, Cole, I'm going to come in one day and you'll have turned into a cow."

I'D PLANNED on kicking around the house until mid-evening, then driving down to the club where Hyun-Shik had died. Then the phone rang, and I found myself being talked into having a quick beer with an ex-cop I'd worked with. I'd missed getting the shit beaten out of me that morning, so I thought I owed Bobby at least a crack at my brain. Hell, I couldn't even begin to tally the debts I owed to Bobby. Stopping off to spend some time with him seemed like a very small price to pay.

Robert Dawson was a burly, twenty-five-year veteran of the Los Angeles Police Department. He was winding down his career while I was coming up. We worked together on some cases, and then after I got shot, he'd come by every once in a while to check up on me. There was a solid friendship between us, something I was grateful for as I fought through the pain. Bobby was there with bad jokes and smuggled-in hamburgers. I decided, after two weeks of broth and Jell-O, that a true friend was worth his weight in rare, greasy food.

There were always rumors going on around the departments, tidbits of gossip that no one really paid attention to. I had my own problems to deal with. I never hid my sexuality. If someone asked if I had a girlfriend, I'd respond no, because my boyfriend would be pissed off. Eventually, people realized I wasn't joking.

Bobby took a different route. He lay low, keeping any relationship he had hidden, even from the closest of his friends. My getting shot affected him probably as much as it did me, and he took it upon himself to change things. Putting in for retirement, he opened the door of the closet he'd hidden in for decades and stepped out, never looking back. He lost a lot of friends after that, and to this day, he says he has no regrets, other than he should have done it sooner.

One afternoon as he sat next to my hospital bed, a grey-flecked, muscular older man whose face was creased from squinting against the sun and laughing, he asked me if I forgave him for not being open sooner.

I told him there was nothing to forgive. We both knew there wasn't a lot of room for a rainbow behind the blue line. He'd done what he felt he should do, and I'd made my choices. At that moment, I wasn't so sure my decision had been the right one. Bobby said, after everything that happened, he could say the same thing about himself.

"You are a sight for sore eyes, boy." Bobby stretched his arms over his head, resting his boots on the edge of the low table between our seats. "About time you decided to spend some time relaxing."

"You saw me a couple of days ago. Shit, we're not married or anything." I sniffed at the nonalcoholic beer the server brought me. It wouldn't have been my first choice, but I wanted my head clear when I drove down to Dorthi Ki Seu. "What's up?"

We'd fallen into a routine of sorts, boxing on some days and sharing a round of beers at a bar near my house on others. Sometimes we were joined by other mutual friends, but today it was just me and Bobby taking up residence in one of the corners.

"I expected to at least see you this morning in the ring," Bobby said, watching a much younger man asking the bartender to refill his drink. "Then I noticed you limping and figured you might have caught some tail last night and overdid it."

"Oh, I caught tail. I just had to throw it back," I joked. I spent a few minutes telling Bobby the story of Mrs. Brinkerhoff and her shotgun, not skipping over the gory details of me running through the lawn with my tail tucked between my legs.

His booming laugh echoed against the walls and made me smile. On the job, he'd been so tightly controlled, I often wondered if he even had a heartbeat. Breaking years of silence was good for Bobby, and I enjoyed being around to see him laugh as hard as he did. It was like he was making up for lost time.

"God, stop talking, kid." He rubbed at his face with a napkin, wiping his mouth and mustache. "You're going to make me pee my pants."

"That's what happens when you get old." I nodded sagely. "Next we'll be fitting you for a diaper and feeding you baby food."

"Keep it up and I'll make sure you don't have enough teeth left in your mouth that the boys will be lining up for blocks to date you." I earned the stinging punch on my arm, and I was sure it was going to bruise beautifully come morning. Lifting his empty mug for the server to see, he ordered himself another beer. "So what are you working on now?"

"Suicide case," I said, setting my bottle down and following Bobby's gaze. The young man turned, meeting Bobby's eyes and smiling. "Don't you have enough phone numbers by now?"

"One can never have too many phone numbers," he retorted. Bobby became all business, his face turning solemn. "Tell me about your case."

"Young Korean man killed himself at a sex club called Dorthi Ki Seu. Mike asked me to look into it for the family." It felt good to talk about the Kims and what happened. I missed having a partner to bounce ideas off of, and Bobby was the closest thing to a partner I had these days. He bent forward, listening intently and letting me ramble until I eventually got to Jae-Min.

"You should see him, damned pretty. Not feminine, just... I don't know, sexy. There's this thing about him. It's like he's just a bit feral." Exhaling, I ran my finger along the rim of the bottle, listening to the sing of my wet skin on the glass. "And I swear to God, I could hear him purring underneath his words. Smelled good too. You know how I am about guys and how they smell."

"Yeah, I know." Bobby looked bemused, and I quirked an eyebrow at him.

"What?"

"It's good to hear you talk about a guy. Nice to see you getting back out there."

"No... no." If I'd shaken my head more, it would have fallen off. "I'm not interested. Hell, I don't even plan on seeing him again for the rest of my life."

"Cole, he's good-looking and made you laugh. What more do you want? You don't have to marry the guy. Just go grab a burger or something and see where it goes." The bar's noise suddenly dropped, and Bobby leaned in closer, keeping his voice low. "It's been a couple of years now. Almost three, yeah? Isn't it time you started to look at guys, at least?"

"I look at them all the time." Protesting didn't seem to help my cause. He just sat back and nodded at me like I was some wayward child he needed to save. "Hell, didn't I just check out that kid at the bar?"

"You looked at him like you were trying to decide if he was going to hold the place up." A sip of beer left foam on Bobby's mustache, and he licked it off with a swipe of his tongue. "Cole, you were never apologetic about who you were, and then after that thing with Rick, you shut down."

"I'm not ready. It's too soon." It was all I could give him. Not much, really, but it was all I had. Jae-Min had been pretty to look at and dangerous because he made me want. He kindled a thirst in me that I'd thought had died along with my lover, and I wasn't sure I was ready to have that kind of desire back in my life. "Bobby, he was good-looking and exotic, but that's the end of it. Something to share with a friend over a beer. Just a story."

"All I'm saying is, you should start doing something with yourself other than digging into other people's problems." He drained the rest of his beer, setting the mug down a little harder than he needed to. "Or pretty soon, all you've got left is those stories to tell and an empty house. Don't make the same mistakes that I did. Live a little bit, kid, before there isn't any more life left in you."

CHAPTER FOUR

DORTHI KI SEU wasn't like any other gay bar I knew. The first time I'd been there, I'd been amazed at how clean and, for lack of a better word, civil everything was. I'd been a part of a task force, a junior member but still apparently high enough up the food chain to warrant a field trip. It had been a good experience, and in more ways than one.

Getting in was easy. There wasn't a cover charge, although I got a thorough looking-at by the young man at the door. Stepping inside, I could see why I'd gotten such close scrutiny. If my light brown hair and height didn't stand out, then the lack of business attire did me in. Dressed down at Dorthi Ki Seu meant taking off your suit jacket and hanging it from the back of the chair.

The interior décor leaned heavily toward what I imagined a Victorian gentleman's club looked like, expensive wall paneling and small clusters of leather chairs. There was a definite Asian flavor to the furnishings, discreet, tasteful, and at odds with other gay clubs I'd been to. I could barely hear the murmur of conversations around me, and the lighting was dimmed down to a nearly intimate level.

Waiters attended to individual parties, sometimes a single man or, at other tables, a pair. The exclusively male crowd ignored me, a politeness I guessed was more cultural than lack of interest. I was lucky I'd found a table, even one as far from the stage as possible. The place was packed, and it showed no signs of letting up.

I was quickly measured up by the white-shirted waiter who'd come to see what I wanted to drink. He was young, fresh-faced, and good-looking enough to make a man look twice. After staring at him for a moment, I realized I was comparing him to another Korean man I'd just met.

Tapping at the order pad with his pencil, he tilted his head to look at me. "Something from the bar, hyung?"

The *hyung* word confused me. To my untrained ears, it was the same word that Jae-Min used for Hyun-Shik.

"I'd love a whiskey." Whiskey not only sounded good, but there were some bottles I'd seen at the bar that I lusted for and sticking to the no-alcohol rule I'd set up a few hours ago nixed sampling. "Just a diet Coke, please."

"Is diet Pepsi okay?" His smile was warm, an underlying promise of sex in his voice. "I can add lime if you want."

"Thanks." I watched his ass move as he walked away. Whoever did the hiring knew what they were doing.

The room smelled of cigarettes and expensive booze. I knew there were private karaoke rooms off the main room, usually rented by drunken, middle-aged Korean men for God knows what, but apparently singing was involved. Even more private rooms were upstairs, and by all accounts, these were for exclusive members of the club. Just small getaways where they could relax, or so we'd been told.

It was only considerate that these rooms had beds or pillow pits in them.

When I was a junior detective, Dorthi Ki Seu had become a place of interest for a multi-city Vice shakedown. There were other spots that were more lucrative, but Dorthi Ki Seu was a holy grail for one of the senior guys I worked with. That was how I met Scarlet.

The detective eventually arrested Scarlet and a few of the other main floor entertainers, cross-dressing gay men who worked the stage of the club either singing or dancing. She'd been attractive then, and I didn't expect her to have changed. When I placed the cuffs on her, I apologized when I cinched a wrist too tightly. I loosened it and asked if she preferred to be addressed as a woman or a man. Her smile was brilliant, making her already gorgeous Filipino face heartbreakingly beautiful.

Scarlet spent less than an hour in the holding cell after her phone call. I never knew who she called, but within twenty-four hours of her arrest, all charges were dropped against the Dorthi Ki Seu staff, and the task force's head detective was reassigned. Last I heard, he was manning an information substation on the pier.

It'd been made clear to us that Scarlet had very powerful friends, friends who would move heaven and earth for her. Or at the very least, make her problems disappear. But I liked her. She was sweet and funny, not to mention in possession of a wicked sense of humor. And I admired the comfort she had in her own skin. I envied that. I've still not found it.

I'd given her my card when she was released, asking her to call if she needed anything. She called casually, more to keep in touch and maybe pump me for information about what was going on in the world of vice and cops. Scarlet was always good for a laugh. I'd just not felt like laughing for a while.

The soft music playing over the club's speakers quieted, and the lights went up on the stage. It was nearly ten o'clock, time for Scarlet's first show. My heart stopped for a brief second as a smoky tune rolled out of the piano on stage, and she stepped out from behind the stage curtains.

She was as seductively gorgeous as I remembered her.

I'd worked Vice long enough to spot a ladyboy, but Scarlet was a different level altogether. As she approached the box-style mic set at the corner of the stage, a spotlight followed her lithe body, and she smiled at the crowd. Even knowing how old she was, Scarlet was flawless, showing miles of café au lait skin, and her luminous black eyes were expertly rimmed with a dark kohl to emphasize their almond shape.

Red sequins flashed under the lights, her slinky gown slit up past mid-thigh and down to her belly button. Her glossy black hair was up, very Audrey Hepburn, and studded with large diamonds near her right ear. She looked expensive, like the kind of woman none of us could afford. I certainly couldn't, even if I leaned that way.

"*You look at me and smile.*" Sex oozed from Scarlet's throat.

There was no other way to put it. She might be a man under the dress, but she knew how to cast a pure womanly spell. Playing with the Etta James tune, she worked the stage, leaning over to croon at a pack of suited men sitting at the edge of the lights. They loved it, grinning back like schoolboys who'd earned a gold star from their teacher.

"Miss Scarlet got your message. She said to come to the back when she's done." A large hand clamped down on my shoulder, and I found myself looking up at a Korean version of one of Claudia's mountainous children. If ever I spoke to my father again, I was going to have a talk with him about the lack of enormous in our gene pool.

Not wanting to startle him into stampeding, I replied, "Thanks."

There were a few more songs, and I listened with half an ear, more interested in secretly watching the men who approached a wide doorway cordoned off with a thick velvet rope and protected by the much larger older-brother-in-arms of the man who gave me Scarlet's message.

An older Korean man, conservatively dressed and immaculately groomed, approached the man, standing by the rope. He was let in with a respectful nod, and continued through the door and up the stairs. Another followed a few minutes later, and then a pair of men, speaking to each other as if they were headed to have dinner.

A round of applause jerked me back, pulling my attention to the stage, and I clapped loudly. Scarlet took a bow, then another, sweeping her arm back to include the piano player in her due. The mountain stood nearby, watching me stand up and finish my soda.

"Just go through the door?" I rattled the ice in my glass and left a five on the table for my server.

"I'll take you." He didn't grab my elbow, but his massive paw brushed at the back of my arm as if he was used to steering people around.

I left the sedate nightclub atmosphere as a troupe of dancers took the stage, the slender men dressed in brightly colored robes that slightly resembled kimono, but not quite. One smiled at me, bowing his head slightly so as not to dislodge the elaborate wig he wore.

Like most entertainment clubs, backstage was chaos. Clothes and lights were fighting for space with a sea of men in various stages of naked. Several were sitting in front of long mirrors, trying to apply makeup, while others jostled and elbowed to get into costume. A hallway continued past the main room, and I hugged the wall when an older man wearing a tight, black-fringed dress sashayed out of a dressing room. An envious chatter from the others followed him as he headed out to perform.

The mound of muscle took me to a room at the end of the hall. A sparkling gold star was stuck to the door, a spatter of Korean boldly painted beneath it. I couldn't read it, but I guessed it was Scarlet's name. I knocked and turned the knob when I heard Scarlet give me the go-ahead.

Her dressing room was an oasis of fabrics and color. Overwhelmed by the glut of sequins, feathers, and frills, I almost missed seeing Scarlet wiping pancake makeup off her face, the bright lights of her vanity mirror turning her skin a white-gold.

"Hey, Scarlet." Even close up, she was flawless. I knew a lot of women who wanted to look as good as Scarlet did right now. Sadly for them, they couldn't even come close. "I see you're still gorgeous."

"Honey, you are sweet. I haven't seen you in a while." She stood, tightening the sash of an orange satin robe around her narrow waist. Leaning over, she brushed a kiss over my cheek, patting at my chest as she sat back down. The sultry torch singer, for the most part, was gone. The only trace of her remaining was the diamonded sweep of black hair arranged on Scarlet's head. "How have you been?"

"Nothing worth mentioning." I settled into a chair, watching as Scarlet made short work of her face, layering a more sedate foundation with a flick of delicate fingers.

"You've come for something, no?" Dark eyes met mine in the mirror. "I saw the card you gave the doorman. You're a private investigator now, right? Did you get tired of being a cop?"

"Cops got tired of me being a cop," I said. It was the only concession I was going to give the past. I had other things I needed to deal with. "I'm here about Hyun-Shik Kim's suicide. I thought maybe you'd be able to talk to me about him."

"Hyun-Shik?" Her fingers stilled, and the ghost of her Adam's apple bobbed in her throat. "Oh, you don't want to sniff around the Kims, honey. Big teeth lawyer."

"Papa Kim is the one who hired me. My brother, Mike, does some work for him."

"Mikio McGinnis is your brother? Ah, I should have known." She turned, her eyes wide with surprise. "You're prettier than he is. He must be jealous."

"You know my brother?"

"He does some work for my lover, sometimes. Nice man. I've met him a few times. Hyung hires his men to take care of driving me if someone else can't." She pushed her vanity bench back, stepping behind a dressing screen. The robe was flung up over the edge, a splash of tangerine against the brown wood. "Do you have a Japanese name too? Or just Mikio?"

"It's Kenjiro, but I never use it," I called out over the screen. "Mike's first name is Colin. He hates it."

"Colin's a nice name." She stepped back out, dressed in a pair of black pedal pushers and a white man's shirt. Leaving the tails out, she fluffed at the back, satisfied with how the fabric fell over her trim backside, and sat back down at the vanity to undo her hair.

"I used to call him Colleen." The memory was a good one. Nothing infuriated my brother like minimizing his masculinity. "Probably why he hates it."

"But you're here for Hyun-Shik, not small talk, yes?" Scarlet plucked the diamond hair picks from her hair, setting them into a velvet case. "I don't really know what goes on upstairs, baby. Not really."

"Scarlet, I know how these places work. I'm sure you know something, maybe?" She gave me a glance in the mirror, briefly meeting my eyes before she plucked at the bobby pins along her sweep. I pressed closer, leaning in until we were almost touching. "I'm just looking for some information. Something about Hyun-Shik's death doesn't work for me, and I want to know why."

"Boys like you are trouble, dongsaeng," she said. "You poke at things you should leave alone. What happens when it comes back to you?"

"Is there something I should be worried about?" I tried for a reassuring smile but wasn't so sure I pulled it off. "Hyun-Shik killed himself, or someone helped him do it. Either way, I was hired to see what I could find. What can you tell me? Anything?"

Scarlet pulled her hair free, letting it fall in a black wave down her back. Working her fingers around her temples, she undid the last of the bindings and picked up a hairbrush, separating out hanks of hair to finish untangling the strands. For a minute, I thought she wasn't going to say anything to me. Then, with a sigh, she began to talk.

"Hyun-Shik started coming here when he was in college. His father bought him his membership," she said, waving the brush at my reflection, warning me to shush.

"Kim bought his son the membership? The same man that insists his son wasn't gay?"

"Anything I say to you here isn't going to go anywhere, yes? You keep it between us. I like you, honey, but I'm not going to start trouble for the Kim family. Hyung depends on the father to do business for him." Waving her finger under my nose, she nearly hit me with the end of the brush.

"Not a word to anyone," I replied, running the tip of my finger over my mouth in a show of silence.

"Mr. Kim knew his son was iban. It wasn't a surprise to him. Maybe the mother didn't know, but the father did." Emotions flitted in her moist, dark eyes. Whatever Scarlet was thinking, it wasn't just about Hyun-Shik. "A lot of fathers try to help their sons in some way. Mr. Kim probably thought that a membership for Hyun-Shik would be a good idea."

"Membership gets you what upstairs?"

"Dorthi Ki Seu membership only gets you upstairs. You have to pay for everything else." She kept her attention on her hair, brushing at tangles. "You can get a lot of things upstairs: drinks, drugs, and boys. Most men go up there for the boys, but they do other things too."

"Hyun-Shik's father was okay with him spending money on that?"

"Maybe he thought if Hyun-Shik had a place to… dabble." She paused, thinking of how to phrase something. "Dabble is a good word. If he dabbled upstairs, he wouldn't be out cruising like some of the others his age. No one sees what happens upstairs. No one comments. Everyone's reputation is safe, and everyone is happy."

"Hyun-Shik couldn't have been too happy," I commented. "He killed himself upstairs."

"Most men come here because they're sad inside, and for a little while, they can pretend that loving men is normal. In here, it is normal." The brush stilled, caught in the length of her hair. "I am so lucky, honey. I have a man who loves me, but he cannot love me in the sunlight. Not if others are around. Most of the men here don't have that kind of freedom. They cannot even love in the darkness. Hyun-Shik was one of those men."

"But in here, he was normal," I murmured. The walls held too many secrets, hidden things that crackled over my skin. To me it was simple. I was going to be who I needed to be to survive. Not being gay wasn't an option. It wasn't easy, but it was better than living a lie.

"Why get married if you're—" I was cut off by Scarlet's trilling laugh.

"Ah, so easy for you, honey. Everything is black and white." She worked at the hair at her neck. "Asian men have to get married. It's what they do. You are born, go to school, then you get married. Next, you have children, then take care of your parents while you bully your children through school. After you are done with that, it's your time to be taken care of. Everything is a cycle."

"So he got married and kept coming back to get himself off? Maybe just enough to blow some steam?"

"It's common. Usually after the first child, maybe the second. It depends on the man." Her shrug was a practiced, elegant lift. "Some men never come back. Duty to the family comes first for most Asian men, and shame can make a man go against what he wants."

"Did he have a regular? Did Hyun-Shik see someone here all the time?"

"He came to visit Jin-Sang Yi." She spelled it for me as I took out my notebook. "Hyun-Shik didn't visit as much after he got married, but when he did, he usually had Jin-Sang sent to him."

"Any of the other boys get jealous about that?"

"No, it's very... practical upstairs." Scarlet moved on to another section. "Well, sometimes. I think Jin-Sang would be upset if Hyun-Shik didn't send for him, but that's probably because of the money. I can't say it was for love. Upstairs boys make a lot of money, baby."

"How much is a lot of money?"

"The popular ones can make about five thousand a night, depending on what they're being paid for."

"Five grand?" I was in the wrong business. Catching a glimpse of my face in the vanity, I didn't think I could pull in that kind of cash. "Jin-Sang is one of the popular ones?"

"Popular enough, I think." She shrugged. "Sometimes a new boy comes, and one of the favorites goes away. It's how these things are. Like I said, dongsaeng, I don't pay much attention to what goes on up there. I'm an entertainer. I don't do those things."

"Did he kill himself before or after he saw Jin-Sang? Do you know?"

"Had to be after. I think the upstairs manager refused the payment in respect to Mr. Kim," Scarlet murmured. "It would have been bad to take money for Hyun-Shik's entertainment."

"So Hyun-Shik went upstairs, had a little fun, then killed himself?" I sat back in my chair. Stranger things had been known to happen. Some suicide victims killed themselves after a good meal while others were too distraught to think beyond doing the act. People were crazy things, but paying for sex and then taking a handful of pills seemed strange. "You mentioned drugs upstairs. Is that where Hyun-Shik got the pills?"

"Oh no, honey." She shook her hair out, setting the brush aside. "Upstairs doesn't do pills. Mostly jutes or sometimes nga nga. Pills take too long, and they're not good with whiskey. That would be too many problems."

"He had to have brought them with him, then." Things were getting complicated. "The biggest question that I can't seem to answer is, why? And why here?"

"That I don't know, honey," Scarlet said with a shrug. "His note said what? He was ashamed? Of loving men? Then why kill himself here? Pfah, your questions make things worse."

"That's why I'm asking." Her cell phone rang, a snippet of a song I didn't recognize, vibrating the tiny silver device across the vanity table. "You want some privacy?"

"No, stay there," she ordered, poking at my chest with a sharp fingernail. Answering, she sighed, hearing someone's voice on the other end. "Hyung! Yes, I am done. Just one show tonight."

The rest was in Korean, a bubbling flow of words that I didn't have to understand to know what was being said. Cooing was universal, and Scarlet's coquettish laughter made me smile. It'd been a long time since I'd sat and chatted someone up on the phone, not since Rick and I were first dating.

I stood, stretching my legs. The drive up and down the coast was hell on my belly, the scar tissue knitting together the nerves of my abdomen muscles. I was beginning to cramp up, and reached around to work the kink loose. Twisting around, something caught my eye, a familiar face smiling back up at me from a silver frame.

Sneaking a peek at Scarlet, I made sure she was still deep in conversation before I walked over to the tall dresser sitting in the corner of the room. Many of the photos were of Scarlet, some vacation shots with a solemn-faced, older Korean man and others with young men who were obviously entertainers. The one that caught my eye was larger than the rest and placed to the side with the smaller shots around it.

I knew the honey-brown eyes that stared up at me, and seeing his face hit me in the gut. Jae-Min was younger in the photo, a few years maybe, at the most. His hair was longer, fringed around his face, making his features nearly gamine, but the sensual pout of his mouth was the same, a hint of a smile dimpling his cheeks.

Cracking the back of the frame to see if there was a date on the back of the photo probably wouldn't be a good idea. Scarlet sounded like she was wrapping up her call, a final coo into her phone and then a throaty tenor sigh. In that small exclamation of passion, I heard the man Scarlet hid inside, so proud of the love he shared with another man.

Scarlet came up behind me, her chin resting against my upper arm to see what I was looking at. I tilted the frame so she could see the picture I was looking at. There was another whispering murmur, lighter and sweeter this time.

"Ah, my musang." She touched Jae-Min's face with the tips of her fingers. "He's Hyun-Shik's cousin. Is he on your list of people to talk to?"

"We've had our talk." I put the picture down. It was hard. For some reason, letting that piece of time go made me shake. "I saw him at the Kim house this morning."

"Aish! Hard to believe that he was there. That woman treats him so badly." Her disgust was palpable, nearly sticky with distaste. "I wouldn't have gone back there."

"Looks like you know Jae-Min well."

"Ah, our Jae." Scarlet smiled as she took the frame from me and put it back on the dresser. "He's one of my favorite people. Have you seen his photographs? I have some he took of me at home. You should see them. They are beautiful but so very raw. He's very good."

"How did you meet him? Did Hyun-Shik bring him here for an evening?" I had a tickle of jealousy in my chest. Somehow the thought of Jae-Min coming to Dorthi Ki Seu for a round of sex and games while his cousin watched disturbed me, and I couldn't figure out why.

"For an evening?" Scarlet padded away, bending over to retrieve a pair of bright red pumps from under the chair I'd been sitting in. "Hyun-Shik didn't bring Jae-Min here as a guest. He brought him here to work."

"What? Jae-Min worked here as a waiter? He didn't tell me. For how long?"

"A waiter?" She was an elegant line, graceful as she slid her foot into one shoe. "Oh no, honey. Jae-Min wasn't a waiter."

My chest constricted, and a numbness crept over my jaw. I didn't want to hear what she was saying. The rush of blood in my ears was like a tidal wave, blocking out my senses. I needed to ask Scarlet to explain, but I knew I wasn't going to like the answer. "What did he do, then?"

"Jae is much too pretty to be a waiter. No, honey, Hyun-Shik brought him to work the rooms. That's how I met my musang," she replied, checking her appearance once more in the mirror and patting at the edge of her lush mouth. "Our Jae-Min became one of our upstairs boys."

CHAPTER FIVE

"THAT son of a bitch played me! He worked down there, and he didn't say jack shit to me about it."

My living room was large, nearly half of the building, but it was still too small to work off a good rage. I kept bumping into one of the sofas and hitting my shin against the coffee table. At past midnight, it was too late to start pushing furniture around to make room for my long legs. More importantly, shoving the couch to the wall would disrupt my bleary-eyed brother's perch.

"Cole, I've had a long day, my beer is half empty, and I have no idea what the hell you're talking about." Mike yawned, more for show than anything else. He usually went to bed at two in the morning, so showing up at my house to talk about the Kim case was well within his working day. Snorting derisively at my growl, he picked at the remains of his carne asada burrito, stabbing at chunks of meat with a fork. "Mr. Kim played you?"

"No." I was disgusted, trying to sort out my confusion. The one thing I was clear on: Jae was at the center of my anger. "Not Mr. Kim. I'm talking about his nephew, Jae-Min."

"That's the guy that stayed with them for a year, right? The second or third cousin." Mike picked at his teeth with the tine of his plastic fork. "What's he got to do with Henry?"

"Henry, huh? I'm sticking with Hyun-Shik. You can call him Henry." I stopped, standing in front of my brother. "Yeah, let me tell you some things about Mr. Kim's little boy."

I spent a few minutes outlining the deceased's connection to the club he'd died at, including his pimping his younger cousin out to the management. Mike absorbed the information without commenting, letting me talk myself out.

"So, you're pissed off because Mr. Kim's son is gay?" Mike asked finally. "Or because he set his cousin up as a whore?"

"No," I said, plopping down on the couch next to my brother, nudging his leg with my bare foot. "Okay, kind of. Why didn't the Kims just tell you some of this up front? They probably didn't know about Jae-Min, but the rest of it. His father knew some of it."

"Because for a traditional Korean family, being gay is very shameful," he replied. "Just be discreet."

"Who am I going to tell?" I exhaled hard, letting my temper ride over me. "Shit, the widow. I've got to talk to her. Does she know?"

"Probably not before, but considering where he was found, she does now."

I took out another copy of the suicide note from my stack of case papers, staring at the scribbles as if I could somehow glean what had been going on in Hyun-Shik's mind when he'd killed himself. "Scarlet said that they don't distribute pills there. What was on the autopsy report? Anything come back from tox?"

"Nothing yet." Mike shrugged, pushing away the paper plate that held his dinner. "They took some tissue and blood, and the body was cremated right afterwards."

"If you were running a whorehouse, wouldn't you keep track of all of the rooms?" I cocked my head at my brother. "I mean, that's your income there. How long did it take before someone noticed that he wasn't coming out of the room? And who was with him? That guy Jin-Sang, or someone else? Do you know?"

"Nope, it didn't come up. I couldn't get a lot out of his father, but to be honest, I didn't try. His son just died." Another shrug, this one more troubled. Mike hated mysteries, where I loved to hammer at them until I found an answer. For my brother, the perfect life included no surprises. "The only thing I can do is ask his father, but I can't guarantee that I'm going to come back to you with answers. They tend to be very close-mouthed about personal things."

"So then why did Jae-Min tell me he was gay?" Grabbing a throw pillow, I shoved it behind my head, leaning back on the couch arm. "Is that a lie he's telling so people think that Hyun-Shik was there because of him? Or maybe to excuse what he did in that club?"

He smirked at me. "Maybe he likes you and wanted a date."

"I'm going to beat you until you cry," I growled under my breath. "He's the one I'm pissed off about. He stood right in front of me and didn't say a damned thing to me about Hyun-Shik. He said he knew about the club but not that he'd worked there."

"Cole, if you used to be a whore, would you tell an investigator which street corner you worked? He didn't know you knew Scarlet, so he probably figured you'd get a few short answers from the club's management and that would be the end of it." Mike raised his head, meeting my eyes. "Why are you picking so hard at this? Is there something really here to look into, or are you mad because this Kim kid couldn't take being in the closet and killed himself?"

I opened my mouth to answer, then stopped. Why was I pissed off? Hyun-Shik's death was stupid, but more stupid was the web of lies that surrounded his suicide. If Scarlet was telling me the truth, then there were a lot of people who might have wanted Hyun-Shik dead, maybe even his cousin, Jae-Min. So a stupid death, to me, was beginning to look like murder.

"Stay with me for a bit, Mike." I took a breath, spinning out my thoughts. "Hyun-Shik was a closeted gay man. He marries a woman and has a son. By his family's thinking, he's done his duty, right? So does he go back to his old ways, or is his death in Dorthi Ki Seu hiding something else?"

"Okay, suppose someone killed him," Mike said. "Who killed him? And how?"

"Several people." I looked over the remains of Mike's dinner, picking out larger pieces of meat and shoving a few in my mouth. Chewing, I refused the napkin he held out for me with a shake of my head. "This Jin-Sang guy might have found him with someone else."

"So he gave Hyun-Shik something in his alcohol?" Mike pursed his lips, thinking. "Maybe he didn't mean to kill him. Just give him something to scare him or make him sick?"

"Still would take some planning, though." I mulled it over. "Unless Jin-Sang is a regular user and had the pills there at the club."

"Jealousy? Didn't want to share his lover?" Mike tossed in. "But you're assuming that Jin-Sang and Hyun-Shik had more than a money thing going."

"Once again, we're back to what Scarlet said: the hired sex toy and Hyun-Shik Kim had an understanding."

"How credible is Scarlet?"

"Credible enough that she's the only person in this mess besides you whose word I can trust." I returned to the burrito corpse, picking at its flesh. "How fucked-up is that? The only truth I can depend on comes from a man who lives lying about what he looks like."

"What about the cousin? You said Hyun-Shik started him working there?" Mike shoved my foot off his leg. "Maybe it finally got to him and he wanted revenge."

"Maybe," I said. "It just doesn't feel right."

"No, why would he wait this long? Unless Jae-Min was being pressured into something." The overhead lights cast shadows over my brother's face, his black hair a glossy sheen beneath the glow. "There's only so much a guy would do for money."

"Wait, you said Jae-Min stayed with them only a short time." I thought back to what he'd said to me in the Kims' kitchen. "He came down here for high school. How old was he when he started working for Dorthi Ki Seu?"

"I dunno. I just found out he was a whore." Mike drained the rest of his beer.

"Don't call him that." I was surprised at how much heat was in my voice. "Just don't."

"If you're going to fall for someone after Rick, don't go for a Korean boy-whore, Cole." My brother's tone was flat, nearly as flat as his nose was going to be, once I was done with it.

"Don't start on me, Mike. Not about Rick and not about this." I warned him off. "Jae-Min's...."

"You're the one who brought up the whoring," he pointed out. "Either he's someone you're spitting on or someone you're defending. Which one is it?"

"I don't know, Mike." I finished off my beer and gathered up the mess of our dinner. After dropping the paper plates into the kitchen trash, I wandered back into the living room. My brother watched me closely as I entered, his face inscrutable. Never good at reading Mike, I slouched back into the couch's soft cushions, irritated that I couldn't guess at what was going on in my brother's mind. "What do you want from me, huh?"

"I think this Jae-Min guy is clouding your brain." He poked at my stomach, leaving behind a bruise I was probably going to find in the morning.

"So what? You think I should just fuck him and get him out of my system?"

"It's bad enough that you have sex with guys. I don't want to hear about it. I don't want to imagine you doing it." Mike made a face. "And I really don't want to get details."

It hurt. Hearing those words from Mike hurt. There was only so much support I was going to get from my brother about how I lived my life. Even if I wasn't planning on hopping into bed with Jae-Min, or anyone else for that matter, I missed being able to talk about everything with my brother. But then again, I thought, I'd never really had that level of trust with my family. If I had, it wouldn't have taken so long for me to come to grips with who I was or who I wanted.

I did what I always did, ignored it.

"Look, I've got to go home. Maddy's probably hoping I'll actually come home in the same day I left." He stood, straightening the legs of his pants. He made a futile attempt to brush the wrinkles out of his shirt, stuffing his tie into his pocket and grabbing his keys from the table.

"You're already too late for that." I walked him to the door, opening it for him to leave.

He stopped, half-turned so I could only see the darkness of his profile. "Cole...."

"It's okay, Mike." The last thing I wanted to hear was my brother sounding like my father. I needed him in my life too much. He was one tie I didn't want to sever over pride.

"No, it's not okay." We'd never spoken about things like relationships. Both of us grew up too Catholic, or maybe too Irish for that. I'd strayed a bit, searching around for where I fit in. Mike had never had that problem, and for him, his little brother's quirks were sometimes too much to deal with. "I keep telling you to get back out there, but then I shut you down when you start talking about it. I'm sorry I can't be there for you with that, Cole."

I stared at him, wondering where he was going to go with the conversation.

"You're my brother, and I love you," he said softly. "But there's a small bit of me that hates what you are. I can't get over that, but I still love you. A lot."

I wanted to tell him I loved him, but the words stuck, choking my windpipe until my chest hurt. He faded when he stepped off the side porch, plunging into the pitch dark until he reappeared in the pool of light from the streetlamp. He gave me a casual wave before getting into his car, as if that was going to make everything all right between us.

"Love you too, Mike," I whispered, too late for my brother to hear, but still, it helped wash away some of the pain. I closed the door, locking it behind me.

BY LATE afternoon, I'd done enough research on Jin-Sang Yi to make my head hurt. Claudia stopped in for an hour or so, begging boredom, but I knew her curiosity had gotten the best of her, and she listened while I spoke about what I'd found out. She'd given me some respite from my research, plopping a pastrami sandwich on sourdough onto my desk with a baleful glare. I was going to object about the lettuce on it, but her lifted eyebrow gave me pause, and I shut my mouth with a bite of the sandwich.

"You going to go see him?" Typing slowly on the keyboard, she leaned forward, staring at the screen. "What are you going to say when you get there?"

"Well, I probably won't ask if he's killed his ex-lover," I replied. "But I have two options right now: talking to Yi or to Hyun-Shik's wife."

"You've got a third one." Claudia hit print and turned her chair to wait for the paper to be spat out. "You can go back and talk to that boy you spoke to yesterday."

"Scarlet? I think I bugged her enough for a month."

"No, not that one." Rolling her eyes, she gathered up her report. "The other Kim boy. The one from the kitchen."

I'd only mentioned Jae-Min in brief passing, so now I was beginning to doubt my poker face. Playing it smooth, I asked, "Why talk to him?"

"Because he seems like the one that knows something." For an amateur, Claudia was pretty good at picking out lies. Probably because she'd raised eight sons. "I'm all for not getting into someone's business, but if this were one of my sons, I'd be banging down every door I could find to get some answers."

Claudia left a few minutes before I was ready to go, cheerfully bullying her youngest son to stop at the store before they went home. He waved at me through the open door, then followed her down the stairs, agreeing with whatever his mother said as she headed toward their car.

Los Angeles's freeways fought me all down the coast, throwing up traffic snarls indiscriminately where I didn't need them. The sun played hide-and-seek with me all the way down, peering out from between buildings to burn its light into my eyes. Rolling the window down, I let the freeway breeze hit me, its unique perfume of rubber and overcooked cement. Billboards kept me company until I turned off toward the coast, hitting the off-ramp at a respectable speed and barely making the light. The Rover's engine hiccuped a bit as I gunned past the white stop line, the yellow light ghosting over to red as I made the turn.

Jin-Sang Yi lived in one of the many cardboard-box-looking condo complexes that had popped up all over Southern California in the '90s. I had to circle the block to find off-street parking, the single guest spot taken up by a gardening truck. I ran a gauntlet of leaf blowers, nearly falling into the low-grade bushes that served as landscaping. Considering what Jin-Sang supposedly made a week, he certainly wasn't spending it on his accommodations. The fake adobe walls were painted a shit brown, a half-assed attempt to provide some sort of California style to the squat condos.

Children shouted obscenities at each other as they played around the complex's swimming pool. A few women sat nearby in the shade of an overgrown tree. No one gave me a second look, and I wasn't expecting one. Living in each other's armpits went a long way toward ignoring people as they walked through what was basically their backyard.

Somewhere inside an apartment, a small dog yapped continuously, the sound bouncing off the maze of buildings. Nearby, a man screamed in Spanish for someone to shut up. I wasn't sure if it was the dog he was talking to or someone else only he could see.

Jin-Sang lived in an upstairs apartment, located as far from the pool and where I parked as possible while still remaining in the same complex. Sweat stuck my shirt to my back, and even though night was close by, the oppressive heat of the day refused to give up its grip on the city. The whine of an air conditioner echoed from the apartment beneath Jin-Sang's, its rattle sounding its furious charge as it battled the afternoon sun.

A car parked in the space marked for Jin-Sang's apartment stopped me dead in my tracks. It was an older white Explorer, the same one I'd seen parked in front of the Kims' house. The interior of the SUV was nearly spotless, just a few pieces of paper on the front passenger seat, nothing to tell me who owned it.

Still, I had a good idea about who owned the Explorer.

I tried to be as quiet as I could, climbing up the cement steps to the apartment. With any luck, I would be able to overhear them through the door. Places like these didn't invest in heavy sound-blocking doors. Tenants were usually lucky if there was a peephole to look through.

There was a sliver of a shadow along the seam of the door. It was open a crack, nearly wide enough to stick a few fingers through. The space wasn't wide enough to allow any airflow through the apartment, and I could hear the air conditioner set into the wall straining to cool the open space. Stepping onto the landing between the two top-floor apartments, I glanced down the stairs to see if anyone was watching and slowly pushed the door open.

I smelled the blood before I saw anything. Nothing smells quite like cooking human blood on a sunny afternoon. Taking a deep breath, I stepped carefully into the apartment, and my stomach churned into a knot.

Splatter covered the wall by the front door, streaking the off-white paint with red. A couple of bullet holes punctured the drywall, exposing the framework underneath. I revised my opinion of the apartment's construction. Whatever the shooter had used to kill his victim had left a huge mess, but the damage didn't go through to the other side, or I would have spotted it when I walked up the stairs.

In my mind, the wall became brick, bleached from years of sun. It was night in a blink, a soft evening where my belly was full and I was looking forward to the taste of Rick's mouth on mine. In an instant, it was gone, taken from me in a spray of blood and bone.

Closing my thoughts against the memory didn't help. All it did was remind me of other things, the taste of Rick's brain on my tongue and lips, then suddenly pain grinding through me as other shots deafened the air. I'd fallen, holding him… crying for him. Then the world folded in on me.

That night echoed around me, hidden in the blood and the afternoon light.

Two bodies lay on the living room floor, sprawled where they'd been shot. I didn't recognize the one on his back, the remains of his face broken by a gunshot. Whatever hit him had taken out most of the right side of his skull, a flap of skin holding what looked like his ear sprawled on the carpet next to his body. I was careful to step around him. Pieces of bone were on the tile entryway, bits of his brain caught under the door, smeared when I'd opened it to go in.

I checked the one nearest the door. The carpet was matted with blood under his body. Whatever happened here hadn't occurred too long ago. The bodily fluids were still liquid, and the telltale stink of his body releasing its remaining refuse had just started to smell the place up. Swallowing the bile at the back of my throat, I turned to the other man.

My fear choked me as I looked at the man lying facedown on the carpet. He was closer to the kitchen alcove, nearly hidden behind a thick-legged table. His features were hidden from me, but a pool of blood had leaked out of a wound I couldn't see, spreading over the stained beige carpet. I didn't want to touch the body, but my brain screamed to know if that was Jae-Min lying motionless and dead.

The black hair I'd wanted to run my hands through only yesterday clung to his neck, weighted down with blood. He'd fallen like a broken doll, legs cocked as if in mid-turn when some god had decided it was done with its toy and cut his strings. Crouching, I forced my heart to keep beating as I reached down to brush away the hair that had fallen forward and covered his face.

And I had to stop myself from sobbing like a girl when I saw Jae-Min's beauty under the veil of black I'd pulled back.

My hands were sticky, the lines on my palms clotted with Jae's drying blood. There was so much of it, leaking out of someplace that I couldn't see. I was afraid to turn him over, afraid to touch him in case he fell apart when I held him. I wasn't going to let him die, cold and untouched.

He was warm to the touch, too warm it seemed, even taking into account the sweltering heat of the apartment. A flush colored his pale skin, a blush of pink across his high cheekbone, and then his mouth moved, giving me a start. Jae-Min moaned softly, and his breath skittered over my fingers. My chest began to thump again as my blood moved through my veins again.

"Don't move," I said, reaching for my cell phone. "Stay where you are, Jae. I've got to call the paramedics."

He either couldn't hear me or was too stubborn to listen to common sense, because the first thing Jae did was shift his body and try to get up. Pushing himself onto his hands, Jae's eyes were unfocused as he blinked, unable to see me or his surroundings. Gagging, he choked on the thread of vomit that dribbled from his mouth, retching violently.

"Cole?" It was too much to be elated that he knew who I was, but I took what I could get. It was followed by some Korean that I didn't understand, but I didn't care. It wasn't rational. I'd just met him, but hearing him croak my name and maybe even swear at me was a relief.

"What part of 'don't move' didn't you hear?" Moving my arm underneath him, I held Jae close when he reached for me again. Resting his head on my jeans, he lay still enough for me to check for where he'd been hit.

Dried blood closed up the tear in his scalp where a bullet had torn past his head. Hidden under his hair, a large lump had formed on his temple, probably from hitting his head either on the heavy wood table I'd found him near or the kitchen counter. Either way, I was guessing he'd been knocked out and now was suffering from a concussion.

Someone answered the phone, and I went into automatic, dumping out information. Jae shivered, his shock setting in. I'd have to find something to wrap him in if they were too far out. I didn't want to risk him falling unconscious as we waited.

"Baby, stay still." I froze, hearing that word come from my mouth. Whatever my brain was cooking up, it was going to have to stop. Jae-Min Kim was the last person I'd want to get involved with. "I need you to stay still until someone comes to look at you."

I was firm on that resolution until his lashes fluttered open and his dark-honey eyes found my face. He didn't smile, not really, but a ghost of something tugged at the corners of his full mouth, and Jae relaxed against me, letting me hold him up.

"Cole, Jin-Sang... is he okay?" Jae-Min shifted, trying to turn around. His back was to Jin-Sang's corpse, and I wanted to keep it that way. I should have backed out of the apartment as soon as I'd seen them lying there, but I hadn't. There was going to be hell to pay, but I was willing to take it. The warmth on my leg was enough to make me feel good about that decision.

"Don't look, Jae. You don't need to look." If he was going to talk to me, I should keep him focused on what had happened while it was fresh. "Did you see who did this?"

"Someone came out from the bedroom. I didn't know they were there." He flinched, and his hands grabbed at my thighs. Pain jerked at his mouth, peeling back another layer of his carefully controlled emotions. He was afraid and hurt, biting at his lips to not cry out. It was the face of a man who had no one around him to console him, beating back any sign of vulnerability. I knew that face. I'd worn that face too many times to count.

"It's okay, honey." His shoulder blades dug into my arm when I cradled him. "Try to keep awake."

"Jin-Sang's dead, isn't he?"

"Don't think about that right now, Jae," I said. Something hit me, hard between the eyes. Looking down at him, I searched for any flinch across his features when I asked, "Do you love him?"

If he answered yes, it would break me. His maybe-lover was splattered across the apartment walls and floor, and I knew how that felt. Life would be filled with guilt and what-ifs. Nothing good ever came from what-ifs.

And if he said no, then I wasn't sure what I was going to do, but I had a feeling that it would untangle the sour knot resting in my chest.

"No." His voice was soft and rough. "Not Jin-Sang. Never him. I came here to get him to talk to you."

"Talk to me?" That was more of a shock than finding Jin-Sang dead.

"I wanted him to tell you about Hyun-Shik." The sound of sirens bounced around outside, coming through the open door. "I needed to talk to you again."

"Yeah?" It seemed disrespectful to feel elation hearing Jae say that, especially as we sat in blood and with Jin-Sang's dead body nearby. Voices echoed in the stairwell, and I called out to the paramedics coming up to the apartment.

"Yeah." He touched me, running his fingers along the inside of my thigh. A medic headed straight over to Jae, and I moved away, sliding him onto the flat carrying board they'd brought up with them. He grabbed at my hand, snagging my fingers and holding on tight. "Don't go anywhere, Cole."

"No problem," I said. Even with the medic glaring at me with his disapproving eyes, I wasn't going to go anywhere. "Won't let you go. Promise."

"Cole?"

"Yeah?"

"I don't mind baby. It's nice." Yelping, he jerked when the medic stuck him with a needle. Pain shot up my wrist, his fingers digging into my forearm. "But don't call me honey. That's my mom's dog's name."

CHAPTER SIX

"Yeah, how do you spell that, again?"

The detective had taken my name three times now. I wasn't sure if he was singularly stupid or just giving me a hard time. Spelling it again, I enunciated each letter until I was certain he'd gotten it right. The sun had set, but there was enough glare from the parking lot lights that his forehead bounced a sheen back at me.

Jin-Sang's body was still upstairs, people walking about his apartment and wondering at his lifestyle. Our hands and clothes had been tested for gunpowder residue before Jae was hauled into the back of a waiting ambulance. So far, from the heated mumbling I could hear coming from the paramedic working on him, things weren't going well. I wanted to commiserate. Things generally didn't seem to go well when Jae-Min Kim was involved.

"McGinnis, Cole." He stopped writing, looking up at me, realization dawning on him. "You're the one that got shot. You worked a house up from here, didn't you?"

"I'm working here, too," I replied. My attention drifted to where the medics were working on Jae. They'd moved us downstairs, closing the apartment off to wait for forensics and whoever else wanted to stomp over Jin-Sang's cooling body. "I do private investigations."

"Didn't the city pay you enough money that you could sit on your ass?" His partner, Branson, joined us. I knew him from work. We'd crossed paths a few times, and never for the better. He was one of those muscle bunnies who swaggered through the locker room, his ebony skin oiled up to emphasize every bulge along his arms and thighs.

"Maybe his ass is just too sore to sit down on." Now that his troll of a partner had arrived, the detective found some backbone and sniggered, snorting a whistle of air through his mustache and into his nose.

"Great. Good to see cops are still attending those sensitivity sessions." I was tired of answering questions and didn't want to start playing games. Jae-Min was too far for me to hear him clearly, but I could tell from the displeased look on the medic's face that he was getting a ration of shit about something from Jae. "We done here?"

"Your boyfriend can wait a little bit, McGinnis." Detective Branson noticed my attention drift. His face soured, wrinkles forming over his shaved head. "I've got a few questions for you myself."

It'd been a few years since I'd last seen Branson, but he hadn't changed much. Maybe got a bit wider in the gut, and the small fuzz of hair he'd been nursing along had receded far enough back that it left a shadowy line under the lobe of his skull. He'd been curt in his past dealings with me, but there'd always been a simmering, hateful veil on his words. Branson didn't have to be careful anymore.

"You hard of hearing? I'm talking to you, McGinnis." I jerked my eyes back to him, pulling away from what was going on by the ambulance.

"Sure, why not?" I'd already gone over everything a few times with Thurman, but I understood the process. "Shoot."

"Did you?"

Oh, clever. I wasn't going to be impressed by his wit. He was going to have to work for anything he got from me. I hadn't seen anything other than Jae on the floor. "Did I what?"

"Shoot the victim. So what really happened, faggot?" If Branson got any more ticked off, he was going to end up looking like a Shar-Pei. "You walk in on them fucking each other and shot them both? Maybe felt bad about it, so you and your lover make it look like a home invasion?"

"A home invasion from inside the bedroom on the second floor?" I asked sarcastically. Like Branson, I had nothing to gain by being nice. I'd had enough of his kind of crap when I'd worked for the force. "Or do you think they let me in to use the bathroom so I was all fresh before I killed them? I already told you. I never met Yi Jin-Sang. I was here to ask him a few questions about an investigation I was hired for."

"Mr. McGinnis, we're just looking for some clarity," Thurman said. He was switching over to the conciliatory tone Bobby used when he wanted to coax something out of someone. Anyone who had to prod a suspect used it or the rough, harsh, I-don't-give-a-shit-about-you voice. "Usually the person who calls in something like Yi's murder is connected to the scene. We have to ask questions to determine that you had nothing to do with his death."

"What were you going to ask him about?" Branson interrupted. "Yi. You came here to talk to him about what?"

"I'm investigating a suicide," I said. "He was a friend of the deceased."

"Friend as in boyfriend or just someone the suicide fucked?" The large cop folded a piece of gum into his wide mouth. He made smacking noises as he chewed, wetting the stick until it was soft enough to mangle against his teeth.

"I didn't get a chance to ask," I said with a smile. "He was dead before I got here."

"And what was your boyfriend doing in there?"

"Again, not my boyfriend. And when I walked in, he was busy bleeding." Jae-Min's voice got louder and very Korean with not a spit of English in it. From the looks of things, he was tired of being poked and prodded. I sympathized. I was feeling the exact same way about Branson and his pet sycophant.

A bruise was forming on Jae's cheekbone, a purple splotch spreading under his pale skin. He'd pushed away the medic, wobbling on his unsure legs. The man swore at him, a spate of Spanish to go along with the languages that had been thrown at him already. They went at one another again, the man insisting on something that Jae wasn't going to agree with. The paramedic threw his hands up and began packing his equipment, grabbing a piece of paper and shoving it at Jae-Min.

"You've got my contact info. Call me if you need anything else. We're done here." It wasn't a question this time. I was finished with them and headed over to rescue the paramedic. Branson swore after me, but I kept walking.

In hindsight, I could pin down the moment when my life went to hell. It was when I walked over to Jae-Min and said, "Wait here. I'm going to take you home."

WHY the hell was I driving Jae-Min home in evening rush-hour traffic? Because the idiot refused to go to the hospital. The medic spat at me in disgust even after I said I wouldn't let him behind a steering wheel. Not that he was going to drive anytime soon. The cops had cordoned off his Explorer as a part of the crime scene. I think the paramedic was hoping he could tail Jae and wait for him to pass out, then drag his unconscious body to the hospital.

From the way Jae was leaning on me as I dragged him out of the car, I would have said the medic's plan wasn't a bad one.

He smelled of blood and citrus. And trouble, if I was going to be honest with myself. Jae-Min Kim reeked of trouble, and it was rubbing its stink on me.

After trying to push me away, Jae jerked his arm free of my hand and nearly tumbled to the cement sidewalk. We weren't in a nice part of town, and even if he was tough enough to laugh off a concussion, scraping open his skin on the sidewalk guck would kill him. I caught him before he hit the ground.

"You fight me even when you don't have to. Come on," I said softly. There were shapes moving along the dark alleyways around us, ominous human shapes lurking outside of the bright pools coming down from the two working streetlights. "Where's your place?"

"We're in front of it."

The building had seen better days. I couldn't make heads or tails out of what it had been before, maybe a long strip mall or a warehouse that someone bought and converted to apartments. Either way, the place was now a tall, whitewashed, brick block with stacks of glass jalousies running along under the eaves. Someone had tried to make the exterior more attractive, adding a decorative cinderblock enclosure around each doorway. Dried ivy strands clung to some of the scalloped stone. It didn't do much to provide privacy. The dead plants only made the place look sadder.

"It looks like a prison." I was being nice. The place looked like bird shit on a hot windshield.

"It's cheap." He struggled to get his keys out of his pocket. I snuck my fingers past his, struck by how cold they were. "The one on the end."

"Let's get you inside."

Jae shivered against me and glanced up at me from under his lashes. My body growled in response, a primal goad into taking what was in front of me. I wanted him. Covered with his own blood and chilled from probable shock, I still wanted him underneath me. Every ounce of common sense in my brain told me I was an idiot, but guys are often idiots. "Tell me there's hot water in your shower. You need one."

"Yeah." The color was gone from his face, turning his already pale skin to porcelain. "I've even got a toilet in there."

"Good, because you're probably going to want to throw up in it." I opened the heavy metal door and grabbed at his waist before he slid down the wall. "You've got a concussion. You should be flat on your ass in a hospital bed."

Light came through stacks of windows along the back of the wall, illuminating the wide space. If I hadn't been so concerned about carrying him over the threshold, I would have dropped Jae when I saw the enormous black and white photos leaning against the wall. He pulled away from me, staggering off toward a door in the side wall, waving off my half-mumbled offers to help. I didn't offer out of kindness. I, like most men, was a pig. The thought of seeing him naked under a stream of hot water would go a long way in paying me back for the anger I was still nursing against him.

He disappeared, closing the door behind him as I found the switch to the lights. The space was larger than it looked from the outside, cleaner than I'd expected too. The furnishings were Spartan, a pair of futons around a low, flat-topped wooden chest pocked with water rings. An enormous unmade bed against one wall, a nest of pillows imprinted with the shape of a long, lean body.

Most of the floor space was taken up by mismatched tables, a few groaning under the weight of electronics and digital cameras. Long lenses sat sentinel on cheap shelves, accompanied by other equipment. I couldn't even begin to guess at what it was used for.

The photos still held me. I saw Scarlet's face in one, stripped of makeup and pretense. This was the man under the makeup and smiles. A sadness clouded her dark eyes. Not loss, I decided. No, this was the face of a ladyboy who loved deeply and wanted the world to know that kind of love. She was still beautiful. Even naked of any pretense, there was a beauty there that I couldn't deny.

There were other images, starkly beautiful and sweepingly tragic. Flipping through them, I was walking into Jae-Min's world, seeing private moments caught between his hands like short-lived fireflies. It hurt something inside of me. I couldn't understand the nearly manic laughter captured in the back room of Dorthi Ki Seu, black and white portraits of men turning themselves into another man's fantasy.

He'd taken other pictures, pieces of urban life seen through unforgiving eyes. Jae-Min imprisoned his life in flat images. I wondered if he was trying to make sense of things or just showing the world what he saw. Either way, looking through the mounted photos made me ache and feel slightly ashamed, as if I was prying into his secret diary.

A furry demon exploded into a hissing fit above my head. I fell back, almost knocking over a few cameras from the table behind me. I fought to catch them before they hit the ground, shoving the equipment back as the cat spat at me again.

She jumped down, giving me a twitch of her tail as if she was dismissing me as a threat. Barely bigger than a small bag of chips, she bounced along the edge of the table, a black poof of chinchilla fur edged with fangs and claws.

"That's Neko."

I'd not heard the shower turn off. Jae stood with his hands clenched over the edge of the couch's back. Dark circles were forming under his eyes, and he seemed to be straining to stay on his feet, weaving back and forth as he fought to stay upright.

"Neko?"

"It's Japanese for 'cat'. Her full name is Koneko-chan, but mostly I just call her Neko."

"You named your cat, Cat?"

"She came that way," he said, shrugging. The white T-shirt he'd put on hung on his body, too big for his slender torso, and the pair of loose, thin sweats he'd tied around his hips weren't much better. I wondered if they were something left by a former lover. Crossing over to where he stood, I grabbed at him before he toppled over. "Wasn't like I was expecting her to come when I call her."

"You're bleeding." I sighed, easing him back into the bed. He fought me, a brief tussle, before I shoved him down onto the pillows. "Stop it. Fuck, for once in your life, do what you're told."

"That's all I do." I didn't understand the bitterness in his laugh, short and cutting, but it was there. In spades.

"Do you have bandages? Anything?" The cat jumped onto the bed and glared at me as if I'd been the one to peel apart Jae's temple. Her opinion didn't matter to me, but she had obviously put me on her short list of people to flay as soon as she grew thumbs.

"In the bathroom." He reached for the furry demon, cradling her petite body against his chest. A light purr started up in her chest, but there was no warmth for me in her cold, orange-yellow eyes. His tawny gaze didn't hold much hope for me either, but I had questions for Mr. Kim, and I wasn't going to leave until I got a few answers.

Coming back with a handful of gauze and medical tape, I sat on the edge of the bed, keeping out of paw-strike distance in case his guard-cat decided to take me down. Peeling off the plaster he'd gotten from the paramedic, I winced at the blotches of blood seeping through the bandage.

"You should have gone to the hospital." Opening one of the sterilized gauze packages, I folded the bandage over and placed it on the crease along his head. "Hold this while I cut some tape. It's not too late to take you to the emergency room, you know."

"Who's going to pay for it?" he asked as I taped the bandage down. It would stay long enough for the gunshot-burnt flesh to heal over, maybe even leave a rakish scar, unlike the rough starbursts that mottled my body.

I'd hoped that, being this close to him, I'd find a flaw or two, perhaps even a pockmark, but God wasn't a kind God. Not to me, anyway. It was getting harder to stay angry at him, especially with the vulnerable, broken look in his eyes. It didn't help that Jae's warm breath ghosted over my neck when he spoke.

"I would have paid for it if I had to. You look half-dead. Hell, a few hours ago, I thought you were dead."

"I'm not, so no hospital." Short and sweet, his voice had a cut of steel to it. There wasn't going to be any arguing with him on the point.

So of course, I wasn't going to back down. "And I don't take money from people."

"Why not? From what I've heard, you've taken money before." I bit the inside of my mouth as soon as I heard the words leave my tongue. I wanted to take them back, or at least soften the sting in them, but the damage had already been done. His mouth tightened, and the ice returned to frost over his face.

"Get the fuck out." Jae's hands pushed against my chest. I was heavier than he was, broader and more muscled, but he had a fury that I couldn't ignore. A familiar feral gleam returned to his eyes, and if I stayed sitting next to him, there was an unspoken promise in them that I would pay dearly.

Once more, men are stupid. I stayed.

"No." I pushed back, pinning him to the pillows. The cat fled, voicing her disgust at being dislodged with a low miaow. Jae felt fragile under my hands, his leanness an unfamiliar landscape under my fingers. It didn't fool me into thinking he was soft. There was hard muscle lurking under his oversized clothes, and his twisting away nearly unseated my grip. "Stop it. Shit, look, I'm sorry, okay? That was an asshole thing to say. I'm sorry."

He looked at me, untrusting and unwilling to give me even the smallest of openings. I was going to take what I could get, even the slight nod and his shoulders relaxing against the bedding was a victory as far as I was concerned. I almost didn't hear his whisper, barely louder than the sound of traffic outside. "What do you want from me?"

If I were brutally honest, my answer would include something about him being on his stomach and holding onto the sheets, but since he'd just been shot, I was going to be a bit more gallant. "Did you lie to me about why you were at Jin-Sang's?"

"I didn't go over there to kill him," Jae replied softly. "I went over there to talk to him. There was a loud boom, and then the next thing I knew, you were pulling me up. I don't even know what happened. I don't give a shit if you don't believe me, but that's all I was doing there."

"I believe you." Strange thing is, I did believe him. I was going to chalk that up to lust more than any real gut feeling, but even in my more stupid moments, my instincts didn't normally lead me astray. "Why didn't you tell me you used to work at Dorthi Ki Seu?"

"Would you tell someone you worked there?" He arched an eyebrow at me, a black sweep of sarcasm nearly lost under the razored edges of his hair.

"Okay, I'll give you that." I nodded. I pulled my hands off of him, not trusting myself with touching his warm skin.

"I figured you'd head down there, but no one would talk to you about me. Everyone down there is Korean or Filipino. We don't talk to people we don't know. Hell, we don't talk to people we do know." Shrugging, he winced with the effort. "Who told you?"

"I saw a picture of you in Scarlet's dressing room. I'm a little dense sometimes, but I can put two and two together and come out with four." I grinned at him.

"You know nuna? Shit." He eyeballed me. The shoe was now on the other foot, and he was wondering if I was lying. "How do you know Scarlet?"

"I kind of arrested her once when I was a cop. She was out before they did the paperwork, but we kept in touch, and I thought I'd hit her up for information since Hyun-Shik died where she worked." The cat had come back, kneading Jae's thigh and looking at me with narrowed, suspicious eyes. "She didn't bring you up, I did. I saw the photo of the two of you, and she told me you were close. Don't be mad at her."

"Nuna probably thought you already knew me," he said with a tired sigh. "I'd never be mad at her. Are you kidding? I'm closer to her than my family."

"It looked that way," I replied. "I need you to be straight with me, Jae."

"No pun intended, yeah?" He moved the cat off his leg and onto his chest. She settled down into a loaf, closing her eyes and purring as loud as her little body let her. His long fingers stroked at the cat's petite head. Each time he ran his hand down over the back of her neck, it was giving me naughty thoughts. About him. Not the cat.

"Yeah." Shifting on the bed, I drew away slightly. I was going to have to ask some hard questions, and the way I was feeling, I'd do more consoling than getting answers. "I know Hyun-Shik took you there to work at the club. Why did you agree to do it?"

"I needed the money." He looked at me like I was crazy for asking.

"You were living with the Kims. They didn't give you money?"

"No." Jae pushed himself up until he rested against the pillows, moving slowly to keep the cat steady. "Auntie kicked me out when I was a junior in high school. She said I was a bad influence on Hyun-Shik. I couldn't go back to NoCal. I needed to have money to finish school."

"You were a kid. How much of a bad influence could you have been?" I swore under my breath. "You were underage. Do they still have kids working there? Shit, we should have shut that place down when we had the chance."

"Good luck with that." He laughed. "Scarlet's lover wouldn't let you. She likes it there. It makes her happy. Hyungnim will do anything to keep her happy."

"What does that mean?" Now was the time to ask him. Like the cat, he seemed calm, willing to be stroked into purring. "Hyung. I keep hearing all of you say that."

"It's like… sir?" He cocked his head, thinking. "Not really, but kind of. You say it when a man is older than you."

"You used it for Hyun-Shik. He wasn't that much older than you. What? Five years?"

"About five," Jae agreed. "But it doesn't matter how many years. Older is older."

"Okay." I wasn't going to go any further. Respect from me had to come in both directions. It didn't seem that way for Jae-Min. "How long did you work at Dorthi Ki Seu? Did you know Jin-Sang from there?"

"I worked the rooms for…." His eyes grew distant, thinking back. "A few years. Maybe four? Jin-Sang was there for the last three years. As far as I know, he never stopped working there."

I'd worked Vice. I knew whores from all walks of life. As he spoke about a life he'd once led, I heard the street-tough remoteness in his voice, and I grew more pissed off at Hyun-Shik for giving up a young boy to other men for pleasure.

"You told me your cousin wasn't cheating on his wife."

"He wasn't," Jae replied. "He'd broken it off with Jin-Sang right after he got married. Hyun-Shik wasn't seeing anyone. He wasn't even going to the club for sex. Maybe a drink once in a while with a friend, but he didn't go upstairs. Not that I know of."

"Was he with you?" I pried.

"Like sex? Not me." He laughed at me. "Hyung wasn't into me. He was done with me right after I went to dance in Dorthi Ki Seu."

"Dance?" That was a new one for me. "What do you mean dance?"

"Yeah, dance. Music playing, wearing underwear or something for them to stick money into." Propping himself up on one elbow, Jae looked at me curiously. Realization dawned on him. It crept into his face, and it looked like he didn't know whether to laugh or get pissed off. "What did you think I did upstairs? Shit, you thought I fucked up there? You thought I was one of the rent-boys?"

I threw it back into his face, hard and fast. "Why else would you be ashamed of working there?"

"Because people react like you do when they find out." The bitterness was back, coloring his words. "You're like all of the rest of them. That's why I didn't say anything. Who the fuck are you to judge me?"

"What did you expect me to think?" I asked, pushing for a moment. He was angry, I got that. I had my own anger to work through. "You hand things off to me in bits, and I've got to piece them together. I was pissed off when Scarlet told me you worked upstairs. I figured Hyun-Shik dragged you over there like a piece of meat and offered your ass up to whoever wanted it."

"Hyun-Shik brought me there to see if they would let me dance for the upstairs clients." He spoke slowly, as if I were an idiot, which, by all accounts, I seemed to be. "They pay money to have guys dance for them while they sing karaoke. Sometimes they want sex, but sometimes they just want to act stupid and get drunk. Jin-Sang did sex. I didn't."

"Never?"

"It's not any of your fucking business, but no, never," He growled at me, sitting up and shoving my shoulder. "You just met me yesterday. What the hell do you care?"

Yeah, that's what I was asking myself too. I just didn't have an answer. "Maybe because you were a kid."

"Hyung, I was never a kid. I knew what I was doing. Hyun-Shik didn't force me into anything." For some reason, that seemed sadder to me than the outside of the building. He meant it. There wasn't any apology in it. For Jae, it just was. I think that made it all the sadder still. "I needed the money to live on. Then I went to college, and I had to pay for that too. I quit as soon as I started doing well with my photography. I don't make as much, but hell, at least I don't get shit thrown into my face."

"Then why did you go to Jin-Sang's?"

"I thought you needed some help. That's why I went to Jin-Sang." He continued working the sheets around his fingers. When I touched his arm, Jae didn't pull back immediately but edged away after a few seconds. I wasn't sure if he'd forgiven me or just was too used to people treating him like a whore. "I knew he wouldn't talk to you unless someone asked him to. Even then, he might not have, not without wanting money for it. He didn't do anything without first getting paid for it."

"What did you think he knew about Hyun-Shik's death?"

"The note was bothering me." Jae-Min pointed toward the crate he used as a table. I could see the copy of the note I'd given him lying with a stack of papers. "I thought I'd seen that before."

"That same note? Your cousin didn't write that?"

"No, he wrote it," Jae said with a shake of his head, and then winced, pressing the heel of his palm against his forehead. I reached for him, but the look he shot me warned me off. "Hyun-Shik wrote something like that to Jin-Sang when he married Victoria. I thought it was the same note, or at least a part of it."

"Hyun-Shik was refusing to answer his phone, and one night, Jin-Sang came home from the club and found the key to his apartment holding down a note," Jae murmured, rubbing his hands into the sheets to warm them up. "He was drunk and yelling at me like I had something to do with it. I don't remember all of it, but I think that piece you gave me was at the bottom."

"That phrasing you talked about." I thought back on what Jae-Min had said in the kitchen. "It wasn't regret over killing himself. It was about giving up Jin-Sang?"

"Jin-Sang was a whore my cousin fucked. Hyun-Shik liked him, but he screwed a lot of people. It's what he did. He wasn't giving up

Jin-Sang. He was giving up everyone." Jae smirked. "He had to stop when he got married. Victoria would have his balls if she caught him. Have you talked to her yet?"

"No," I replied. "I didn't think there was anything here but a suicide. Now, I'm not so sure."

"So you think someone killed Hyun-Shik? Really?"

"Yeah and my gut tells me Jin-Sang's death is connected to it too," I said, nodding my head. "So I guess I'll have to see what Victoria has to say about her husband."

"She's a bitch. Don't let her good manners fool you." His face turned waxen, and he turned his head, struggling to keep his nausea down. "I don't feel good."

"It's the concussion. Let's get some soup or something into your stomach." I stood up, and he grabbed at my hand. "What?"

"Why don't I call Scarlet? She'll come over and take care of me. She's not working tonight."

"I don't mind." He didn't look good. Not bad, because someone as pretty as he was never was going to look bad, but there was a need for sleep and food on his face. "I can crash on the couch. You shouldn't be alone. Remember?"

"I know," he said with some regret. "But you're going to have to go."

I waited for a heartbeat. Mike always said I was slow about catching on and often expressed surprise that I'd made detective. "You don't want me here? Okay, no problem."

"No, the problem is, I do want you here. Too much." He let go of my hand, pulling back into the pillows. Regret curled his mouth, and I wanted to kiss the wickedness back into it. "You're hot, and you're taking care of me even when you're pissed off, which kind of gets me off. So yeah, I'm going to call Scarlet, and you're going to go home. Now."

CHAPTER SEVEN

"SO HE kicked you out?" I wasn't going to give Bobby the satisfaction of teasing me, but sometimes, after a few beers, my tongue doesn't do what I want it to. "Because he was turned on by you?"

"Yeah, pretty much." I counted glass bottles, soldiers I'd lined up on the bar, wondering if the bartender was going to cut me off soon. I got my answer when I signaled for another and he tipped off the bottle cap without even flinching. The bartender was elevated to archangel status. I reminded myself to leave adequate tribute.

"Did you tell him you were gay?" I saw Bobby smiling around the lip of his glass. "Although I think that horse has left the barn. I'm pretty sure he already knows."

"Nope, I was too...." I couldn't think of the word. It was on the tip of my tongue, but I couldn't reach it. "Yeah, I don't think I need to tell him."

"Chickenshit?" Bobby offered up. Always helpful, that Bobby.

"No," I denied emphatically, then shrugged. "Maybe. I met him yesterday. It's not like we have a relationship."

"Cole, we're guys. We fuck first and then look for happy ever after." He drained his whiskey and sighed before asking one of the guys behind the bar for a club soda. "That's the best part about being gay. We don't have to deal with all of that crap women bring to the table. We screw and then see if we like each other. That way, if the sex is bad, we're not stuck with someone we don't like."

"That's what I love about you, Bobby. You're a romantic." Tipping the bottle back, I doused my face with beer. Somehow my mouth moved when I wasn't looking. Wiping off the foam, I muttered at him, "Laugh and I'll kick you in the nuts."

"You couldn't find my nuts right now if I had my pants down and was waving them in front of you." Hooking his hand under my arm, he pulled me off the bar stool. "Come on, I'll walk you home, Princess."

"I'd like to see you say that to me when I'm sober." Thinking hard, I remembered he sometimes called me that when we were boxing, usually when he was pounding the crap out of me. "Never mind. Forget I said that."

"I'm pretty sure you will." Bobby paid for the last of my beers and hustled me outside. I struggled to get back in. After all, I'd promised to leave the bartender an angelic tip. "I left him something extra. Home you go."

The cold air hit me hard, and I drew in a lungful of ice. With no cloud cover, the basin's heat had fled to the stars and the night sank its chilled bite into the city. After the searing day, the desert grew cold. By one in the morning, there'd be frost on the grass that would be dew when the sun rose. It was no wonder I kept losing some of the bushes in front of my place.

Compared to the Chicago winters I'd endured as a teen, I'd take Los Angeles's chilly nights during any drunken stumble back from a bar. I felt the urge to break into song, probably my father's Irish blood.

"I should learn the words to 'Danny Boy'," I mumbled.

"God no," Bobby said, guiding me around a lamp pole. "I've heard you at karaoke. You utter one note, and I'm leaving you in a pool of your own puke."

"I don't puke." The beer was making it hard to think. "Okay, I've puked once or twice, but that was a long time ago. I was thinner then."

"And you're mountainous now." He snorted as he turned me up the walk. My legs were firmer than they'd been when I'd slid off the barstool but still a bit weak. "Sleep this off. Go dream of your pretty-faced little boy."

"He's not a boy." The crafty bits of my mind sent me images of Jae's pale body stretched out onto a soft bed, one leg crooked and that damned mouth of his open just wide enough for me to slip my finger into. Swallowing, I tried to push away the image, not liking where I was going. Sure, I wanted Jae's body under me, his sleek skin glowing with a sheen of sweat. I wasn't dead. He turned me on. For some reason, there was something about his feral, lying sweetness that made me twitch. "Trust me. You'd want him too."

"Yeah, from the sounds of it, I would." Bobby deposited me on my front stoop, waiting for me to open the door and get inside before he left. "Get some sleep. Skip the gym tomorrow. I'm giving you a get-out-of-a-beating card."

"Yes, Master," I burbled, and he laughed, slapping me on the ass.

"If only you played those games, Princess." Kissing me on the back of my head, Bobby pushed me into the hallway. "Don't forget to lock the door. I'll see you later."

I fumbled with turning the deadbolt when I got inside, certain that someone had come in and moved it an inch or two to the left since I'd used it last.

"Or could be the six beers you drank, dork," I mumbled, tossing my keys on the table where I'd have to hunt for them in the morning. A shower sounded both nice and disgusting. I wanted to get the smell of alcohol off me, but it would sober me up too much. I compromised with a quick splash and a scrub, dousing my head with cold water before staggering over to the bed.

And of course, sleep eluded me. My brain was too busy circling back to Jae's mouth and the line of his body against rumpled sheets. My alarm clock mocked me, taunting me with its glowing numbers and illuminating my cell phone, which had its own silent sneer going.

"Fuck it." I had his number. I'd even programmed it in. A punch of a few buttons rolled over into a purring ring, and a sultry voice answered the line, husky with fatigue. "Jae?"

"No, baby. This is Scarlet." The purr wasn't for me. It was one Scarlet always had in her voice. She probably practiced it in the echoes of a bathroom, listening for the right pitch that could curl the hairs on a man's belly. It did nothing for me, but I had to appreciate the seductiveness in that rough velvet purr. "Is everything all right?"

"I was… calling to see if Jae was doing okay." I could lie. I was a trained liar. Scarlet's tsking chuckle made me feel like I was three years old again and caught stealing a cookie. Feint, my brain screamed, dodge! "Is he asleep?"

"Yes. Let me go outside. I don't want to wake him." I heard movement on the other line and then the sounds of faint street traffic as

Scarlet stepped outside of Jae's stone fortress. "Hold on. Aish, you're an idiot."

There was some discussion, a heated exchange between Scarlet and a deep-voiced man. She was shooing him away from the front door, first in English, then with a flare of hot Korean. I was imagining the worst when I heard another rumbling argument from whoever was outside of Jae's door.

"You okay?" I didn't like the neighborhood Jae was in. I was liking it even less with what I was hearing. "I can be over there. Get inside. I'll have someone come around."

"I don't need saving, baby." She murmured into the phone, laughing at me over the line. "That was one of the boys hyung sends with me. Believe me, honey, the last thing they want is going back to him with a hurt Scarlet. Nice Korean boys, thick in body and sometimes in the brain too. Just told him to go sit in the car with the other one, not stand on the doorstep."

There was a flick of a lighter and then Scarlet's inhale on a cigarette. I could almost see her standing in the cinderblock enclosure around Jae's front door, her hip tilted against the wall as she angled the phone against her chin, exhaling a cloud of smoke before returning to the half-drunken pest on the line.

"Honey, why you calling so late?" The polished exotic English she'd spoken at the club blurred under the weight of the hour. Her Pinoy accent was richer now, a darker, earthier sound to her voice. When I didn't answer immediately, she filled in the silence with a low murmur. "Ah, so that's how it is."

"How what is?" Even in the haze of what beer I had left in my system, I had an inkling she wasn't just guessing at the fire Jae stoked in me. Hell, she made a living at stroking men's egos and tickling that nerve in our brains that went straight to our dicks. I wasn't hiding anything from Scarlet.

"I thought you were liking men. I guessed but weren't sure," she said. "Most men like you at least look at the boys, but no, none for you. Before Jae, I thought maybe you were funny kind, and not in my way. Not liking either boy or girl."

"Hey now!" It kind of hurt to have my sexuality stripped away, even if it was imaginary. "I do okay."

"Honey, I'm sure you do fine," she said. It sounded like she'd said those words a million times. Probably had. "So you're gay. Who isn't right now?"

"Did you tell Jae?" I asked around the lump in my throat. It was one thing to be taunted about being gay, but to be asexual was too much of an insult. "About me…."

"He probably knows. He's not stupid." Another drag on her cigarette made a hissing noise in my ear. "I saw when you were here. You want him. Hovering and checking on him, like he was something you couldn't have right now, but in a little bit, maybe, he give you some honey. I know men. I know how they are."

"Scarlet, I just called to see how he was doing, not date him. He got kicked in the head pretty hard today."

"Like I said, honey, he's asleep now." Scarlet sighed. "I'll tell musang you called to see how he was. You go back to sleep now and try to pretend you didn't call for something different."

I tried protesting. I even made a few noises that sounded like I meant to grumble at being shoved aside, but her tsk pierced my eardrum, and I had to hold the phone away from my head.

"It's not wrong to want him. My Jae-Min is pretty, and maybe you both can kiss each other's boo-boos away." The traffic noise subsided, followed by the solid clunk of the heavy metal door. "Go back to bed, baby, and dream of something really good."

MORNING did not come gently to me. In one of life's ironies, there were songbirds outside of my open bedroom window, trilling away at the sun that seared my eyeballs. Blinking away the crust on my lashes merely allowed more light to hit the back of my aching skull. Mumbling, I tried to make the morning go away with a pillow over my head, but the songbirds were soon drowned out by the ringing of my phone.

"You up, boy?" The crackle on the other side made my teeth ache, and I debated hanging up to avoid any long-term damage to my fillings. On a good day, Claudia's voice had an edge to it, a matriarchal, authoritative ring. In the state I was in, I recoiled from the shrill she put into it.

"Yeah, I'm up." Struggling to find the alarm clock, I captured it before it slid off the nightstand and reassessed my morning to early afternoon. "Did you want something?"

"I'm leaving," she announced. "Figured I'd check to see if you were dead before I left."

"Kind of you," I mumbled around a mouthful of foul breath. Sometime during the night, my tongue had decided to lick the inside of a sneaker, and it was all I could taste. "Isn't it Saturday? You're not supposed to be at work."

"I needed my pay, so I called you up, but you didn't answer, so I came over to check. I don't want to come to work for a dead man. They don't pay," Claudia said. "I wrote myself a paycheck, and your brother called. He said you can call that Kim woman if you wanted to. He talked to her already, and she's fine with talking to you. He left you her number on your phone, but since you didn't call him back, he called me."

"Thanks," I said with a nod, then immediately regretted it. I was hoping Mike was talking about Victoria Kim and not Hyun-Shik's mother. Of course, I'd not spent any time with any Kim other than Jae, so it could have been anyone. "Have a good afternoon."

"Get out of bed, boy," she ordered before she clicked off. "And take a shower. You must reek to high heaven."

I stumbled in and out of the shower, washing off the night sweats and the filth I'd picked up in my mouth. As I toweled off, my fingers brushed against the whorl of scars on my side. It was larger than the others, the bullet tearing through more skin and muscle.

Of all of my wounds, that one hurt most often. The tangle of nerves worked through the scar tissue sometimes misfired and cramped up my side. The pinkish pucker was still raised, smaller tears working out from the epicenter to form a starburst pattern over my ribs. The doctors had worked hard to get my heart going again, stitching up the veins and arteries torn apart from the piece of metal that had rattled against my ribs. By the time I'd woken up from the drugged daze they'd put me in, the world had gone on without me.

When I'd left the restaurant with Rick, things had been pretty good. We'd shared a house and a life. Even his small runt of a dog had begun to take a liking to me. I'd just been assigned my first case as lead, and the dinner we'd shared was a kind of celebration. If someone could celebrate being handed a drug dealing case. I'd kissed him goodbye, holding his face in my hands and tasting his mouth before heading to the car where I'd thought my partner, Ben, was waiting.

"Yeah, he was waiting," I muttered around a mouthful of toothpaste, spitting out the minty froth into the sink. The bitter taste was back, but it had nothing to do with beer or anything else I'd swallowed. Staring at my reflection in the mirror, I said, "Is that what happened to you, Hyun-Shik? Were you at Dorthi Ki Seu thinking things were good and the people you trusted had your back? Is that why you went there? Did someone call you over, or did you go looking for someone?"

Clothes were simple. Jeans, a black T-shirt, and a pair of leather boots I'd scuffed into a workable softness. Grabbing my phone and wallet from the nightstand, I stopped in front of the Art Deco armoire I'd gotten from a consignment store in San Diego. I'd fallen in love with the golden tiger oak piece when I'd first spotted it amid the other furniture. I'd given Rick a hard time about doing the gay thing while on vacation. I was too butch to go antiquing, and he'd never let me forget that I'd been the one who ended up paying someone to deliver it to our house in Los Angeles.

The armoire wasn't just a pretty piece. It also had a concealed drawer at the top where I kept my gun. After what happened to Jae and Jin-Sang, I wasn't going to go out without a bit more protection. Bobby had pulled strings to get me a Concealed License, and I'd never really had a need to use it, but after yesterday, sliding on a shoulder harness seemed like more than just a good idea.

Some cops were in love with their guns. I liked them well enough, but I didn't need one on me at all times. My father schooled both Mike and I on how to handle a firearm, when we were young. Mike loved them more than I did, but I was the better shot, much to his disgust. I blamed it on his wimpy stance and unsteady hands, but only if I wasn't within reach. I might be taller, but my brother still could kick my ass if he wanted to.

It'd taken me a few months to get over the flinch when I heard a gunshot, and I still felt the echo of a recoil on my face when I pulled a trigger. Bobby helped me work through that on the range. Nothing like blowing away a few targets to help with controlling my rage, he told me.

He was wrong, but I wasn't going to argue. At least I'd put away the gun-shyness I'd developed.

I rigged up, tucking in the Glock Mike had given me for Christmas. I gave him a singing fish, three video games, and a couple of ties. After a few rounds of country-western tunes, we were ordered to take the fish outside and drown it. His wife didn't have much of a sense of humor, but it made for great target practice for the Glock. Shooting up a robotic fish on Christmas Day is one of the best memories I have.

I called Victoria Kim and got a snot-voiced woman who informed me that Mrs. Kim would be available to me between the hours of three-thirty and four that afternoon. The address she gave me wasn't far from the elder Kims' abode, and its proximity to Mommy and Daddy made me wonder if Hyun-Shik hadn't fully untied the apron strings.

"Half an hour isn't a lot of time to talk about your dead husband, Victoria." I pondered the timing of the interview.

The neighborhood was nearly cookie-cutter identical to the one Hyun-Shik's parents lived in. Perfect lawns with two-inch grass blades were studded with flower beds and the occasional tasteful statuary, a fountain or two to break up the monotony of green and color. Houses here ran into the millions and were strictly kept in line by association rules.

The snot-voiced woman answered the door, a tall, scrawny rail with saline blobs perched squarely on her chest. Her face went along with her voice, pinched and thin with narrowed eyes that looked me up and down. I gave her a smile and faked some pleasant social twitter as I introduced myself. She wasn't buying it, and her sniff told me as much.

"I'll tell Victoria that you're here." She sniffed again, toddling off on break-neck stilettos. "Wait in the living room."

If femininity could be sterile, Victoria's house did it. Every wall was covered with a subtle wash of color, blush white that ran dull when the light hit it. I looked at the furniture, spindly upholstered things that wouldn't hold my weight. One of the couches looked promising, a bit sturdier than the rest. I kept it in mind as I looked around the room.

There weren't any personal touches among the still-life paintings, except for a single photograph of a little round-faced boy dressed in a bright red robe. I'd seen the same picture in the Kims' gallery, as well as a flurry of others. Strange that the mother of the child would only have one image of her kid.

"Hello, Mr. McGinnis."

She was taller than I'd expected, coming up to my chin, and had the perfect rosy skin and long waves of blonde hair that someone would expect from a Californian beauty. Turned out in a high-waisted, black pencil skirt and button-up white shirt, she sauntered in, taking advantage of being the prettiest thing in the room. Perky breasts and slender waist coupled with long, tanned legs, she looked more like one of Mike's naughty-secretary fantasies than the grieving widow.

If I were into women, I'd have been all over her.

Luckily, I wasn't into women.

"Please, call me Cole." I made some noises about how lovely her house was, and she gave me a thin smile, as if she believed me but I was taking up her time. I added another mark to my not-liking-women checklist. "Thanks for seeing me. I know this must be a hard time for you."

"We're getting through it. I'm sorry I can't offer you much in the way of refreshments. No one's really been to the store other than to get food for my son." Her nearly tear-filled eyes were practiced, almost flawless except for the telltale pinch of her cheek between her teeth. I had a boyfriend once that mastered crying at the drop of a hat, and she looked exactly like he did when he was trying to pull one over on me. "Please sit down."

"I won't keep you long. I've only got a few questions." The couch held up, but my legs were too long for it, and I ended up squatting like I was sitting at a preschooler's desk.

"I don't know what I can tell you." Victoria sat in a chair right next to me, crossing her legs and leaning forward to give me a bit of cleavage. I played her game and gave them a bit of a glance. "I don't know what I can say about Henry's death. It was all such a shock to me."

The tears were gone, replaced by a slight widening of her eyes and a sliver of a pout on her lower lip. It looked good on Jae, a natural slope to his full mouth. Victoria stocked it in her arsenal, along with her tears and breasts.

I wondered if I was being too hard on her, not giving her the benefit of the doubt, when an Asian man came down the foyer and walked into the living room. He was built like one of the bouncers at a trendy nightclub, his thick chest packed into a dress shirt that buttoned up to his neck. His features were coarse, like God hadn't quite finished with him before he'd wandered off to be born. A thick bristle of black hair stood out on his square head. It was so much like Mike's and Hyung-Shik's haircuts, I almost asked him if it was just a number you picked on a menu at the stylist, but the grim set of his face gave me pause.

If I were a betting man, I'd say he wasn't happy to see me there. When he thrust his jaw out at me, it was like I'd won the jackpot.

"Who's this?" He remained standing, spreading his feet apart and looking down at me.

"Cole McGinnis. I'm investigating Hyun-Shik Kim's death." I did the obviously male aggression thing to do. I stood up and offered my hand to him, looking down at his shorter height with a half-smirk. "And you are?"

He didn't take up my offer of a handshake, turning instead to the grieving widow and placing his palm on her shoulder. Victoria turned slightly, angling her knees toward him, and I watched their eyes dance together for a moment before she tilted her head toward me, sweeping her hair behind her shoulder with an elegant push of her hand.

"Mr. McGinnis," she said, ignoring my offer to use my first name. The heat of her body language cooled down considerably toward me as she focused her wiles on him. "This is Brian Park. He's... was... one of Henry's coworkers."

"Coworker?" I kept it a question. "Nice of you to come by and help out."

"I'm more of a family friend, really." He shot her a look, his fingers working into her shoulder like a cat kneading a lap. "I met Henry through work, but we became close friends. Of course I'd be here for Victoria." She perked up a bit, brightening back into the feminine archetype I'd first met.

"Huh." I took out my notebook, scribbling down some nonsense. "Park, that's Korean, isn't it? And you work for Mr. Kim, Hyun-Shik's father?"

"Yes, I work for his firm. Hyun-Shik was my manager, but we became friends," he said. Crossing over behind her, he leaned against the back of the chair, placing Victoria between us. "I don't see what being Korean has to do with anything."

"I was just wondering if you'd seen the note he left and if you could read it." I drew out a copy I had tucked into the notebook, offering it to Park to read. He shook his head, not taking the paper. "No, you didn't read it, or you can't read it?"

"I didn't read it because it's a private matter. A lot of our clients are Korean." He pursed his lips. "Being able to understand hangul is a job requirement."

"Did either of you have any idea that Hyun-Shik was going to Dorthi Ki Seu that night?" I asked, watching their faces.

"No," Brian responded firmly. Victoria remained silent, clasping her hands in her lap. "He kept that part of his life secret. Neither of us even suspected he... liked men. He kept it hidden from me. Maybe someone in his family knew, but I didn't."

"If I'd known, I wouldn't have married him," she finally spoke up, clearing her throat. The wash of tears was back, swimming just on the edges of her lashes. "I hate that he made me live a lie."

Funny how she slid him so easily into the past tense when Jae-Min still had difficulties acknowledging his cousin's death. Brian circled around to sit in the chair next to her, reaching for her hand. They were the picture of grief, his rough face softened with concern for her. It was almost believable, except for the flit of her fingers along the inside of his thigh as he pulled her hand into his lap.

"No one blames you for how you feel. He probably felt guilty about it all," Park said, patting her arm. "That's why he killed himself. He loved you, Victoria. He loved you and Will."

"Actually, that's kind of why I came by." I sat back down, ignoring the fact that my knees nearly blackened my eyes. The couch groaned its displeasure at my weight. "His death. Not about how much he loved you."

"That's what you said." Victoria made a show of dabbing the edges of her eyes. "To talk about Henry's suicide."

"Yeah." I went back to my portfolio, sliding Hyun-Shik's note back into the side sleeve. "Sort of."

"Sort of?" Park frowned, creasing his eyebrows together until they were a solid black caterpillar crawling over his forehead. "He committed suicide at a sex club. He left a note. What else is there to talk about?"

"Brian!" Victoria hissed. "Will is upstairs! Keep your voice down."

"Sorry," he said. I doubted his apology. It was easy to doubt with his thumb stroking the inside of her wrist. The heat of his caress kicked up a wave of her perfume, a floral, musky scent that lingered between them. Nope, I wasn't convinced at all that he was sorry Hyun-Shik had died—or about where he died.

Maybe it was just me, but it seemed like Brian Park was more interested in the Widow Kim than he should have been. She pulled away from him, wringing her hands together. Her mouth slimmed into a thin line, creasing her pink lipstick.

"Mr. McGinnis, the fact is that my husband Henry killed himself in some disgusting place that he crawled off to have sex with other men." Victoria's façade cracked, showing me a glint of the ice she had hidden underneath. "I loved Henry, the Henry that I thought I knew. The man who died was a stranger to me, and I'm not ashamed to admit that I hate him for that."

"See, that's what I have a problem with, Mrs. Kim. I don't think your husband killed himself," I said softly. "I think he was murdered."

CHAPTER EIGHT

I HAD to give Victoria this. She had more balls than Brian. There wasn't so much as a twitch on her face when I announced that I thought someone had killed her husband. Brian Park, on the other hand, turned the color of a well-done pork chop.

"What the hell are you talking about?" Suddenly the family friend was no longer concerned about consoling the widow as much as he was about tearing me apart. A vein popped up along his forehead, throbbing violently as he stood up. "You think this is a joke?"

"No, I'm quite serious." I watched Victoria's expression change from placid grief to a more stricken alarm. She glanced up the staircase, and her face calmed when she saw no one there. "I think Hyun-Shik... Henry... was murdered. The note he left wasn't an apology about his suicide. It was a part of a note he wrote to someone who was shot to death yesterday."

"Who? It couldn't have been his whore cousin, Jae-Min," Victoria spat. "If it was, I'd have heard Mama Kim's screaming for joy from here."

"No, it wasn't his cousin." I didn't have Victoria's fortitude. I winced when I heard her talk about Jae like that. He'd been right. There certainly wasn't much love for him at either of the Kim households. "The note was for one of the club's employees, a man named Jin-Sang Yi. He was a... friend of your husband's."

"I don't need to know the name of my husband's whores, Mr. McGinnis." Victoria was done being warm. She eyed me carefully, measuring something she couldn't put her finger on. From the tightness in her face, I was fairly certain I wouldn't be getting any invites to any of her upcoming tea parties.

"I think it's time you got out, McGinnis." Park paced, shoving his fists into his pockets. A rush of anger made his face a deep red, and it mottled at the lines on his high forehead. "Just get the hell out and leave her alone."

"Victoria, don't you want to know the truth?" I kept an eye on him, but I wasn't going to budge from the sofa. He didn't come any closer to me, but the threat of violence lingered. "If Hyun-Shik didn't kill himself, wouldn't you want to know that?"

"As far as I'm concerned," she said calmly, "Henry killed himself as soon as he set foot inside of that disgusting place. Even if he didn't love me, Will should have been enough for him. Enough to keep him from going to some boy to suck him off."

Her beauty was gone, replaced by an ugly temper. With her lips curled back, she looked like a cornered dog defending a bone it had found in the yard. I could almost taste the hatred she had in her heart. Hyun-Shik Kim would get no sympathy from his wife if ever he met her in the afterlife. The most he could hope for would be the tip of her stiletto heel into the base of his skull, and that would be if she was feeling generous.

"You can leave now, Mr. McGinnis," Victoria said, smoothing her skirt as she stood. "You can tell the Kims that they can chase after ghosts if they want, but I'm going to move on with my life. I married a man who used me. Henry told me he loved me, then snuck around behind my back to fuck other men. A woman I could have at least dealt with. But men?"

"You don't know that he did that," Park said. His fingers circled her wrist lightly, drawing Victoria to him. "We don't know that he was unfaithful to you, Vicki. Don't do that to yourself."

"How can I ignore that?" Her voice pitched up, a shrill cut to it as she turned on him. "All those late nights when he was supposedly working? How the hell am I supposed to trust that now?"

"You have to trust that he wasn't going to endanger you or Will," he insisted. "That boy was his life."

"Do you know the most disgusting thing about this, Mr. McGinnis?" Victoria pulled herself up, squaring her shoulders. The temptress was gone, and in its place was a hard, strong column of a woman. "I had to go to my doctor and ask him to run tests on me so I could make sure that Henry hadn't brought home some disease from his screwing around. I had to subject myself to the looks that I got from the nurses there because my husband couldn't stop himself from sticking his dick in some man's ass. God help me if he got Will sick."

"Vicki, don't say that." Park gave up the illusion of friendship and folded her into his arms. "Will's fine. You're fine."

"The only reason I might be fine is because Henry and I didn't even touch each other for the last year." She laughed, a sour vinegar of a sound. "I used to think it was because I'd gotten soft after Will. That it was something about me, that Henry didn't find me attractive anymore. Now I find out that the problem was that I didn't have the right parts for him. So you tell me, Mr. McGinnis, how the hell am I supposed to care about a man who lied to my face about loving me?"

"I don't know," I answered truthfully.

"If he was murdered, it was probably because he pissed someone else off," Victoria whispered. She struggled to contain her anger, restoring the iciness she'd worn earlier. "I'm not going to lose sleep over him. I can't. Now, if you excuse me, I'm going to go check on the one real thing Henry left me. Brian, can you see him out?"

We both watched as she headed to the staircase, her heels clicking on the floor when she reached the foyer. The sun from the tall windows turned her hair to a bright honey, and she stood for a moment in its warmth, tilting her chin up when she turned toward me.

"I don't want to see you again, Mr. McGinnis," Victoria said, gripping the banister tightly. "If I do, I'm going to call the Kims and tell them that they won't be seeing their grandson anymore. And honestly, considering how Henry turned out, I'm beginning to think that not having them in Will's life would be the best thing for him."

I SAT in my car for a bit, resting my forehead against the steering wheel. Curtains fluttered in a window on the second floor of the Kims' home, so I knew someone was watching me, probably waiting for me to take my suspicions off down the road. I believed Victoria when she said she didn't care how her husband died. I heard the hatred in her voice and the trembling fear she'd tucked away when she'd spoken about her son being sick.

"I hope to fucking God you used a condom, Hyun-Shik," I said, turning the ignition key. "Because if she catches anything, she's going to piss on your ashes and serve it as soup to your parents."

My head hurt, a gentle throb to let me know that not only had I skimped on restful sleep, but also that the beer I'd drunk lingered somewhere in my body, its yeasty goodness muddying my blood.

"Getting too old, McGinnis," I sighed, turning my blinker on and waiting for the light to change. "Used to be you could drink all night and wake up a few hours later all fresh and ready to go. Now look at you. Having a few beers and lusting after some young Korean boy. You should know better."

I called Mike up as I maneuvered the Rover through the lower canyons. Listening to the chirping ring through my earpiece, I scanned the hillsides, not pleased with the sagebrush choking the landscape. It was looking to be a dry year, perfect conditions for wildfires. After the last wave of firestorms that had ripped through the district, the canyons were preparing for another hard burn.

"Yeah?" My brother answered the phone through a mouthful of something. "What's up, Cole?"

"I just left the Widow Kim." A truck slowed in front of me, and I tapped on the brakes, keeping the Rover at a distance. "I shared the good news that maybe her husband didn't kill himself."

"And let me guess, she wasn't too happy about it?" Mike swallowed, a gulping noise that buzzed the phone's speakers.

"Was that a lucky guess, or did she call you?"

"Called me," Mike laughed. "You pissed her off. Started making noises about suing me, which I shut down fast enough."

"She didn't waste any time." I wasn't surprised. Victoria Kim seemed like the type of woman who could quickly put her ducks in a row and then blow them away with a .22 handgun. "Mrs. Kim wasn't too happy about Hyun-Shik being gay. I think the dying part of the equation was a bonus for her."

"Think she had something to do with it?" he asked. The sounds of papers being shuffled around nearly drowned out Mike's voice, and I waited a moment until he was done. "You there?"

"Yeah, I was listening to you do origami boulder, there," I said, then told him about the original note Hyun-Shik wrote Jin-Sang and walking in on Yi's death. Mike's low whistle was enough to sink any doubts I had left over. "I'm kind of worried about Jae-Min. We should keep an eye on him in case someone moves in on him."

"Wanna just move him into your place? He could be your houseboy." No one could leer like my brother. It was a disgusting trait he shared with my father. I'd hoped that it had skipped me, but some of my former boyfriends assured me that no, I definitely was a McGinnis in that regard.

I was about to answer when I felt a tap on my rear bumper. It was normal, really, considering the uneven flow of traffic on the freeways. Usually someone who'd gotten a new car and hadn't quite broken into the rhythm of driving it. The Rover could take most hits without even a blink, so I wasn't all that worried. Besides, I'd dented it often enough on my own, driving through the hills on camping trips.

I was debating pulling over to see if there was any significant damage when there was another jolt, harder this time, and I glanced up, staring into my rearview mirror. Once was nothing to worry about, but twice seemed aggressive. My mirror was filled with the hard-lined front end of a new Econoline, its windows tinted much too dark to be close to legal. Pound for pound, I'd have to give the Ford the upper hand over my battered Rover. The sun glinted off its chrome, burning my eyes. I blinked, and my vision watered, then cleared right as the van surged again, slamming into the back of the Rover.

The hit jerked me forward, snapping my head back. I lost my earpiece when it hit again, a hard shove with its front bumper against the Rover's back end. My tires squealed as I was shoved across the roadway. Mike's voice screaming my name was lost under the crunch of the van hitting the Rover with a hard determination. I heard my rear quarter panel give under the impact, then my forehead hit the steering wheel, and all I could see were stars.

My back end slid out to the right, pushed by the van's momentum. I fought the spin, trying to straighten the Rover out. I gunned the engine, turning into the spiral. Another hit slammed the side of my head into the car door. More stars, and I tasted blood in my mouth.

"Fucking son of a bitch." I swallowed, gagging on the taste on my tongue. Mike's yelling got louder, and the panic in my brother's voice was palpable. I shouted down at the passenger well, hoping he could hear me, "Shut up! You're not helping!"

My brother has always been a master of cursing. He didn't fail me now. The words that came out of the headset were very clear. It was as if he were sitting right next to me. Next to his ability to burp the alphabet, it was one of his greatest talents.

"Screw this." The other driver brushed up against the Rover, and I hit the brakes hard, letting it rush past me. "Let's see how you like it."

I kept the van to the right of me, edging the Rover's formerly pristine front end against its rear. Accelerating, I hit the van's back end, shoving it forward. The canyons flew past us, purple and grey lines of brush dotted with yellow. The scent of rubber and acrid smoke filled the Rover, and I choked on that more than I did my own blood.

Blinded, I gassed the Rover again, hoping to hit the van hard enough to push it into the median. The Rover's front end gave, hooking into the Ford. The other driver slammed on his brakes, a flash of red lighting up the van's rear, then the crinkle of plastic as the Ford's taillights broke. I couldn't stop fast enough, tangled into the other car's backside, so I twisted the wheel, hoping I could at least put the side of the Rover into the van.

My world tilted sideways, then stopped. Sparks of light burst along the edge of my awareness, and then I choked, feeling blood fill my nasal cavities. Something gave way, the sound of metal tearing drowned out the rushing in my ears, and then there was a muted hum of noise that echoed through the Rover. I realized the sound was the running engine, punctuated by the rush of cars passing by. A few cars slowed to avoid the debris we'd left behind.

Mike's yelling was a tin mosquito in my ear, and I fumbled to reach the headset lying on the carpet. I coughed, spitting mouthfuls of mucus and blood, and the throbbing in my face turned to a roaring pain. Swallowing, I tried to clear the viscous liquids at the back of my throat, trembling as I brought the earpiece up to my cheek.

"Mike, shut up. It's okay," I said, blinking to clear away the haze from my vision and waving aside the acrid smoke from the burning tires. A hand reached through the open window, and I jerked away, thinking it was the driver of the van coming to finish off the job.

"You okay, man?" Unless the owner of the Econoline was a dreadlocked woman, I was safe. She cocked her head at me, giving me a wide-eyed once-over. "You need an ambulance?"

"Nah, I'm good." I must have sounded convincing, because she went back to her car and took off. My face hurt from where I'd hit it on the steering wheel, and my shoulders were wrenched from trying to keep the Rover upright. The Ford was long gone, leaving a trail of smashed plastic and glass in its wake.

"Cole, stay there. I'll get someone out there to you," Mike practically shouted into my ear. His voice only served to make the ringing bells in my temple take up another chorus.

"No, really, I'm all right." I tested my teeth with the tip of my tongue. "Car's a bit banged up, but I think it's drivable."

My brother's heavy sigh reminded me of my father's. I'd heard a lot of my father's sighs in my lifetime. Mike's was a nearly exact mimic. "What the hell happened? Did you roll the car?"

"No, I think someone's not happy with me," I said, hawking out another mouthful. It was more spit-colored this time, splattering on the scrub grass growing against the side of the highway. The Rover pulled forward without any issue, and I sped up on the shoulder, easing back into the flow of traffic. Mike buzzed in my ear, complaining about my stubbornness.

"Get to the doctor," he scolded. "Or better yet, get over here and I'll take you."

"Nope," I refused, listening to the Rover creak a bit when I switched lanes. The front end made a little noise, but nothing I was too worried about. "I've pissed someone off, and I'm going to find out who. I need to make sure that Jae's okay. Someone's going through Hyun-Shik's friends, and sooner or later, they're going to get to him too."

I ENDED up in front of Jae's squat brick apartment. If anything, the early dusk light made the place look even more depressed. I parked the Rover, easing the seat belt off. A sharp pain darted through my belly, and I gasped, swearing at the tightness curling the scar tissue under my shirt. Pressing my hand on the tear, I hissed through the pain in my side.

Around me, people continued their lives, televisions blaring and screaming at children who wouldn't eat their dinners. It was early enough that the evening news filtered through the noise, a steady droning update on the price of being human. The neighborhood was like one of many in the county, a collection of poor on the edge of desperate.

Before I'd left the force, I'd been working on establishing contacts in a community like this one, spackled together homes bursting with families too large for their walls. It made for a tense living, and despite the glowing stories of success that occasionally surfaced in the news, most of the time, life here was a brutal, hard ride where violence was fed to a child in its breast milk. Death was a common visitor for one reason or another.

I'd worked a more Hispanic neighborhood, but except for the language on the signs here, it looked the same. The bubble-slash Korean on the barricaded storefronts was foreign to me, but I guessed they announced the same types of specials that would draw in someone with a tight fist on their wallet. The air smelled a little different, less oil than the streets I'd been learning on but harder spiced, a lingering anise undercurrent that soon was lost under a rush of coppery stink when I sniffed.

Blood burbled in my nose, and I reluctantly touched the bridge. It was tender, but there was no crackling rice sound that I could hear. I chanced a look at my face and winced. A bit swollen where I'd bashed my cheek against the frame, but the bruises forming under my eye and across my nose gave me pause. They promised to be a brilliant black and purple if given a few minutes. If Jae-Min had ice, then I would profess my undying love. When I almost lost my footing on the curb, I gave up ice for the hope of a strong shot of any kind of root alcohol.

The door was sadly lacking a large doorknocker, so I leaned on the bell, feeling the warmth of the light beneath its rubber surface. The door creaked open, and a flustered Jae-Min appeared, his dark hair ruffled as if he'd spent more than a few minutes running his fingers through it. My body responded first, a stirring of my sex inside my boxers. He looked too damned good, lean and sensual in casual cotton pants tied at his waist and a thin white shirt that turned transparent under the porch light. His mouth was wet, drops of water trembling on his lower lip, and my teeth ached anew, less from the rattle of being broadsided by the van and more from wanting to sink into his full lips.

"Hyung!" The feel of his arm around my waist blotted away the pain in my side. It felt good to be touched. I didn't realize it until just then, but I'd missed being touched by someone other than family. Stumbling forward, I let him catch me, his hands sliding down over my hips as he shut the door behind us. He was smaller than me, slighter in body, but he certainly was strong enough to hobble me into the apartment.

"Am I old enough to be called that?" I mumbled, the ache in my nose beginning to spread across my face, lodging in my cheekbones. "Don't I have to be at least twenty years older than you? How's your head?"

"I'm fine, but you look like shit. What happened?" Jae smelled good, a blend of citrus and sex. I might have been imagining the sex part, but the green tea and grapefruit scent was real. Even through the cloud of blood I was trying to breathe through, I could smell him. Being bashed about apparently made me horny. "Who did you piss off?"

"You've known me for, what, three days and you think I pissed someone off?" I tried to sound incredulous, but he rolled his eyes at me and dumped me on his couch. My elbow hit the frame, and it stung up to my shoulder. "Ouch. Fuck."

"Stay there," Jae ordered before he disappeared into the bathroom. "I'll get something to wash off your face."

His cat took a leap from the counter and landed neatly on the coffee table. She pulled her feet under her sleek body and squatted, staring at me with her orange-yellow eyes. A bit of fang slid from under her lip, the barest hint of a threat in case I moved wrong. I shrugged off my jacket, silently hoping that the show of a gun in my shoulder holster would give her pause, but the fang only got longer. Sighing in defeat, I attempted to make some show of affection toward her.

"Neko, right?" I called out to the man making noises behind me. "The cat? Her name's Neko, right?"

"What?" Jae came back, spreading out gauze and tape on the table and sitting down next to his cat. She mewed at him, a pleasant, sweet sound that belied the evil I suspected lurked within. He stared at my shoulder, edging slightly back on the table. "You've got a gun. Why do you have a gun, and why is it in my house?"

"I thought it would be a good idea, considering someone shot at you yesterday." I drew the Glock out and tapped the bullet load out of it. Checking the chamber, I was satisfied it was empty before taking off my gear and stowing its ammunition in one of the jacket's pockets. "There, better?"

"Yeah. Thanks." He scritched at the cat's ears before handing me a couple of aspirin. I was about to dry-swallow them when he handed me an open water bottle. "Don't do that. They'll stick in your throat."

"Thanks." Putting the rim to my mouth, I watched his hands as he opened a package of antiseptic wipes. The bottle tasted as I imagined he would taste, spiced sugar and a hint of candlelight, as well as the flat taste of recycled Los Angeles tap water.

"What did you do?" His touch was light as he dabbed off crusted blood from a cut near my eye. I knew from the quick glance at my face in the Rover's side mirror, Jae couldn't be very impressed by the battering I'd taken. The car was in better shape, its solid metal body easily shaking off the brunt of the Ford's assault. "Hold still. It's dried too much. This is going to hurt."

"I went to talk to Victoria. You're right. She's a bit of a bitch." I swallowed the girlie scream that scrabbled along the edge of my tongue. The sting from the salve crept slowly over my skin, and I bit my tongue so Jae wouldn't hear me make noises I preferred to make in bed with company. "That hurts like a motherfucker, just so you know."

His fingers were warm on my face, the edges of his palms brushing along my lips. My tongue darted out before I could stop it, skimming over his skin. He stopped dabbing at my face, pulling back slowly. I smiled, wondering if the pain was making me bolder or I was just tired of fighting the want of him.

"Did she beat you up? What did you talk to her about?" He pressed back in, nearly straddling my leg when he moved forward. "Hyun-Shik?"

"First, all of this was from someone tailgating too hard," I said around my gritted teeth. The scrubbing was hopefully working loose any blood, because it felt as if sheets of my skin were being lifted off. "Yeah, I talked to her about your cousin. She held up the 'poor me' bit until I started talking about Dorthi Ki Seu. And she really doesn't like you."

"I don't like her, so it's fine." Jae shrugged. I played with the hem of his shirt, my fingers brushing along the flat of his belly. His fingers stopped, then started again, his breathing turning shallow. "You're distracting me."

"I like distracting you," I whispered into his palm. "You shiver when I do this."

Bobby was right about so many things. Somewhere in the drunken haze of last night, I'd made up my mind not to fight what I felt about Jae-Min. I wanted him, and it wasn't as if I'd been celibate my entire life. I'd just not been with someone since Rick. I was getting tired of satisfying myself, and Jae's mouth and slender body seemed to be perfect to slake the want in me.

"Don't tease me." His voice dropped, a husky, slithering sound that made me harder. "I'm not something for you to play with. Sit still. I'm not done. Tell me about what Victoria said to you."

"Pretty much nothing. And I'm not playing with you. I'm pretty serious." I lay there under his hands, wincing when he scraped at my face. Jae sighed, and I gave up my halfhearted attempt at flirting for the time being. "I told her I thought Hyun-Shik was murdered, and she kicked me out. Flat out told me she was glad he died."

"I think she is," he said, nodding. Dabbing a new gauze with alcohol, he returned to abrading my skin. "With Hyun-Shik gone, she doesn't have to bring Will around to the Auntie or Uncle unless they do what she wants. They're worried that he's not going to be Korean enough."

"Not Korean enough?" I cocked my head back to look at him, curious about what he was talking about. "What do you mean? How can he get less Korean?"

"Like you," Jae said, as merciless as he was about scrubbing my face clean. "You're Japanese but not Japanese. You don't know even the simplest things about being Asian. There's no connection to your mother's family or blood, is there? They're dead to you."

"Hold up," I protested, grabbing at his wrists and pulling his hands away from my face. "Just because I wasn't raised by my mother doesn't mean her family's dead. They're still in Japan being as Japanese as they want."

"They might as well be dead." He shrugged, the white shirt catching on the rise of his chest. Jae's nipples poked ridges into the fabric, momentarily distracting me from what he was saying. "It's not a bad thing, for you. For Will, his family is right here. Koreans live for their children and their grandchildren. It's what makes the family go on. Having Will was the only reason Hyun-Shik got married; not because he loved Victoria, but because he had to provide family to live on."

"So he decided he wasn't gay anymore because he needed a kid?"

"He wasn't going to stop loving men but couldn't afford to be that person anymore." Jae didn't struggle out of my hold, settling his knees on either side of my legs. "It was time for Hyun-Shik to grow up and have a family. If he was smart, he would have married a Korean girl, but Vicki was good for Uncle's business. She came with a lot of connections."

"You couldn't have told me this before I headed over there?" I let go of one of his arms, holding the other loosely. Putting the bloodied bandage down on a torn wrapper, he shook his head at me.

"Hyun-Shik put that behind him," he murmured, dropping his eyes. "Hyun-Shik's son has to be… sheltered from who his father was. It's better that way."

I wasn't sure if the shyness was real, but the contrite glance he gave me from under his lashes did me in. Victoria had nothing on seduction, compared to Jae-Min. If it was artificial, then he was damned practiced at it.

My hands were in his hair before I even thought about wanting to touch him more. Scraping back the black strands, I paused when I saw the small plaster bandage on his temple. Jae's eyes widened, and he gasped, unsure of what I was going to do. I had to admit, I wasn't certain myself, but in the middle of trying to figure out if his cousin had killed himself or if he'd had help, I'd tossed aside my feelings for Rick and was falling for a lying, sleek Korean man. Guilt ate at me, worms of censure working through my thoughts as my thumbs ran over Jae's cheekbones, bringing a blush to the surface of his pale skin.

"Don't," he pleaded. There wasn't much conviction in his voice. It sounded more like a please than a stop. "You don't want this."

"Want this or want you?" There'd been other men who'd caught my interest, but none had really made me lust before. Not like this. I needed to push Jae down and make him scream my name. I wanted his hands on my back and to feel him around me. "No one's made me need them more since Rick."

"Nothing good ever comes from it. Not for me," he said, shaking his head. Jae trembled under my fingers, and the tremor ran down his skin and into mine. "Look at what happened to Hyun-Shik."

"Is that what this is all about? Do you think you're going to end up like your cousin?" I pressed my hands lightly on his skull, holding his face up so I could watch his expression. Jae didn't resist, but he didn't look pleased at meeting my gaze. A thought surfaced in my mind, bubbling up from a blackness I couldn't name. It sprang from my mouth before I could stop it, flung out into the open in sharp accusation. "Did your uncle kill Hyun-Shik because he was gay?"

"No!" Jae nearly jerked free from my hold. His hands pushed at my chest, his palms flat against my shirt. "Uncle would never have killed his son. Never. He loved Hyun-Shik."

"People sometimes kill people they love." I moved my hands down, running over his shoulders and then down to the small of his back, sliding him forward until he was nearly in my lap. "Trust me, Jae. I've seen that up close. Nothing kills like someone who wants to keep someone they love from making a mistake."

"Why did you come here?" Jae-Min tilted his chin up, a challenge if ever I'd seen one. A tiny scar ran under his left eye, and it made me grin to see the imperfection.

"I came here because someone tried to run me off the road today, and all I could think about was, what if they got to you," I said. "I think you're trouble, and I should be kicking myself in the head for wanting you, but here I am, drinking from your water bottle, listening to your cat hiss at me, and letting you peel my face raw."

I didn't give him much time to respond. Cupping his face, I bent forward to take a taste of that mouth, drawing out a slow moan when his tongue briefly touched mine. It was a small kiss, and I wanted more.

I pulled him off the table completely, sliding him down against the arm of the couch, and covered him, stroking at his face with my fingers. A press of my thumb on the edge of his jaw parted his lips for me, and I dove on him, drowning in the taste of him until I didn't have an ounce of air left in my lungs. When I pulled back, he was gasping as hard as I was, shivering under the stretch of my body. Rubbing my mouth against his cheek, I skimmed over the fine down on his skin and sought out one of his earlobes, suckling it onto my tongue.

The dark swallowed up the honey of his eyes, and he panted when I pulled back to stare down at him. Giving him a quick peck on the end of his nose, I said softly, "That's why I came here."

"Want you," he murmured, spreading his hands over my chest. "And you piss me off."

"Yeah, I piss a lot of people off," I agreed, licking at his mouth. "But I want you too. God help me; you make me nuts."

CHAPTER NINE

"LIFT up your arms," he said softly, tugging at my shirt. "I want to see you."

For a moment, I was unsure. I knew what my chest looked like. The starbursts of scars weren't pretty. I was toned and hard, my muscles firmed up from pounding the bag and running, but no amount of time in the ring with Bobby would do anything to lessen my scars' ugly color or dimpled skin, but I let him lift my shirt up and pull it off.

He didn't flinch when he saw the damage, and I watched Jae through my lashes as he traced out each keloid, his fingers leaving a whispering tingle on my skin. Bending closer, he kissed the one near my heart, then licked the longer jagged ruin on my ribs.

"What happened?" He stared straight into my face, and I flinched, unable to take the brutal honesty in his eyes. He wasn't asking what they were. I knew it from his voice. He was asking how it happened and who put them there.

"I was shot." It sounded so simple. I didn't have words for the disintegration of my life or the loss of my lover. "A few years back. My lover, Rick, and I were shot. He didn't make it."

He stared at me, and I couldn't guess what he was thinking. A small snippy part of my brain told me never to play poker with Jae, not unless I wanted to be humiliated, because nothing showed through his expressionless face. Then a drop of sadness touched his eyes, and I had to look away. Seeing his iciness fade hurt something inside of me, something fragile that would break if I stared too long.

When his mouth closed over mine, it nearly ruined me.

He slowly explored me, a soft kiss that gentled the fear in my chest. I tasted the wildness in him, a fierce erotic spice that my gut told me would burn if I took a bite.

I'd never wanted to bite into someone like I wanted Jae.

"Am I the first one?" He tilted his head, cupping my face to look at me. His hands felt strong, long fingers caressing my temples as his thumbs traced over my bottom lip. "Since him?"

"Yeah," I said, shuddering at his touch. "And I feel like shit for wanting you, for needing you."

"Wanting me doesn't mean you don't love him," Jae replied, a lopsided smile quirking his full lips.

"I think I more than want you," I said, holding him tightly before he slid away from me, but he stayed, regarding me with a thoughtful expression. "My brain tells me to run because you're trouble, but my gut tells me something different."

"What does your gut tell you?"

"That you're a lot of trouble," I muttered, and he laughed, a joyous sound that had me chuckling.

"Well then," Jae said, shifting on my thighs. "Maybe you should decide if I'm worth the trouble?"

Straddling my legs, he watched me, cautious and controlled, waiting for me to make the first move. It's always a fallen angel who waits for a man to open the door to hell, and if I was going to be damned for pushing Rick aside, I was going to taste Jae on the way down.

"Yeah, you're worth the trouble." He left me for a moment, and I lay there aching until he returned, holding a small bottle of lube and condoms he'd retrieved from a nightstand. Grabbing him by the waist, I pulled Jae back into my lap. Easing his knees on either side of my legs, he bent forward and leaned in for a kiss.

The flat of my tongue fit against the upper curve of Jae's mouth. With a dipping movement, I traced the sweet pink bow. Slowing my possession, I licked at the corners of Jae's mouth, sliding the tip of my tongue past its part. Jae moaned, letting me take him, sliding his own tongue against mine in a seductive dance.

A hint of heat curled in my belly, and Jae grew wilder, angling his head so I could kiss his face. His hips moved, rocking against my thickening cock, and I moved my hands down to cup him closer. I felt every languid twitch of his cock through the thin fabric of his drawstring pants, encouraging him by kneading his ass. Digging my fingers into Jae's hips, I pulled Jae tight against my erection.

"That's it, baby. Keep rocking me," I murmured, breaking off our kiss to lick his throat when Jae leaned his head back. The air trapped between us grew hot, smelling of arousal. "God, you feel so good."

Jae sighed, rubbing his own sex with the flat of his palm. I pushed his hand away, digging past his waistband. My fingers were much cooler than Jae's hard shaft, and he hissed at the contact. Using the flat of my thumb, I smeared the drop of pearly seed I found at the tip, rubbing it around the head. Velvet soft, it swelled, parting the pout so it wept again.

"God, I love that I can make you do that," I said, catching the dew on my pad and sucking my thumb clean. Jae groaned, his backside thrusting up with need. He'd growled when I'd pulled away, his honey-brown eyes going dark with lust. Grinning with the sexy man I had in my lap, I tucked my hand back down the front of his pants. "Get up a bit, babe. I need to get under you."

Jae lifted, moaning when my fingers slid under his sac. Rolling his balls in my palm, I used my thumb to stroke Jae into a ready hardness, watching the flutter of his eyelashes when I brushed around the man's entrance. He leaned back, shifting his legs until his knees were on either side of my thighs. The hard mounds of his ass parted, and I felt his cock heat against my body.

"Push into me." Jae lowered his mouth, digging a bite into my throat. He captured my pulse between his teeth, and I felt the tip of his tongue on my skin.

"Hold on. In a second, baby," I promised. I was already on fire, and Jae's small wiggles on my crotch were doing things to me that made me want him more. Tucking the bottle of lube between us, I twisted the cap off, flinging it aside. Bringing the bottle up, I kissed Jae's trembling lips. As I warmed the cold oil between my fingers, I drank from his mouth, swallowing Jae's moans as our tongues met.

"I don't want to wait," Jae said, his voice rough.

"Me neither," I murmured, moving my hand down to the pucker between his spread cheeks. My fingers tested the man's pout, pushing and teasing the rosy ring. Able to dip the tip of my finger in, I pulled down, getting a long, shuddering moan from Jae's panting mouth.

"Where are you going?" he growled, rumbling a warning when I pulled my fingers back.

"I need more lube. It's by my leg." I laughed when Jae's fingers fumbled at his knee, searching for the vial of gel. "The other leg, baby." I leaned back and held my other hand up for Jae to coat, but he shook his head.

"No," he murmured harshly. "You'll just tease me. Use that hand to get your pants undone. I want you to feel me when I do this."

I frowned, wondering what he was up to, when Jae tilted his hips forward and the cold, slippery feel of lubricated fingers joined mine at his entrance. Working his hand down the back of his pants, Jae arched his back, thrusting his trapped cock into the flat of my belly, and rocked a finger into his entrance. Thick with gel, it slid in, taking my fingers with it, and Jae panted, his mouth open with need.

Groaning at the sudden contrast of heat and cold on my hand, I pushed up, flattening Jae's balls into the hollow of his thigh as I dug my fingers deeper into Jae's passage. The man's tightness resisted the intrusion, then suddenly gave way, sucking me in. A few strokes and my wrist ached, throbbing from the unnatural angle, but the discomfort was easy to stand, especially when Jae's mouth fell open and his eyes rolled back, glazed with sexual tension.

I tugged at Jae's pants, freeing his erection with a pull of his loose waistband. Hooking my hands into his pants, I pushed them down until his ass was exposed and rocked Jae forward so I could get the fabric halfway down his thighs. Tearing open the wrapper with my teeth, I spat out the foil and shook out the condom. My cock was unwilling to stay still, and it bobbed about as I struggled to get the sheath on with one hand.

"Hold on, baby." I couldn't keep stretching him and get my cock covered at the same time. Reluctantly, I pulled from Jae's body, more than a little aroused when he whimpered with longing. The condom finally stretched over my cock's head and down my shaft, and I moaned, biting at Jae's neck. "Come on, baby. I need to fuck you."

Shivering, Jae slid his fingers free from his hole and gripped my shoulders. The small sounds coming from his throat grew intense, driving me wild. I gripped Jae's hips and guided the man up, angling him until the tip of my cock brushed over his tight entrance, but I wasn't ready to take him yet.

Sweat dampened Jae's shoulder blades, making his shirt stick to his back, and he groaned, trying to pull me closer. As I pushed into him, he gasped and held steady, working his fingers into my hair. He rocked with need, mewling and begging as I played with him, my fingers parting his ring and applying a thick line of lubricant around his pout.

"Go easy. Please. So big," Jae breathed, nibbling at the tip of my ear. He tightened his knees around my legs, canting his hips down until he rested on my cock's head. "Push in. Now. God, please."

The thrust of my cock head against Jae's entrance breached the first ring, and I waited for his body to adjust before I went further. Forcing himself to relax, Jae arched when my fingers ran under his shirt, finding his hardened nipples and pinching them tight. Gasping, he thrust down, riding the slight pain until he found the pleasure of being filled. I entered him carefully, stretching him until I thought he would burst, but Jae wanted more.

Pressing down on my shoulders, Jae steadied himself with his hands and pushed down, engulfing me fully into his heat. The brush of my groin against the cup of his ass was what Jae needed, the pressure of my heft against the nearly too-taut skin of his rectum. I felt the bittersweet tingle of his body closing in on me, the slither of his passage rubbing on my shaft, and I gripped his hip, angling him slightly so I could hit the sweet spot I knew lay inside of him.

"Baby, you are so tight... so hot," I mumbled, forcing myself to stay still until Jae grew used to me. Jae was forcing himself down, needing to feel me buried deep inside of him. A ripple of stimulation against my shaft, and I bit my lip, nearly drawing blood as my control was tested. Keeping my hands on Jae's hips, I breathed out hard, cooling the damp sweat on Jae's neck.

Raising the hem of his shirt, Jae hooked it over his neck and shoulders, exposing his chest to my mouth. I took up the invitation, leaning forward and pushing myself further into the tight channel. With a flick of my tongue, I tasted one dusky nipple. When Jae moaned with pleasure, I licked again, swirling my tongue around his chest. A nip of teeth on the areola drove Jae's hips into motion, and he began to rise along the length of cock, plunging back down with a slow glide.

I suckled, drawing the nub out until I could pull it, and dug my teeth in deep, reveling in the shiver of Jae's warmth rippling around me. I twisted his other nipple slowly around and scraped at it with my nails. Digging his hands into my shoulders, Jae rode me slowly, undulating forward with a rise of his hips backward before drawing back down again. I let his ass press on my thighs, holding him in place before letting Jae start again, wanting to be in as deep as he could take before pulling up.

"Keep going, baby," I said, biting and nipping a trail down from Jae's chin to his shoulder. The feel of Jae's ass around me drove me wild. I thrust up, meeting Jae's hips when they lowered. Spanning Jae's ribs, I stroked the soft skin there before moving down to cup Jae's erection. "I'm going to make you insane."

"I like this." He panted into the hollow of my throat, his teeth scoring my skin. Nipping at the tender flesh on my collarbone, he bit harder, suckling at a spot until the pain drew tears into my eyes. Licking at the spot, he moved on, cupping one hand behind my head while using the other to balance himself against the couch. Stretched out in front of me, he glistened, a long stretch of muscle and skin I couldn't get enough of.

The heat of our bodies warmed the gel to a liquid, and it pooled down my shaft. Wiping at some of the gel, I rolled my fingers into the lubricant and reached behind to finger Jae, pushing first one digit and then another alongside of my sex, driving hard into Jae's soft warmth.

Surprised, Jae toppled forward, panting at the stretching. Unable to stop himself, he quivered, quickly surrendering control as I twisted my fingers up to hit the soft bundle of nerves along Jae's core. Stroking hard, I pounded his hips up, hitting the round of Jae's ass and filling him to the top. Thrusting harder, I slid to the back of Jae's channel, hitting the ridge of his body over and over until Jae's mumbling cries grew louder with each grunting twist.

"You like that, baby?" I gasped, breathing hard. I kept up the pace, driving into him until Jae could do nothing more than hold on, pushing down to grasp my cock with a tight clamp of his muscles.

We rode one another hard, feeling the pleasure build up. A touch of my palm on Jae's too-sensitive head made him jerk, and then the world spun out of control. Gushing, his cock spurted its release, a trail of spicy salt liquid hitting my chest and stomach, curling into the faint whorl of hair along my navel.

I quickly followed, my balls cupping tight, and I jerked with the feel of Jae's climax. Jae's velvet heat drank me, pulling my seed from me. Exploding, I kept thrusting, pushing in as far as I could as my body spilled out its heat.

Jae's shuddering spasms eased; then he twitched. When the head of his shaft brushed over my belly, he hissed, his skin too sensitive to be touched. Clamping over my lessening erection, he milked me with easy, slow rolls of his hips, and I watched the fire fade in his eyes and a languor slip into their brown depths.

"Was I worth it?" Leaning his head on my shoulder, Jae panted, breathing in my sweaty scent and the masculine aroma of our sex. Jae blinked, and I felt a hot wetness on my skin. "The trouble, I mean?"

"You are more than worth it," I said softly, realizing I meant it. I felt way too much guilt to be healthy, but having Jae around me felt good. "Worth any trouble you might bring."

CHAPTER TEN

"IT'S about damned time. I was beginning to wonder if you were going to turn into a monk." Bobby handed me an open bottle of sparkling water, a wedge of lime shoved into its neck. My living room was big enough to seat ten people, and he still squatted on the couch next to me. He'd brought a beer for himself, one of the dark stouts I'd gotten from a local brewery. "You just left afterwards?"

"Not immediately. Shit, wasn't like I shot off and then split." I sipped at the green bottle, making a face when I got a mouthful of pulp. "He had to get up early for a photo thing. If I stayed, he wouldn't have gotten much sleep."

"I would have at least stayed for dinner." Bobby laughed when I flipped him off. "You've got it bad for this one."

"This one?" I shuffled through the papers I'd spread out on the table. "He's got a name."

"Jae-Min Kim. Don't get me wrong, Princess, I'm glad you're back in the game." He grabbed the copy of the suicide note, turning it around. "It took you long enough."

"So?" I frowned. The second sip was more palatable after I worked the lime down the neck and into the water. "I wasn't ready before. I'm not so sure I'm ready now, but God, I want him. I just wish I could stop feeling like I'm cheating on Rick."

"It's been years since Rick... since Ben," he said softly. "When are you going to forgive yourself for that? I watch you smile and then shut down when some guy smiles back."

"Rick's dead because of me."

"Rick died because of Ben." Bobby cut me off. "Not because of you. Not because he loved you and because you had a life together.

He's dead because of Ben. That doesn't mean that you can't start living your life again."

"I thought you weren't the girly-talker type." I poked back.

"I'm not, but who the hell else is going to listen to you?" He pulled the papers away from my hands.

"Not the voices in my head, that's for sure."

"Fuck him, Cole. Fuck him and enjoy it." Bobby went straight for the kill. "I'm not saying that you didn't love Rick. Hell, I didn't even know Rick, and I know you loved him, but Cole, you've got to go on."

"I tried, Bobby," I admitted. My face grew too tight, and I rubbed at it. "I kissed him, then fucked him, and it was *so* damned good. So why am I thinking, 'how can I be doing this to Rick'? Isn't that stupid?"

"Did he kiss you back?" he asked. "Before the sex?"

I had to stop and think about it, then regretted even doing that. Jae's mouth on mine was an erotic slide into need, and reliving it wasn't going to make my life easier. I'd felt the tip of his tongue on my teeth, then on my lower lip, his mouth opening wide enough to let me taste him. There was a hint of the cloves he smoked and something promising in his kiss. My body burned where his hands explored my ribs, stroking at my sides as he made soft kitten noises under me. I was surprised at how much happened in those few seconds, and then the cold air between us when I jerked away.

"Yeah, he kissed me back," I said from behind my hands. "Next thing I knew, I was… you know. Then I left."

"You've got to be the most fucked-up guy I've known." Bobby took a swig from his beer bottle. "And I'm including myself in that. What the hell were you thinking? You should have stayed, and damn the job."

"It's his *job*, Bobby. And he needs some room," I replied. "We're not… good for each other. He's some loose idea of what the truth is, and I'm poking around his family and stirring up shit. Not a good way to start a relationship. Wait. Sorry, I forgot. We can't have a relationship because he's got to go off and get married soon. Because he's Korean."

"Okay, you lost me," Bobby admitted. "What the hell?"

"No, apparently that's how it works. You can be gay until a certain point. Then you have to go off and have kids," I said, turning the bottle around in my hands. "That's what Hyun-Shik did, and Jae-Min's probably going to do the same. It's what they all do. Have to have a kid for the family."

"And that leads us to his cousin's bitch-wife, yes?" he mused. "So this kid decided to pull off the rainbow panties and go have a straight het life?"

"Poetic. You should write that down."

"I'll jot it down when I write my memoirs." Shuffling through my notes, Bobby pointed to the now-familiar suicide note. "So who ran you off the road? The sobbing widow?"

"She wasn't sobbing." I recalled Victoria's grief crumbling away under her anger. "Well, she was, but it was as fake as her boobs."

"You noticed her boobs were fake?" He shook his head, swishing a sip of beer in his mouth, and swallowed. "I worry about you sometimes, Princess."

"Concentrate less on her breasts and more on why she'd want Hyun-Shik dead," I said.

"But we don't know that for sure," Bobby pointed out.

"No, we don't," I agreed. "But that's as good a place to start as any."

"Nothing big on the insurance take. Everything goes to the son. It's a big something, but she can't touch it." He dug through the paperwork spread out on the coffee table. "House and finances revert to our dear enhanced-boobie widow. She had money when she came into the marriage, so he's not that big of a leap on the economic food chain. Our Vicki-girl scored big when her parents died a year ago."

"I checked that out. They were in a car accident in Italy. I don't think she had anything to do there." I checked the notes I'd gotten from Mike. "Hyun-Shik made out better in the marriage. Her dad was connected, and the Kims' law firm benefited from that."

"You said something about a guy. That family friend." Bobby sat back, leaving his beer bottle on the table. "He could have done Hyun-Shik to get him out of the way and make time with the wife."

"Who says 'make time' anymore?" I asked.

"I'm old. Cut me some slack." He reached across the space between us and jabbed me in the chest with his index finger. "We've got the friend who's sniffing around her. Maybe he took care of Hyun-Shik with Jin-Sang's help, then scratched him off next?"

"So it was him in the van?" The couch cushions let go a sigh of air when I leaned back into them. There were times when I wished I had a dog. Right about now, scratching a Labrador's wide head would go a long way in the thinking process. Glancing over at Bobby, I guessed he'd draw the line at that kind of affection.

"This would have been easier if you actually saw the guy."

"Sorry, I was busy trying to stay on the road, and then I got kind of consumed with knocking him out of commission," I replied. "It was bad enough being rescued by a hippie chick in a sports car."

"Takes all kinds in California," Bobby reminded me. "What's the friend's name?"

"Give me a minute," I said, scrambling through my half-assed notes. "Brian Park. Works for Papa Kim's law firm. Hyun-Shik was his boss, but Brian assured me that they were all buddy-buddy."

"Buddy-buddy as in fumbling in the closet together?" Bobby's eyebrows crawled up his forehead and wiggled at me with a lewd shuffle.

"I don't know. I don't think so." Park hadn't seemed to have it for his dead boss, but I'd been wrong before. "He seemed to be more interested in patting Victoria's hand than sobbing after Hyun-Shik. He did say the gay thing was a shock, or words thereof."

"So not so close friends that he knew our boy was dipping himself into other guys," Bobby mused. "What about the cousin? The one you have the hots for? Are we sure that Hyun-Shik wasn't doing him?"

"Jae wasn't seeing his cousin." If I didn't know better, I'd have said I was becoming territorial. From the look on Bobby's face, he seemed to share my opinion. "Sorry, it's been a rough day."

"Yeah, what with being run off the road and getting some."

"We're back to that, then," I said slowly. I was getting tired of the people around me who seemed very willing to toss that last handful of dirt onto Rick's grave. "I'm still working through this shit. I don't appreciate my friends sticking their faces into my business."

"Yeah, we're back to that." With a nod, Bobby squared his shoulders, preparing for a fight that I knew I was going to lose. He went gentle with his next ripping off of mental bandages, but the sensation was no less painful. "Rick's not coming back, Cole. I already told you, it doesn't have to be forever with this Jae kid, but hell, it's something. I don't think Rick would expect you to spend your entire life alone."

"Depends on how generous he was feeling at the time." I laughed, mostly to blot out the sorrow choking my throat, but also because, while I loved him, Rick wasn't the easiest person in the world to get along with. But he purred like a kitten when stroked the right way, just like Jae had when I'd held him against the couch and sucked on his mouth.

"Did you ever talk to someone? I mean, since the shooting?" Bobby pried carefully, edging closer.

"Like a shrink?" My laugh this time was much more bitter. "Yeah, the department sent one as soon as I woke up. He wanted to make sure I didn't go on some revenge rampage against other cops."

"No, about Rick." The verbal jab was as sharp as his finger, poking at healed-over scars. "Your brother, maybe?"

"Dude, Mike wants to hear about my sex life as much as you want to hear about his," I responded. There was a burning along the edges of my eyes, and I pressed my lips together, biting at the inside of my cheek. We were getting too close to things I avoided, and despite my brotherly affection for Bobby, I didn't want to tumble into some crying jag. "I don't want to talk about Rick. He's gone and buried someplace his family guards like it's the Hope diamond. I can't even fucking visit him there. They even took the goddamn dog."

"Okay," he agreed. "Then how about Ben?"

"Jesus fucking Christ, Bobby!" I was across the room before I knew it. The table lay on its side, and the paper stacks we'd pulled apart were on the floor, flat victims of my anger. I wasn't prepared for Bobby's feint, but then I never am. Stuttering, I struggled to regain my mind and failed. "Why the hell would I want to talk about Ben?"

"You talk about missing Rick, but you never talk about Ben," Bobby said, grabbing at my shirt as I stalked past him. I resisted, but he wrapped the shirt around his fist and pulled, dragging me down onto the couch. Staring down at me sprawled out next to him, Bobby patted my chest, unerringly finding the knots of tissue under my clothes. "You lost two people you cared about that night. Maybe you don't need to talk about Rick as much as you should talk about Ben."

"I can't." It was hard to admit pain, even to someone like Bobby. While I was busy fighting for my life, Ben's life was bleeding out in the front seat of the car we often bantered in. His body was being interred, and Rick's brains were already being washed off by the infrequent Los Angeles rains before I woke up from my coma. "Bobby, I don't have anything to say. What the hell can I say?"

"It's okay to miss him, you know."

"Rick?" I was confused. Upside down and staring at the ceiling, I felt like I did when I woke up in the hospital room amid beeping machines and a squishy tube looped down the nasal passage Mike hadn't broken when we were kids.

"Not Rick. Ben." Bobby's hand on my stomach moved in small circles. "It's okay to miss him. You were with him longer than you were with Rick. Hell, you spent more time with Ben."

"It's not okay," I replied. Broken bits of guilt were surfacing, flotsam I'd shoved into a river of grief to avoid looking at them. "How the hell is it okay to miss him after what he did to me? After what he did to Rick? How the hell do I even give him that much of myself? Huh?"

My face hurt, the skin over my cheeks drawn tight as I lay on Bobby. In my mind, I could see Ben's face, laughing at something stupid I'd said as we wandered the streets, looking for something or other. My memories with Rick were too entangled with images of Ben, his face popping up in pictures of backyard barbeques or at a football game, all of us drunk off our asses and grinning like the idiots that we were.

"He never told me why," I choked out. "Fucking son of a bitch never even left a note."

Bobby prodded again, fearless as he walked on the fractured ice of my heart. "What would you want it to say?"

"Something." Frustrated, I sat up, scrubbing at the drying tears on my face. "Fuck, anything, Bobby. You know, something that would make some sense of all this shit."

I didn't hear what Bobby said under the ring of my cell phone. Since I'd already spoken to Mike, I let it go, waiting for it to go into voice mail, when he grabbed it, holding the damned thing for me to answer.

"Might be your Korean boy." He waggled his eyebrows again. "Here, answer it. Might make you feel better."

There was going to be a point in the near future when a bottle of hair remover was going to end up in his shampoo bottle, and I was going to laugh myself to death when those eyebrows floated down the drain of the gym shower.

"Hello?" I didn't recognize the number, but the 714 area code wasn't one I could ignore. It could be anyone from one of the Kims to another of Dorthi Ki Seu's dancers calling to tell me they were pregnant with Hyun-Shik's lovechild. Implausible, but still not outside the realm of bizarre that seemed to follow me around.

A spate of Filipino crackled across the speaker and into my ear. I didn't need to know what the person on the other end was saying to understand that I was being sworn at, and probably more thoroughly that I'd ever been in my life. Spits of words were beginning to make some sense, tidbits of English smattered through the high-pitched screaming. I only knew one person that spoke Filipino, and the street-guttural tone of it was a far cry from the polished silk of her normal voice.

"Scarlet?"

"You come fix this! Come down, buglit, and fix this. You're the reason he is like this, hurt!" There was more swearing, and then suddenly a deeply accented voice replaced Scarlet's, a soothing, authoritative older man who sounded as if he wasn't used to being argued with.

"Is this Cole McGinnis, please?" I grunted a yes and rubbed at my abused ear, trying to work the ringing out of my eardrum. He spoke briefly to someone else in Korean. I was guessing Scarlet by the conciliatory tone of his voice.

"What's wrong?" The water in my stomach came up in a rush of bitter over my tongue. I was already raw from talking about Rick, or avoiding talking about Rick. The mention of a hospital and Scarlet's anger were a kick to the belly. "What happened? Jae?"

"Scarlet's musang was hurt. The apartment he lived in had a gas leak, the police officers tell me." The man went on, but I didn't hear him, not with the pounding of my blood in my face. "Perhaps his oven light was not on and something created a spark."

"Fuck, is he okay?" I cut him off. For all I knew, he'd told me Jae was out dancing, but from the echoes of Scarlet's curse words in my ear, I doubted it.

"He is hurt, but the doctor hopes he will be okay. Sarang, yes, I am asking him to come here." He returned to our conversation. "He is at the Garden Grove hospital. If you are coming down, please understand that Scarlet is upset. She is very fond of dongsaeng."

"I'll be right over." I clipped the phone closed and searched through the mess on the floor for my keys, growling when I came up empty. "Where the fuck did I put my car keys?"

"We'll take my truck." Bobby grabbed my arm, yanking me toward the front door. "What the hell's going on?"

"Jae…." If Scarlet's keeper could be believed, Jae would be fine. Either that or he was lying through his teeth and was only trying to draw me down there so Scarlet could peel my testicles from my body with a melon baller. Either way, I needed to get over to the hospital.

I filled him in as Bobby shut the door behind us, half-running to his truck. My mind raced to catch up with my fear, which had left the ruins of my thoughts with a maniacal glee. I pulled myself into the cab and waited for Bobby to turn the engine over, going through what I'd been told.

"Fuck me, someone's after Jae." I exhaled hard, my fear finally finding someplace in my belly to set up its rave.

"Didn't that guy tell you it was an accident?" Bobby maneuvered around my battle-weary Rover, tsking at the damage left by the white van. "Gas leaks happen, Princess."

"Yeah, but I was in his kitchen. His stove was electric, and so was his wall heater."

Bobby exhaled under his breath. "So whoever it is isn't stopping with that Jin-Sang kid."

"Doesn't look like it." One good thing about being half Irish: while my temper usually got me into trouble, it sometimes saved me when I needed a good kick in the ass. My anger showed my dancing fear to the door and took up residence, firmly staking a claim on what I was going to do next. "Fuck this. We find this asshole before Jae gets killed."

"Best thing I've heard you say in a long time." The look Bobby gave me was long and probably was lewd as well, but I couldn't see his eyebrows do their jig in the dark of the cab. "Come on, Cole. It's good to see you into someone. Admit it, you like this guy."

"Yeah, I do." I fell into watching the lights pass over the glass, the blobs pushing along the freeway in a measured urgency. Jae's ripe mouth and unreadable brown eyes loomed in my mind, fueling my rage. "He's going to probably get me killed, but yeah, God fucking help me, I like him. Worse, I want him."

CHAPTER ELEVEN

"HEY," I murmured into Jae's ear, stroking the pitch-black hair poking out of the bandages around his head. His eyelids fluttered open. Those enticing cinnamon eyes were foggy for a moment as he tried to focus on my face. Awareness sunk in quickly as he recognized me, a slow smile cracking his dry lips.

His face was dirty, and a smear of something viscous clung to his cheek, but he looked better than I'd hoped. The smile he gave me went a long way in dispersing the knot in my stomach.

"Hey, Cole." Watery would be how I would have described his voice, but at that moment, I didn't care. I might not even care later as long as he was talking.

I'd been expecting the worst when I'd seen Scarlet's anguished face, her makeup run off by tears. The Filipino and Korean she shouted at me dissolved as quickly as her foundation must have when she'd grabbed at my shirt and I pulled her small body into a hug. Scarlet was frail under the armor of her personality. Mumbling something about Jae, she cracked wide open and sobbed hard into my chest.

Terror tastes a lot like blood. It lingers on the tongue until all I can smell and taste is metal. Sometimes there's a coldness that crawls over the face, but for the most part, fear resides happily in the senses, shaking loose any stability in the world. My mouth was full of metal shavings, and the shaking in my hands wasn't because I was cold. I'd been scared for Jae all during the drive over to the hospital, and seeing him lying against the too-white sheets that he came close to matching, my dread began a creeping meander along my spine.

"You came," he whispered. "Did Scarlet call you?"

"She called me and mostly yelled at me. Then someone with sense got on and told me where you were. I came right down."

Blood speckled his face, a small cut on his cheek held together with a butterfly bandage. The lines were already dried to black and peeling off when he moved. I wanted to kiss some moisture into the mouth. The crackle across his lips looked like it hurt. I gave in to the joy of seeing him and took a taste, reveling in the subtle orange zest in his mouth and the play of his tongue on mine. Breathing into his kiss, I fell hard into Jae, submerging myself until I felt the wet of tears on my face.

"Hyung, don't cry." Jae's fingers were cold on my neck, then a tiptoe of ice along my face where he wiped under my eyes. "I'm fine. Just a bump on the head."

"To go with the one you already had?" I didn't want to let him go, a warmth spreading down into my toes when I felt his mouth move to kiss the corner of mine. "Most people don't go through life banging their head against things. It leaves dents."

He grumbled at me, "Your hair must cover huge craters on your skull."

The mutter turned into a cough, working up from his lungs and shaking his whole body. The machines beeping around him didn't skip a beat. Tiny lights and sounds continued to measure his breathing and heart rate, ignorant of his distress. When I adjusted the oxygen feed looped around his neck, he grumbled more, low, deep noises that went straight to my dick.

Funny how I could think about sex during the dumbest of times.

"You look bad, Cole," Jae said, blinking. His eyes went unfocused for a moment, and I grabbed at the nurse's call button just in case. Waving his hand, he dismissed my worry with a click of his tongue against the roof of his mouth. "Stop. Just tired."

"You don't look too good yourself, baby." His breathing had improved, but there was still a layer of soot around the edges of his face, and the smaller of the cuts on his chest and arms weren't bandaged. Someone in the ER had tried to remove the black dust from his face, but they'd done a half-assed job, probably more concerned with keeping Jae's lungs going than with how he looked.

I got a wet washcloth from the bathroom and pulled the rolling stool close to his bed, wiping carefully at his face and neck. It took several trips back to the sink to rinse the cloth out and a few wrinkled-nose protests from Jae, but the sticky tar dust came off, leaving a blush on his pale skin where I scrubbed a bit too hard.

"Neko!" My arm ached where he grabbed it. For someone recently on the brink of death, his motor skills appeared to be great. "You have to go find her for me."

"Jae, don't worry about the cat right now, okay? You need to get some rest."

"She's all I have, Cole."

He broke me. Right in half. The plaintive hitch in his smoke-ravaged voice and the pout to his mouth broke me. God didn't play fair when he dealt out manipulation tools. I could barely get Claudia to give me an extra piece of pie by giving her puppy-dog eyes, and Jae seemingly could take down my defenses with a sheer bat of his eyelashes.

"Please."

That was just uncalled for. Like the final nail in my coffin. Nodding, I agreed, wondering how I was going to come back to him with his cat's corpse. Judging by what Scarlet half described, the place sounded like it was leveled. Of course it also sounded like Scarlet wasn't the most objective person where Jae was concerned, but I could understand that.

"What happened? Do you remember anything?" It might have been too soon to press him, but in the coming hours, Jae would remember less and less. I wanted to get some answers while it was fresh in his mind. "They said it was a gas leak."

"No gas in the place. It's all electric." His frown moved the bandages down over his eyebrows, smashing his hair against his temple. "And I don't know what happened. I was cropping pictures, and then I woke up in the ER. I couldn't breathe."

"Did you hear anything? A car outside? Something?"

"It's a brick building, Cole. I heard brick." Another cough shook Jae, and I held up a cup of ice chips. He nodded as he coughed again, spitting up into a tissue. The phlegm was runny and mottled with black swirls. "My chest hurts. Throat too."

"Here, open," I said, holding out a chunk of shaved ice for him. "Get some liquid into you. The nurse outside said you could suck on these."

Next to his mouth, his tongue seemed to be the next deadliest weapon he had in his arsenal. I really didn't need to have it sliding around my fingers and suckling the icy water from my hand. It wasn't that I didn't want it there. I could think of lots of places that tongue could also be, but with Jae lying on a hospital bed, my body wasn't listening to the scolding my brain was giving it.

"Tired." Leaning his head against my arm, Jae closed his eyes, murmuring softly in Korean.

"English, baby," I reminded him.

"Who is that? Is that… your boyfriend? I don't want you to have a boyfriend." His eyes were open again, staring through the open door at Bobby.

Scarlet was in good hands. Bobby was a master at consoling people. My best friend never used that finely honed skill with me because he thought tough love would work better. If that didn't work, he resorted to the tactics of my older brother and pounded the shit out of me until I gave in.

"Oh, um… no," I said. It seemed like as good a time as any to set the record straight. "That's my friend, Bobby. There's no one but… you, okay?"

"Were you scared?" Jae slurred the words together. Exhaustion was spreading through him, leaving bags under his eyes. "I'm sorry I scared you."

"Yeah, I was scared. Hospitals aren't the best place for me, sometimes." I was losing Jae to sleep, and I slid him off my arm and onto the pillow. "Why don't you get some rest? I'll be right here."

"Neko, remember?"

"Yeah, shit. Okay, I'll head down there and see what I can find," I mumbled, rubbing at my face. Bobby had driven us, and I wasn't sure he was up to taking me to a disintegrated building to look for a dead cat in the middle of the night. On the other hand, he owed me one, and it was as good a time as any to cash it in. "I'll be back."

"No, I need to get out of here." Jae strained to reach the call button. "Need to find someplace to go. Can't go with nuna, she's living with… well, I can't go there. Maybe Uncle Kim can put me up."

"Jae, no." I looped the wire out of his reach. "You're stuck here until they tell you it's okay to leave."

"Can't afford it." He was fully slurring now, barely able to keep awake.

"Don't worry about that. I'll take care of it." His pulse beat strong under my thumb as I ran my hand up his neck, cupping his jaw. He set his mouth into a tight line, and I was momentarily thankful that he was too battered to give me much of a fight. I might have outweighed Jae by forty pounds, but I was willing to bet he could give Bobby a run for his money if he was pissed off enough. "I'll be back. Promise."

"Call Scarlet when you find Neko. She'll let me know." Jae nodded off, resting his hands under his face as he turned, struggling briefly for air. "Take care of her. Please, Cole."

I didn't want to leave him. Hell, I didn't want to let him out of my sight. There was going to be the unpleasant task of telling him that he was going to stay with me until we could figure out what the hell was going on, but that was going to be an argument I intended to win, even if I had to drag Claudia in as a proxy. Pound for pound, she could take Jae on, and with luck, Scarlet would side with me.

"Cole?" Jae's soft whisper stopped me before I left the room.

"Yeah, Jae?"

"Agi."

"What?" My head was already throbbing with a headache, probably from the stress leaving my pores, but the word made no sense. "I don't understand you."

"If you insist on calling me baby, at least do it in Korean." He grunted. "It's agi. Now go find my cat."

"EXPLAIN to me why I was stupid enough to let you talk me into doing this?" Bobby stifled a yawn, more for show than sleepiness. I'd been with him on pub crawls that lasted until six in the morning, and he was as fresh then as when he'd started. "The cat's dead. A building fell on it. The only thing left of it should be its ruby slippers."

"Was that a gay joke?" I poked, sipping at the rancid coffee we'd gotten from a convenience store. "Because if it was, it sucked."

"I just don't know why we're going into the wilds of Garden Grove to go look for a dead cat."

"Because I promised him." Pointing out the obvious usually worked with Bobby, so I tried my hand at it. "And because there was that night when you called me at three in the morning to come get you, and then you made me promise not to laugh or say anything when you came out of a club wearing only pink suede chaps and a black thong. That's why."

"I'm never going to call you again. You're going to sit by the phone and wait for me like some lovesick puppy, and I'm going to sit back and laugh at you."

"Right. You have no other friends but me." The coffee wasn't so bad once I shook more sugar into it. I'd already dumped five packets in and was more than willing to sacrifice another five to thin the oil slick forming at the top of the cup. "And I'm taking pictures of your naked white ass the next time it's in those chaps."

"You are a cruel bitch, Princess."

"I learned from the best, old man."

We turned the corner, and my heart stopped. It looked like there was nothing left of Jae's side of the building. Three of the retaining walls were caved in, leaving the already pathetic porch structure standing solo amid rubble. A municipal truck was parked near the curb, workers already trying to establish power to the block. The blast had taken out the lights for at least five buildings, and from the looks of things, the rest of the building hadn't fared well either.

Three police cars sat watch, wide-shouldered patrolmen leaning against a hood and keeping a steady watch on us as we pulled up. A fire utility truck was parked slantways across the driveway, blocking any vehicle from entering the cordoned-off area. All together, it looked like a block party had gone wild, and the city had sent reinforcements to contain the crowd.

"Jesus, it looks like a fucking bomb went off." Bobby whistled, parking the truck. "That kid's damned lucky to be alive."

He wasn't far from wrong about how the building looked. I thought we'd seen the worst of it from the street, but as I stepped out of the cab, the fickle light from the streetlamps turned the place into something I'd only seen in apocalypse movies.

The bathroom walls were blown back against the brick, the gypsum board no match for the force of the alleged gas leak. Most of the ground was flooded, probably from the fire trucks who'd answered the call. I approached the place carefully. Investigators would be crawling over the place come morning, and the last thing I wanted to do was move something. As it was, there were a couple of men poking about the place. They gave us the briefest of glances before they continued walking around the perimeter of the building.

"Hey, boss-looking guy at two o'clock. You go sniff around, and I'll go schmooze." Bobby elbowed me in the gut. "He probably wants to kick us out. I'll do my best retired-cop impression. Try not to look like a looter."

"Tell him I won't touch anything."

There wasn't much to touch. What wasn't sodden was burnt. Jae's photos were black, flat corpses, their edges curled in. I wondered if I could get them to release his photo equipment, but there was no telling where it was. The cinderblock lay in puzzle pieces over the remains of the apartment. It was a wonder Jae had survived. It would be a miracle if his cat had.

"Hey." Bobby joined me, clapping me on the shoulder. "The supervisor said that we can go looking around the edges but not to touch anything. He hasn't heard anything, but things have been pretty loud down here. Neighbors keep yelling that they want their power back on. One of the idiots took a shot at the line crew."

"Yeah, this looks so promising." I stared at the crumbled walls. "Okay, maybe we can take a look and hope we can at least see something."

"Hold up, Cole." He grabbed at my arm, pulling me back. "You hear that?"

"Don't pull this shit on me, Bobby," I said, jerking myself free. "Too long of a night for practical jokes."

"Shut up. I'm serious." Stepping toward the pile of gypsum, Bobby stood with his head cocked, listening intently. "I am telling you. I heard something."

"I am going to break your ass if you start laughing at me." The threat was thin. I was too worn to do any serious damage to him, even if I wanted to. I nearly fell flat on my face when my foot caught on the bed frame. Bobby caught me before I made a total fool of myself, but I could hear the snickers from the cops watching us. "Okay, what am I listening to?"

"I swear to God, I heard a cat," he said, pointing toward the pile of debris against the intact wall. "Over there."

The screaming demand was faint, but I heard it. Lifting a section of wet drywall, I opened up a small hole to peer through. "Shit, it's too dark. You have a flashlight in the truck?"

"Yeah, let me grab it." Bobby nimbly maneuvered through the brick minefield that I'd stumbled over. He was back with a thick, black Maglite, turning the beam on. "Here. Don't let them see you digging."

"What do you do with this thing?" The light pierced even the darkest corner as I moved closer to the mess. "Call down UFOs?"

"I got it because it's heavy enough to whack assholes like you over the head with," he sniped back. "Look for the damned cat."

A pair of orange-gold eyes peered out at me from the hole, her rumbling voice nearly as tortured as Jae's. From the sounds of it, the cat had been crying for hours, probably incensed that her pet human hadn't come for her. Handing the flashlight to Bobby, I reached in, snagging her by the shoulders. She came without a fight, blinking when she emerged into the flashlight-drenched world.

"Fuck me, Cole," Bobby whispered. "You are so going to get laid for this."

"Shut up." I gripped Neko tightly, trying out some baby talk to keep her calm. "I didn't do this to get laid."

"Then I'll tell him I found her," he teased. "What I saw through the door was fucking hot. I want to get laid for finding the cat."

I decided that once I got Jae's cat to someplace safe, my first order of business would be to punch Bobby in the face. Maybe break his nose. I informed him of my plans as we picked our way out.

"Keep dreaming, Princess," Bobby said, unlocking the door to the truck. I slid in, holding the cat tight against my chest. The last thing I wanted was to lose her now.

"Home, Robert," I yawned, trying not to hit my jaw against her tiny head.

"Nuh-uh. I'm afraid our night isn't over yet." Bobby tapped the call button of his navigation system, bringing the information screen online. I groaned when I saw the listings he pulled up.

"Oh, you've got to be kidding. She's fine. She looks fine."

"Hey, last thing you need after rescuing your boyfriend's cat is for it to get sick from breathing in all that smoke," he pointed out. "Dead cats don't get you laid. Here's one close by. Nothing says I want you like a huge emergency vet bill."

DAWN was shaking the world awake by the time I got in. I didn't want to look at the clock because I feared it would tell me I only had a few minutes left of the night before Claudia would begin her round of wake-up-Cole calls. I jostled the cat carrier inside, apologizing to Neko when she screamed her disapproval at the treatment she was getting at my hands. Behind me, Bobby carried the paraphernalia the emergency vet said I would need to make Neko happy while she stayed with me.

I've seen a mother of infant twins carry less shit with her than what that cat scored at the vet.

"Where do you want this?" Bobby asked, scraping off the price tag from the litter box. "Downstairs bathroom?"

"She going to find it there?" I peered into the carrier. Neko spat another demand to be released, and I was fairly certain I heard a death threat included in her displeasure. They'd given her a bath to wash off the soot and drywall debris from her fur, and now she was a poofy black ball of cute. Demonic and possessed, but still cute.

"Doc said she would." He shrugged, ambling off to the bathroom. I left him to assemble the potty and braved opening the cage, belatedly wishing I had a rolled-up magazine to defend myself with when she leapt out to rake my throat open.

My chest smarted where her claws dug into me during her examination, and my thumb throbbed under a thick bandage the vet assured me could come off in an hour or so. I was planning on leaving it as a type of gauze armor in case she decided she wanted another piece of me for a snack. I didn't believe them when they told me cats sometimes got aggressive when they were stressed and was rather insulted when they laughed at my request for kitty Prozac.

She bounced out of the carrier, a gleeful bundle of furred and clawed vengeance looking for my jugular. Stretching, Neko took her time in exacting her justice, sniffing at the couch and then heading over to the bag of food I'd not opened yet. I did her bidding and filled a dish with kibble, then poured water into another one and watched her inhale a good portion of both.

"Okay, I'm going to head out." Bobby stopped at the archway leading into the living room. I finished picking up the last of the papers we'd left on the floor, stacking them as neatly as I could considering I couldn't see more than a few inches in front of me. "Get some sleep, Cole. We'll do this again tomorrow."

"You want to crash here?" I offered, but he shook his head. Grunting a goodnight, I walked him to the door and locked it shut after he left. Turning around, I found Neko in the middle of the foyer, offering me a view of her foot as she cleaned her leg. "You're a very classy broad there, cat. I'm going to bed. Well, right after I leave a message for your daddy telling him I found your scrawny ass."

The water on my skin made the cat scratches itch. I cursed the fluffball under my breath as I dried off, stepping over her sprawled body when I got out of the bathroom.

"You." I nudged her with my foot, a gentle tap that caused her to roll over and offer me her belly. "You are in the way, little girl."

The sheets were cold against my skin, and I luxuriated in the comfort of my bed for a moment. A second later, I felt a weight against my legs and then a heaviness settling on my hip. Opening my eyes, I was treated to the inscrutable view of the back end of a cat. Tentatively scratching her back lightly with my fingers, I used my free hand to dial Scarlet's cell phone, hoping to leave a message.

I was shocked when Jae answered, breathless and worried.

"Hey, what are you doing up?" It was stupid to ask him that. The reason he was awake was currently kneading her pointy little claws into my hip. The blankets seemed not to be a deterrent at all. Shifting, I hoped to distract her, but she mewed in contentment and continued to aerate my skin.

"Did you find her?" His already strained voice was too tight for my liking. "Was she...."

"She's okay." His sigh of relief made me glad I'd spent a good chunk of change for the vet to tell me she was perfectly fine and would probably be terrorizing generations of humans to come. "She's here now."

"You sure it's her? I mean," Jae stammered a bit. "Did she have her collar on?"

"Yep. Trust me, baby," I replied, moving my attention from her spine to her chin. She set up a faint rumble of a purr, puffing her white-starred chest out in approval. "It's your cat. Satan's mistress is perfectly safe."

"Agi," he reminded me. "And don't call her that. She's a good cat."

"She tore me to ribbons." I felt a little bit guilty for lying to him, but I was going to milk my injuries for as long as he would let me. Compared to the dual concussion, being shot at, and then having a building blow in on him, I was far behind on the sympathy list. "You should be asleep."

"Couldn't sleep. I was worried."

"Yeah, I should have called you sooner to tell you we'd found her," I said. "We went to an emergency vet to make sure she was okay. He said she checks out fine. She's already eaten, and I think I'm going to be learning how to clean a litter box in the morning."

Jae's whisper was so soft I nearly missed it. "I was worried about you."

"Hey, I'm okay, ba... agi." It was like being fifteen all over again and having one of the football players palm my ass in the middle of gym class. I wasn't going to be able to sit down comfortably for about a week if he purred at me again. "What are you doing using Scarlet's cell phone? You're in a hospital room."

"Aish, your Korean is horrible. Never mind. Stick with English," he teased, a soft laugh turning into a short bout of coughing. "Nuna is asleep on the chair, and no one knows I answered it. She had it on vibrate."

"Scarlet tell you we decided you were coming here?" I ventured carefully. We'd not talked more than a few seconds, but she'd agreed with me that Jae needed looking after. She even partially forgave me for getting him blown up, although I was disinclined to take full responsibility for the matter.

"Nuna said you decided and that she had nothing to do with it." While he sounded stronger and I was glad for it, the wisdom of having a fully sentient Jae roaming through my house was beginning to terrify me. Neko meowed her opinion, hooking her claws into my sheets one last time before tucking her chin in to sleep.

"Nuna lies," I laughed, startling the cat. She opened her eyes, slits of malevolent gold in her petite black head, then went back to sleep. "Hide the phone before the nurses come in and beat you. I'll see you tomorrow."

"Cole?"

My stomach clenched at the sound of his voice trembling. The teasing flirt disappeared, and in its place was the battered young man I saw on the hospital bed.

"Yeah, Jae?" I wished Scarlet awake or for the ability to crawl through the phone. He ached. I heard it clearly in his splintered, whispering sobs. "I'm here, baby."

"I'm scared," he confessed softly. "I don't know what's going on."

"Me too, baby." The ache in my chest grew. In the front of my mind, I suspected I'd brought this trouble to Jae's doorstep. The last twenty-four hours blew apart any normal that his life might have had. "I don't know if that makes you feel better, but I'm scared shitless."

"You don't act like it," Jae accused with a sniff.

"That's my tough-guy exterior. You should see me right now." I teased at him, hoping to draw him out of his melancholy. "I'm lying in bed on sheets with big roses on them with a cat on my hip. Very macho."

"You're lying."

"About the sheets, but not about the cat," I said. "She's like a lead weight. How can something so small weigh so much?"

"She eats a lot." There was a smile in his words, lightening his mood. It darkened as quickly as when clouds moved over the sun. "Are you going to protect me, hyung?"

"I didn't do such a good job at protecting my last boyfriend, baby." Thoughts of Rick surfaced. His laughter when I blew raspberries on his belly after sex, the horrible omelets that he insisted on making every Sunday morning, the deadness in his eyes as he slid down in my arms. I shut those memories away, concentrating on the memory of

Jae's bright brown eyes. "But I want to try. More than anything, baby, I want to protect you from all this shit."

We lay on either side of the call, listening to one another breathe. It was a glorious thing, the in and out of his breath against the phone. I didn't want it to end, but sleep tugged hard on my eyelids, and I suspected that Jae wasn't long for consciousness if he'd been up waiting for me to call.

"Go to bed, Jae. I'll be there in the morning." Shushing his protests, I listened to his grumbling assent. "I promise."

"Pfah." He dismissed me with a harsh explosion of sound. "Fine, sleep. But Cole?"

"Yeah?" It was like putting a three-year-old to bed. There was always something else a kid wanted: a story or a glass of water.

"I like it when you call me baby," Jae growled through the phone. "But not in Korean. Really, you stink."

CHAPTER TWELVE

THE cat kneaded at my skin, piercing through the sheets and the pajama bottoms I wore. I was nothing more than a prone scratching post, and she mewed her disgust at me when I moved her off me. She was back before I could turn over, tenderizing my body for what I was certain would be her midmorning snack. Being evil took a lot of energy, and something as small as she was probably had to keep up her strength.

It was raining outside, a sound that was drowned out by my doorbell ringing. The bells echoed, deep and booming, through the empty house. It hadn't fully faded when it rang again, and the cat dislodged herself, jumping off the bed in a bounding prance.

"Okay! I'm coming!" I nearly tripped on Jae's cat, goose-stepping around her as I made my way down to the first floor, pulling on a T-shirt. The hall clock chimed at me as I passed, marking off the morning. Rounding the landing, I glanced through the glass window in the door, and my heart skipped its beat when I flung open the door.

An unknown man held Jae tight in a paw of a hand, his thick fingers closing over Jae's upper arm. He was bundled up against the cold, while Jae shivered in what looked like clothes he'd borrowed from a giant. The jut of his jaw angrily challenged me to do something about his firm grip, dark stubble darkening his wind-pinked skin.

I rose to the occasion. Easy enough to do. The sight of Jae's pale face alarmed me. His weaving shoulders downright scared me.

"Let him go." I grabbed at Jae, holding him up. The man tugged, pulling back. I wasn't being menacing enough, so I pushed at the man's shoulder with my free hand, shoving him back down the first step of the stoop. "You're going to lose your fucking hand if you don't let go right now."

"He owes me money for a cab ride." A thick Slavic accent made him almost impossible to understand, and his eyebrows knitted down into a single line over his broad nose, suspicion curling his mouth. "I let go and he goes inside without me getting paid."

"I don't have any money." Jae's breath was cold on my neck, and he shivered when the warmth of the house hit him. "I'm sorry. I didn't...."

"No, it's okay," I said, hoping it sounded reassuring. Turning to the cab driver, I told him to wait a second while I got my wallet from the table in the hallway. Pulling out a few twenties, I shoved them into his hand and closed the door in his face, grabbing at Jae before he slid down the wall in a jumble of bones and bruised meat.

He squeaked, trying to hold himself up with the flats of his hands, but his legs gave out under him. Pitching forward, he made an inelegant tumble into my arms, his knees splayed apart. Breathing hard, he mumbled an apology and tried righting himself, only to fall forward again. Slipping off the pair of oversized flip-flops he wore almost sent him to the floor, and I clutched at him again, catching him.

"Did you tell Scarlet you were leaving? Shit, Jae. What the hell were you thinking?" His hands slapped at mine, warning me off. He was determined to stand on his own two feet, and I was just as determined to help him.

"Nuna knows I'd come here," Jae grumbled, trying to shove my hands away. "And no, I didn't tell her."

"Stop before you hurt yourself." Muttering at him did no good, so I tried scolding. "God, you've got as much sense as your cat."

"Fuck you. I have sense," he shot back, fighting me to stand up. He wove slightly, shoving my hands away when I reached to support him. "Where is she?"

The cat in question miaowed loudly from the landing, screaming her displeasure at me. Hooking my arm under his, I lifted, letting his weight rest on my shoulders. "Come on, let's get you upstairs."

"I can crash on the couch," Jae said, motioning to the living room. "Neek-neek, come."

"Can you let me win one argument? Just humor me and let me get you up there." I was glad to see the cat blissfully ignored him as she did me, sitting down to chew on her toes. "And why the hell aren't you in the damned hospital? Who let you out at six in the morning?"

"I checked myself out," he replied, letting me guide him up the stairs. The cat screamed, a demanding beacon. Either she was playing lighthouse or was giving directions to the bed. Whichever it was, she definitely had an opinion about it. "Hospitals are too expensive, Cole."

The climb up the stairs was tiring his abused lungs, and I stopped at the landing, letting him rest. His black daemon slammed herself into his ankles, and he smiled, an open, bright grin that made my heart stutter. It changed his face, washing away the ice and blooming a warmth over his mouth.

"I told you I'd pay for it." I didn't want to let him go, but he bent forward to scoop Neko up. She glared at me from her perch on his shoulder, rubbing her nose on his jaw and peeling her black lips from her fangs.

"You're crazy. You've known me for, what? Three days? Four, maybe? Bad enough I came here." Jae inhaled hard, getting his breath back. "I can't afford a hospital. I still send my mother money for my sisters, and I'm not going to make any money for a while until I get the insurance money for my cameras. If they give me money. The police said it looks suspicious."

"The police came by?" I slung my arm around his waist, letting him settle against me. "When? After I left or before?"

"After." He shifted the cat, holding her in the crook of his arm. The walk to the bedroom was short, punctuated only by Neko's mew of protest when she was placed on the mattress. "Those two that were at Jin-Sang's. They asked where you were. I don't think they like you."

"No, they probably don't," I conceded. As far as a lot of cops were concerned, I'd asked for what I got. The truth sometimes didn't matter to the boys in blue. "What did they say?"

"They asked me again what I was doing at Jin-Sang's and if I thought someone was trying to kill me." He shrugged as if being questioned by the cops was an everyday thing. "They also asked me if I was sleeping with you."

"What did you say?" I asked through the open door of the bathroom. There were extra toothbrushes somewhere in the linen closet. They'd apparently gone on safari, and I had to find one for Jae.

"I told them we hadn't gotten to sleeping yet," he responded, a teasing lilt in his voice.

"I'm sure that won them over." I placed the toothbrush package on the nightstand, along with a disposable razor, although I couldn't see even a shadow on his face. "I mean about Jin-Sang."

"That I knew Hyun-Shik's suicide note was really a part of the letter he wrote and that he should talk to you." Jae scratched at his cat's belly, a far braver man than I'd ever be to come close to those dainty claws. "They asked me if I saw who shot me, but I told them I didn't."

"Did you?"

"What? See who shot me?" He shook his head. "No. Someone came up behind me and the gun went off before I turned around all the way. I told them that before, but I don't think they believe me."

"If the shooter was in Jin-Sang's apartment already, then whoever it was heard you talk about the note," I said softly. That didn't bode well for Jae. Someone out there knew he had concrete knowledge of Jin-Sang's involvement with Hyun-Shik's death. He blinked like an owl when I told him I thought he was in danger. "Really, Jae. I want you to be careful. It's why Scarlet and I thought it would be better if you were here with me, where I could watch you."

"I thought it was because nuna lived with hyung and he can't afford any more scandal," he said, pursing his mouth. I wasn't sure if he was making fun of me or serious. "Scarlet-ah, everyone knows about them, but me? It won't look good if I stay there with them. Hyung doesn't need that. Nuna doesn't either."

"Probably that too," I said. There were things going on in the background of this whole mess that I couldn't wrap my brain around, culturally Korean things that I was ill-equipped to deal with.

"You have no idea who hyungmin is, do you?" Jae laughed at my bemused look. "He is someone big with the Korean embassy. His wife stays in Korea, but Scarlet-ah is who he takes with him wherever he goes. In their lives, the wife is the mistress, and it is nuna that he comes home to. They are all happy with that arrangement."

"Is that what Hyun-Shik was planning? To turn Victoria into his occasional mistress?"

"Who knows what hyung was doing? I didn't speak to him much. He was busy with work and his son." Jae chuffed under the cat's chin, undulating her disgruntled mews. "She's complaining about the bed."

"Don't listen to her. The bed was fine for her scrawny carcass last night." Giving her the evil eye back, I held out the sheets for him to get under. There were little bruises on his throat, marks from the flying debris of the explosion. "Lie down, and we'll talk in a few hours when it's a reasonable hour. I'll grab some sheets, then turn off the light so you can get some sleep."

"Where are you going?" I almost didn't hear him from the depths of the closet.

"The other bedroom has a Murphy bed. I'll sleep there." Tugging at a pillow on a high shelf, I ducked when a barrage of linens fell on top of me, burying my feet. I left the mess there, too tired to care and concerned about the fatigue in Jae's voice.

Carrying out the lone pillow, I stood by the bed, looking down at his drawn face. Despite the bruised look under his eyes, he took the breath from my lungs. He'd gone past the worrisome point on my radar and shot straight down into hellish trouble.

"Can't you stay here?" His teeth dimpled his lower lip, eyes large and dark in the low light. "Please? I need you to stay."

It was a mistake, but I nodded, sliding onto the bed and pulling the sheets over my legs. "Move over a bit."

Turning the lamp off, I lay back into the pillows, wondering if he could hear the pound of my heart. It seemed very loud to me, nearly reverberating in my eardrums. He stretched out next to me, lying close enough for our bodies to touch. It was a king-sized bed, but the mattress seemed too small, and I felt every movement he made, listening to him breathe.

"Tell me about Rick. What was he like?" Jae murmured, running his fingers along my side. I tensed, unsure about the contact. He traced a ridge of scar under my shirt. Raising the shirt hem, he examined the keloid with his fingers, splaying his palm over the starburst. "If you can."

I didn't want to, but Jae deserved to hear the truth. I tried to focus on the facts, numbing the pain in my heart. "What do you want to know?"

"You said he was shot, but that's all you've said."

"We were having dinner, and I was kissing him goodbye before I had to go back to work. I was a detective then. I worked Vice," I said, trying not to relive the night. Rick's grin was a watery screen behind my closed eyes. I wasn't sure if I was seeing him through tears or time was taking away my memory of his face. "I saw him die before I felt the bullet. He was shot first. Then I was hit and went down."

"Did they catch who did it?"

The question was so innocent, and I didn't know how to respond. Of course he'd want to know if the bad guy was caught, but I loved the bad guy as much as I loved Rick. Ben was my best friend, as much of a brother to me as Mike and Bobby.

"My partner, Ben, shot us." I stumbled over the words, searching for how to talk about losing so much in one night. "He shot Rick in the head first and then me. He emptied his gun out. Later on, another cop found him in our unmarked. He'd killed himself, probably right after he killed Rick."

"Why? I mean, why did he do it?"

If I had the answer to that, I probably wouldn't have spent every night since fighting nightmares and sleeplessness. I'd been Ben's partner longer than I'd known Rick. He'd been a constant in my life, much like Mike. To lose him as well as Rick nearly killed me, and I still had no idea why.

"I don't know." Sheila, his wife, had asked me the same question, then walked away when I had no response. I had no idea where she was or what she was doing. I was the godfather to Ben's oldest daughter. I'd watched their kids on nights when they needed time for their marriage. Sheila cut me out of her life as smoothly as Ben cut Rick out of mine.

"Did he love you?" Jae pushed himself up onto one elbow, dislodging the cat from his leg. "Was Ben in love with you?"

"Baby, Ben didn't leave us anything. Not a note. Not anything." Admitting my helplessness was hard. I'd lost three years asking that same question: why. And still was no closer to an answer. "I went nuts for a bit afterwards. Didn't know up from down. Bobby helped me out. Redoing this place gave me something to do while I tried to figure things out."

"Then you became an investigator?"

"Gave me something to do. I missed working Vice. I thought it would be a lot of divorce cases," I admitted. "Finding dead bodies wasn't on the agenda."

"I didn't want to be one of the dead bodies you found." Jae sighed, pulling my shirt back down. I briefly missed the warmth of his hand. Then he tucked himself against me, hooking his ankle over my shin. I burned under his touch. He was making me crazy with his breath on my neck.

"Jae, why did you ask how Rick died?"

"I didn't. I asked what Rick was like. I wanted to know why you loved him," Jae said, nesting into the pillows. "How he lived is more important to me than how he died. Maybe it should be for you too, no?"

LYING next to Jae was torture. I'd sooner have been able to fall asleep under a water drip than endure the feel of him against me. Every little hitch in his breath jerked me out of my doze, and I turned to check on him, staring down at his prone body until I was sure he was breathing okay. His cat gave me owl eyes from her perch at the end of the bed, and finally I got up and headed downstairs.

"Don't worry. He's safe from me right now," I informed her, sitting on the bottom of the stairs. I tied off my second sneaker when the house phone rang, and I scrambled for it, not wanting the ring to wake Jae up. "Yeah?"

"Hey, Princess." Bobby laughed at my breathlessness. "What the hell are you doing? Wet dreams at your age?"

"Dick."

"And a big one too," he teased back. "What time do you want to head over to the hospital to go stare at your pretty little boy?"

"No need," I said, wandering into the living room. "The pretty little boy checked himself out of the hospital this morning and came here. I've already had a round of why-did-you-do-something-that-stupid with him and lost miserably."

I left out the discussion about Rick and Ben. Jae's words were too raw in my brain still, scraping diligently away at bleeding scabs. I didn't want to admit to missing Ben. Hell, I didn't want to admit to wanting Jae, but I did that. Under duress.

"Nice." Bobby whistled under his breath. "What are you doing talking to me?"

"Small thing called smoke inhalation? Oh, and common sense." I reminded him. "I was going for a run to get the cobwebs out."

"Want me to go with you? It'll take me a few minutes, but I can get over there."

"Nah, I'm okay. Just going around the block a couple of times to work off the edge. Maybe do some thinking." The rain spat at the window, a gentle patter compared to the deluge earlier. It would be a good time to run, cool enough to push myself into a good sweat. "Come by later if you want. You won't be interrupting anything."

"God, you are the stupidest asshole I know." Bobby hissed at me through the phone.

"I seriously doubt that." I laughed at him. "I've seen the guys you take home, old man. I'm going to go running."

My cell phone weighted down a pocket of my sweats, and with luck, I'd be back before Jae woke up. I didn't have a lot of faith that his cat wouldn't chew on the piece of paper I'd left on the nightstand, obliterating the number into illegibility. Closing the door behind me, I shook the tired off my body.

The air outside smelled of asphalt and puke, a perfume wafting over from the bar across the street. Tar glistened from its wash, black smears left on the sidewalk from a failed roofing attempt by the Indian restaurant a few doors down. Hooking my foot against the stoop, I stretched, letting the burn of my muscles try to warn me off, but I sternly told my legs we were going for a run no matter what they said.

I wasn't even going to acknowledge the suggestions my cock whispered at me.

The pound of the sidewalk on my feet felt good. Falling into a steady pace, I let my mind go, feeling only the rush of air in my lungs and on my face. The scar along my ribs started to ache, seizing up. I worked through it, pressing the flat of my hand against my side. A cramp began to spasm under my palm after another mile, and I finally gave in, slowing to a trot before stopping, bending over to gain control of my breathing.

I was just about to head back when gravel hit the sidewalk next to me, popped up by wide tires. Lifting my eyes, I grimaced at Bobby's wide grin and nonchalant wave. The sides of his truck were caked with mud, drying chunks falling off and landing in the gutter by my feet. Dressed in a flannel shirt and ball cap, all he was missing was a coonhound riding in the bed and maybe a gun rack to complete the picture. The passenger window rolled down smoothly, and his grin got wider when I eyed him suspiciously.

"You look like a redneck," I said, steadying my breathing. I wasn't going to give him the satisfaction of seeing me heaving to catch air.

"Get in, Princess. And I come from fine redneck stock," he shot back, reaching over to unlock the door for me. "Nothing to be ashamed of. Peaches and hunting, that's what makes America the fine, proud country that it is."

"You were in the closet way too long." I slid gratefully into the truck's cab. The air conditioning felt good on my heat-soaked skin. Grabbing the towel he offered me, I wiped at the sweat on my face and neck and cracked open a bottle of water he had in the cup holder, draining half of it down my dusty throat. "Next, you'll be listening to country western."

"Young boys don't get as sweaty dancing to country music as they do techno," Bobby pointed out. "Sweaty boys lead to half-naked boys, which is a thing of beauty to a gay man. In case you forgot."

"I haven't forgotten." How could I forget? I had a thing of beauty in my bed which I'd left to go running. "God, I'm an idiot."

"Glad you've finally realized what we've all known." Bobby swore at the Mini that cut in front of him. "Damn specks. Now, why are you an idiot this time?"

"Because I've got Jae-Min in my bed and no damned idea who killed his cousin." I wanted to rub the tired out of my skin, but it was nothing a strong cup of coffee couldn't take care of. "I've got no suspects."

"Did you tell the cops?" Bobby slanted me a look before pulling into a drive-through coffee hut. He ordered two black coffees with sugar, pulling up to the window to pay.

"It was ruled a suicide, remember? As far as they're concerned, he did it to himself," I responded, taking one of the paper cups. The steam smelled great, invigorating my senses. "Shit, I don't know that he didn't kill himself. It's a whole bunch of maybes."

"Those are good maybes." The truck bumbled out into traffic, hitting a speed bump, more than likely dislodging more chunks of dirt. "The suicide note is from a Dear John letter he gave to some Korean boy who then was murdered right after you spoke to the deceased's family. Those are some good maybes, Princess."

"Don't forget the cousin," I reminded him.

"Definitely haven't forgotten the cousin." Bobby took the top off his coffee, blowing on the hot liquid before sipping carefully. "Shot in the head and then blown up. And who is now asleep in your bed waiting for a gentle kiss to wake him up."

"I'm going to kick your ass." Muttering, I slouched down in the seat. "When you're done driving me home."

"Yeah, that's going to happen." Bobby mocked me sometimes. It was a righteous mocking, but it was mocking just the same. He pulled up behind my car and whistled low at the sight of it. "I'll be fucking damned."

My Range Rover sat on punctured tires, tilting to one side where the road sloped in toward the sidewalk. Something red had been splattered over the hood and roof, dripping in long trails down its sides, pooling in the dents. I got out and walked around to the front of the car, shaking my head at its smashed headlights and battered hood.

A tire iron lay on the grass, its blunt end scraped with my Rover's paint. I didn't have high hopes for fingerprints. Its brushed-carbon surface wouldn't hold dust, and the cops wouldn't spend the time or money to drop it off at a forensics lab. They'd write it off as a gay-bashing and go about their business. Maybe even laugh in front of me, depending on their mood.

"That's a lot of rage there," Bobby said, finishing his coffee with a noisy slurp. "I think someone's trying to tell you something."

Panic hit me, closing in the air in my lungs. "Fuck. Jae. I've got to check on Jae."

I sprinted up to the back of the house. The door was unlocked, the knob turning in my hand before I could fit the key into it. Did I leave it open? I didn't stop to check the jamb, scrambling up the stairs and calling for Jae. Bobby was behind me, his heavier footsteps a thunder on the hardwood floors.

"Jae!" I couldn't find him. The bed was empty, the sheets holding his scent. Screaming down the stairs, I headed to the den, praying he'd gotten bored and gone to look for something to read. "Bobby! He's not up here!"

"Cole, he's down here!" Bobby called to me from downstairs. "He's okay."

Relief dried my mouth, and I stumbled to get down to the first floor without falling on my face. Jae stood in the kitchen, a quizzical look on his face and a cup of tea in his hand. His fingers played with the white tag dangling from a string over the cup's lip, folding its edge as he stared at me.

"What's wrong?" Jae stirred the tea with a spoon. His tousled black hair stood up away from his face, a fringe falling over into his eyes, and the damp ends spotted a T-shirt he'd borrowed from my dresser drawer. Its stark whiteness glowed against his skin and turned the bruises along his neck and collarbone a vivid purple. Startled, his eyes got big in his face. "What happened?"

I couldn't answer, not with the panic blocking my words. The cup went flying, dashed to the ground when I grabbed Jae, pulling him to me. I didn't care if the tea made a mess or if Bobby laughed in my face. I needed to kiss him, anything to reassure me that he was real and whole.

He tasted like sex and wonder, his mouth opening under mine. My hand found his hair, cradling his head as he tilted back into my palm, arching his body against mine. With his palms flattened against my back, he molded into me, his hips rocking against me, sliding into me until we fit together. The kiss burned away the taste of coffee in my mouth, leaving Jae behind on my tongue.

"I'm okay, Cole." Jae broke it off first, twisting slightly and touching my face. I held on to his waist, breathing the kiss into my belly where it burned hot. "I'm here."

"You two are so cute," Bobby commented, stepping around the ceramic shards on the floor. "There's a room upstairs. I'll clean up the mess."

I was saved from having to come up with a snappy rejoinder when an enormous boom shook the house. The noise was deafening, rattling the windows in the kitchen. The dishes I'd left in the drainer toppled over, and I heard glass shattering from the front of the building, loud pinging noises followed by the rushing sound of panes falling into tiny pieces. Up and down the street, car alarms started to scream, whooping loudly from the blast.

"You okay, baby?" I checked Jae over, trembling when I ran my hands over his shoulders and arms. "Stay here, okay?"

"I'm not helpless," Jae said, frowning. "I can go with you."

"No." I ran my thumb over the pout of his mouth, taking the taste of him with me on my fingers. "I need you to call the cops. And stay in the house. I don't want anything to happen to you."

"What if something happens to you?" he asked, turning his pout onto Bobby. "Are you going to take care of him?"

My supposed best friend melted under Jae's sensual parted lips and soft brown eyes. He turned to me, halfway beseeching me to help him. He was on his own. After teasing me that I'd gone soft for Jae, I let him stew in that erotic mouth and pretty face. See how he liked it. Scratch that. From the cow-eyed look on Bobby's face, he'd like it a lot.

I poked Bobby in the ribs to get him going. "Jae, find Neko. If we've got to get out, I don't want to hunt for her."

"Cops first, cat next," Jae agreed with a nod. "Go."

Sirens were echoing against the buildings, a fire truck heading in our direction. The Range Rover was a smoking mess, scattered apart into little bits of metal and glass. People were gathering around the carnage, staying a few feet away in case something else happened. Bobby's truck had taken collateral damage. A large piece of the Rover's ski rack jutted up from his hood, a giant phallic kiss-off to the world in general. The blast had shaken off most of the dirt, but the truck's windows were gone, sparkling bits of glitter on the sidewalk, road, and all over the interior.

"Fuck." At times, Bobby's clear vision and succinct words astounded me. I repeated his wisdom with an answering echo of profanity, staring at the shattered windows in the front of the brownstone. He stepped back onto the sidewalk, watching the fire truck pull in next to the smoking front end of my car. "Cole, I think you pissed someone off."

The second explosive went off before the firefighters could get off the truck. A fireball erupted from the remains of the Rover, blowing up the rear axle and shooting flames straight up in the air. The gas tank ruptured, sending me flying.

I hit the bushes hard, tearing through the branches and slamming into the cement facing on the stoop. Tasting blood, I tried to stand, my legs buckling under me. The air was still, a slight wind carrying off the plumes of black smoke rising from my ruined car. People were talking, or shouting by the looks of their faces, but I heard none of it. Their voices were lost in a rush of ocean waves in my ears.

Blinking, I tried standing again, looking frantically about for Bobby. He grabbed at me, nearly yanking my arm out of its socket as he pulled me up. Soundlessly yelling, he furiously patted at me, and a hot sear sliced over my shoulder as he put out the flames on my shirt.

"I can't hear you," I shouted back, wondering if he was as deaf as I was. Except for the tenderness in my knee and the aches forming over my thighs and back, I was in one piece.

The same couldn't be said for the Rover. Or, sadly, Bobby's truck.

Flashing lights cut through the smoke, and an ambulance jerked to a stop. Its siren could have been on full volume for all I knew, but nothing was slicing through the buzzing in my head. My back felt alive with scratches. The mock orange branches had scraped me raw when I'd hit, and my shirt was now beginning to soak through with blood. I tried moving again, felled by the stinging pain in my left knee.

Jae appeared, shoving at Bobby as if his husky body was nothing. Cupping my face, he spoke to me, soundlessly worried and strained. He gave Bobby a poisonous look, and I tried to explain that it wasn't his fault, that we couldn't have known there was another device under the Rover, but Jae wasn't having any of it. I knew what he was saying, his mouth moving around a word that I should have known. I mimicked the motion of his lips, and a wide grin spread over my face. I couldn't help but smile, the ends of my mouth tugging upward until I was sure they hit my eyebrows. If I still had eyebrows.

"Agi?" I repeated, jerking their attention back to me. My voice was probably too loud, but I couldn't hear myself. "Jae, did you just call me baby?"

CHAPTER THIRTEEN

"WHAT are you doing out of the hospital?" Jae met me at the stoop, holding the door open for us as Mike waddled me in. He looked like I felt, drawn and pale, but at least he was on his own power. My leg hurt from walking, and my hearing kept flaring up with a round of cymbals.

"Heh, I said the same thing to you. I'm fine. Just some ringing in my ears." I tried moving carefully. My ribs ached, and the scar tissue along my side twinged every time I took a step.

"They kicked him out." Mike dumped me on the couch, giving my shin a light kick before stepping back. "Dick."

It was good to be home. The smells were familiar, lacking that harsh perfume of sickness, death, and astringent. I was speaking to Mike's back as he headed into the kitchen. "Get me a Diet Coke while you're in there, okay?"

"They kicked you out?" Jae sat down on the couch next to me, stretching out his long legs. "Suppose something is wrong with you?"

His bare feet brushed mine and the warmth in my belly spread down, thickening against my thighs. Feet weren't supposed to be sexy. Bobby was probably right. Jae was getting to me because I hadn't been laid for a while. Another glance at his face brought that argument to its knees. His tongue wet his lower lip, and I pulled my gaze away before Mike learned more about gay sex than he ever wanted to know.

"Yeah, you don't have much room to talk. You left," I said, clearing my throat. The room felt warm, almost a prickly heat on my face. "Really, I'm okay."

"My brother's an asshole. No one wants him to stay." Mike passed me a cold plastic bottle. "Jae, did Bobby leave?"

"Miss Claudia was here for a while," Jae said. "Bobby left a few hours ago but said he'd be back. Nuna said that she wanted to come down before she went on stage."

"Bobby gone is a good thing," I muttered, wincing when my brother poked me in a sore spot. "Hey, I'm injured."

"You going to be okay here?" There were some murmurs of assent from me and a suspicious nod from Mike. "Stay put. No wandering around."

"Yes, Dad," I replied with a false smile.

Jae watched us, silent amid our teasing. A few minutes later, my brother's car started up and left the driveway, leaving us alone. His breathing sounded better than it had that morning, but it was clouded, a faint wheezing sound when he inhaled. I wanted to lean over and kiss him. My body wanted a hell of a lot more. Twisting off the top of the plastic bottle, I took a swig and let the cold bubbles rush down my throat.

"I'm sorry about your car." His touch was gentle. "Do you want help getting upstairs? Maybe get some sleep."

"Sorry, no sleep for me just yet." I handed him my soda and reached for my phone. "I'm going to call Bobby and see if he's up to a little snooping around Jin-Sang's life. When I get back, we can talk about you calling me baby."

"I called you an idiot," Jae snorted, pulling away. "Well, if Bobby goes with you, at least he can catch you when you fall flat on your face. I'm going to stay here and make dinner. There'll be food if you make it back. If you don't, then more for me tomorrow."

"THIS is the cousin's number?" I asked, sitting in the air-conditioned comfort of the rental Bobby had been given. "Joshua Yi?"

"Just dial the damned number." He was grumpy, rousted out of bed and muttering about my ungratefulness. "I'm burning favors for you doing this."

Bobby had done some of the legwork while I was busy being poked by the doctors. Since he'd left the force in much better graces than I had, he still had people behind the badge that were willing to do things for him, small things like peek into an ongoing investigation and see where things were at. Jin-Sang's murder investigation was already stale. Branson and his partner, Thurman, weren't exactly dragging their feet, but there was little to glean from Bobby's peeking. At least it gave us something to go on.

The crime scene had been turned back over to the apartment managers. Businesses usually took precedence over police work, after all was said and done. Once everything vital had been collected, rentals were quickly released back to their owners. Branson was done as far as he was concerned. A few pictures were taken, and pieces of carpet were ripped up. The dead's personal effects were, for the most part, handed over to a relative. The cousin's name and number was ours from the police report, and he'd been more than willing to let Bobby talk him into letting us see Jin-Sang's things for a few hundred dollars.

Yi's cousin answered on the third ring, his voice clipped and hurried. He agreed to meet us at his house, giving me directions at a machine-gun pace. I repeated the address as I wrote, hoping I didn't miss anything. A dial tone joined the persistent ringing in my ears.

"Grab the map book from the back," Bobby said. I moved too quickly, and my head spun, the bulgogi in my stomach threatening to spill onto the car's interior. Glancing at me, Bobby grunted his disapproval. "You should be in bed instead of wandering around Garden Grove. Mike's going to kill you when he finds out you're doing this."

"What can happen?" I asked. Sure, trouble seemed to be following me around, but I blamed that on Hyun-Shik. Once I found out who killed him, all of it would go away. "Besides, I've got a murder to solve."

"A murder you should leave to the cops," he reminded me. "You worked Vice, not Homicide, and you never made lead before... shit, Cole. You scared whores off of street corners and popped kids for carrying pot. Hell, did you ever even see a dead body on the job?"

"Not like that," I said. The demons in my brain whispered: just Rick. "But thanks for your support, Bobby. I feel the love."

"Love for you, I've got. Faith that you're not going to get yourself killed doing this?" Shaking his head, he turned off the highway and onto the surface streets. "That I don't have, Princess."

With nothing to add, I pointed out the next cross street, concentrating on giving directions. I had to agree with him on several points. Murder was outside of my comfort zone. If it weren't for Jae, I would walk away from Hyun-Shik's death, especially since I seemed to be the only one who thought he'd been murdered. My gut told me that I was doing the right thing. Someone had to do right by Hyun-Shik. It might as well be me.

Josh Yi looked nothing like his cousin. For one, he was alive. Secondly, he took the SoCal wannabe thug culture to heart. He wore white socks and flip-flops, long, brown, baggy shorts trailing down past his knees. Yi's head was shaved nearly bald, a scrawl of blue ink tattooed on the back of his neck. I couldn't make out what it said, then realized it was Korean, a pop of circles and lines against his pale skin.

"Yi?" I approached with my hand out, keeping my smile tight. "We talked on the phone."

"Yeah, you're the guy his club hired?" He repeated the lie Bobby had told him earlier. Spitting on the cement, he chin-nodded a greeting to Bobby. "You can take the leftover shit with you for a couple of hundred. The clothes and kitchen stuff are already gone."

"Wouldn't his parents want his things?" I asked as Bobby handed money over to Yi.

"Nah, he's been dead to his parents for years. They don't want his crap. I'm just going to throw it out. You might as well take it." His shrug was a dismissal of Jin-Sang's life. We loaded up the trunk with boxes from the garage, their cardboard sides smelling of apples. Yi stood over us, watching but not helping. Within a few minutes, his cousin's life was on its way to my house.

"It's kind of sad," Bobby said. His rugged face was smoothed with a solemn look that I rarely saw. "Kid's been dead for a few days and he's already nothing."

"Not to me," I replied. "Whoever killed Hyun-Shik probably murdered Jin-Sang, or at least is connected in some way."

"Well, like I said," he grunted. "Don't get killed doing it."

"WHERE'S Jae?" Bobby lugged the last box in from the car, forbidding me to carry anything in my delicate condition. Adding it to the stack on the floor, he flopped down on the couch, gratefully accepting the cold beer I'd left for him. I had to admit, I was ready to call it a day. My body was sore, and the crackling haunted my hearing with a ferociousness I'd not thought possible. Going out hadn't been one of my best ideas, and my bruised limbs were letting me know it.

Jae had dinner waiting for us when we came back, and I resisted the urge to tease him about being domesticated. At least not before I ate. I wasn't exactly sure what we were eating, but it was flavorful and had meat in it, all signs of a good meal. Bobby crooned over the spiciness, and I spent the better part of the meal plotting his demise after Jae gave him a brilliantly warm smile.

"He went upstairs to lie down," I said, cursing the bump on my head. Alcohol was off the menu for a few days, and I grudgingly sipped my water. Then again, a beer would have knocked me on my ass, and we still had boxes to go through. "Said he was tired, but I think he doesn't want to deal with any of this. Considering the last time he saw Jin-Sang, I don't blame him."

"Shit, we probably shouldn't have been doing this here." Bobby exhaled softly. "He's okay with this?"

"He said he was fine. I don't know." I opened a box, hoping Jae wasn't lying to me. "Let's see if there's anything here."

"Do you know what you're going to do with it when you're done?" Bobby cut at the yards of packing tape covering one seam.

"I'm kind of hoping he had some friends down at Dorthi Ki Seu. Someone there might want something. I'll ask Scarlet." I pulled out a stack of papers. The contents were a jumbled mess, as if someone had emptied desk drawers into the box and taped it up.

"Good idea. It would suck if no one did."

We pored through the papers and books. I set aside some letters that were in Korean, hoping to beg Jae-Min for some translating help if he was in the mood. Based on what we found, Jin-Sang had been focused on taking care of himself. He kept meticulous records on spa appointments, noting every dollar he spent on himself. The price of his haircuts made me squirm.

"Vain, or desperate?" I tossed up for discussion after finding a brochure for skin resurfacing. "I don't think I know women who spend this much on themselves."

"Do you actually know any women?" Bobby teased.

"I'll tell Claudia you said that," I shot back.

"Claudia isn't a woman. She's a goddess, and you can tell her that," he replied. "He might have been vain, but look at things from his point of view. He's in his late twenties and still dancing...."

"And doing other things." I held up a handful of condoms.

"It's rough out there for those kinds of guys," Bobby pointed out. "Look at his competition upstairs. There's always someone prettier and younger. He's got to step up his game every time he goes in."

A photo made me stop digging, and my sorrow flared. Red lights provided most of the lighting for the picture, pinking the edges of their mouths, but a flash drenched their faces with a shiny gleam. Jin-Sang looked happy, but there was a tightness around his eyes, and his smile looked forced. The men sitting next to him were what made me stop.

The photos I'd seen of Hyun-Shik were staged headshots and the artfully arranged family shots scattered about the Kims' household. His strong features were different when he smiled, and the casual photo told a different story than the dutiful son and devoted husband he was, as portrayed by the Kims.

This Hyun-Shik was flushed, from alcohol or perhaps from sex, a dominant masculine presence amid the other men. Jae-Min sat on one side of him, leaning into the frame but far enough away from his cousin so the gesture didn't read as sexual interest. In contrast to the warm Hyun-Shik, this Jae-Min was mysterious, a distant iciness warning anyone off before they came too close. A study in human nature, I thought, Jae hiding the fire inside of him while Hyun-Shik seemed to come alive.

"See that other guy?" I showed the picture to Bobby, pointing to the fourth man sitting at the table. "That's the lawyer from the house, Brian Park."

"Really?" He took it from me, turning it over. "Didn't he say that he didn't know Hyun-Shik was gay?"

"Yep." I nodded. "And I think the Korean on the back says Dorthi Ki Seu. I've seen it enough, but I'll check with Jae."

"So another lie, but this time from Park. He *knew* Hyun-Shik was gay." Bobby grinned. "Look at Jin-Sang. He's practically sitting on their laps. Check out where his right hand is. Park looks very happy to have company on his lap."

A noise on the staircase made me turn, and I spotted Jae standing in the archway. I held my hand out to him, hoping he'd join us. "Hey, did we wake you?"

"No, I couldn't sleep. My brain's too busy." Sliding onto the couch next to me, Jae leaned against me, and I tried not to smile. His body was against mine, touching me in a nearly solid line. Bobby's gaze dropped, and he surreptitiously watched us through his lashes.

I wanted to kiss Jae hello but settled for a half-hug around his shoulders, then passed him the photo. "Do me a huge favor and tell me this was taken at the club."

He studied the picture, his expression flat. Nodding, he turned slightly, moving the photo out of his line of sight and settling further against me. Neko jumped onto his lap, settling into a fierce kneading motion while squinting at me. "Yeah, that's upstairs. That was a night I was visiting Scarlet, and hyung was there with them. I stopped by to say hello before I left."

"How well do you know the other guy?" Bobby asked, reaching over to scratch the cat's head. She purred under his touch, a traitorous sound considering all that I'd done for her.

"Brian? He works… worked… for hyung," Jae responded. Bobby mouthed the Korean back at me, and I shook my head, not wanting to get into a discussion about honorifics. "He started coming to Dorthi Ki Seu before Hyun-Shik-ah got married. I wasn't working there anymore, but I think he got a membership. I don't know."

"How much does one of those memberships cost? A couple of thousand?" I asked, then choked when Jae named an amount that could easily purchase a sports car. "What the hell do you get for that?"

The look he gave me was pointed, as was the snort Bobby let out.

"You get company," Jae said, choosing his words carefully. "How much company depends on how much you tip."

"I should never have become a cop," Bobby muttered. "I was on the wrong side of the law."

"I don't think anyone would pay you to give them a lap dance, much less anything else," I responded. Jae's expression turned hard, and he made to get up, cradling the cat against him, but I caught at his waist, pulling him back down. "We're not talking about what you did, Jae. Just about stuff in general."

"I didn't... fuck anyone for money," he spat, but he let me cradle him back into position. "Not everyone who worked upstairs does that. I needed the money, but not that bad. Look what it did for Jin-Sang. Things were never good enough for him. Too hard to live that way."

"Isn't Park into the widow? Victoria?" Bobby said, then rubbed his face when I smirked. "Yeah, I know. You don't have to say it. Not all guys are happy with just one flavor."

"Good way to put it," I responded. "I think I've got to go back and talk to Brian Park."

"Do that tomorrow. Maybe even the day after." Ruffling my hair, Bobby stood and pissed me off by kissing Jae on the cheek. Sidestepping the kick I aimed at his ankle, he tweaked my nose and said, "Try to get some sleep, Cole."

I cleaned up a bit, organizing the things that we'd pulled out, placing the photos someplace that the cat couldn't chew on them. Jae watched me from the corner of the couch, then tugged on a loop of my jeans to make me sit down.

"Stop, leave it. You're too tired." His hands were on my ribs, a light caress before he let go. "You're making me tired. Go to sleep."

"We can go to bed like an old married couple." It wasn't quite ten, but my bruises were mocking my stamina. "God, I hurt."

"You should have stayed home and not gone out to find Jin-Sang's things," he scolded. The long, elegant fingers left off stroking the cat and returned to me, running along my forearm. "You are an idiot."

Flirting was never my strong point, so it wasn't a surprise to me when I said, "But I can be your idiot."

Personally, I put down my horrible flirting to a lack of practice during high school, a key time in social development when boys learn how to talk up the ones they're interested in. Since I'd spent most of high school drooling over the football players and the swim team when they showered, I didn't have much time to develop those key speaking skills. When other boys were learning how to woo the opposite sex, I was mastering the ability to sneak peeks at naked male bodies while no one was looking.

"Stop that," He didn't pull away, but the sheer ice mask I'd seen in the photo fell into place. I hate that look, hated that he felt like he should hide from me.

"Jae—"

"You make this hard, hyung," he cut me off. "Sometimes I think I shouldn't have come here."

"Why not?" I pulled him closer, ignoring the mewls of protest from both him and his cat. Settling Jae across my legs, I supported his back with my arm, refusing to let him go. "I like having you here."

"Staying here is too dangerous for me. It makes me want to not leave, and I have to," Jae whispered, tilting his head back. "It's easy for you to be who you are, Cole. It's not for me. I can't be here with you and not want you."

"Hey, I'm not talking forever here. We can do this and see where it goes." The protest was weak, even to my ears. I realized I did want him longer than a few days. I could see him in the house. Waking up next to him or coming in from snapping pictures of naked businessmen wearing bunny slippers and finding him in my... our bed. Those were easy images for my mind to come up with. Even without having sex, I wanted him.

Much more, I painfully admitted, than I'd wanted Rick in the beginning.

"Where can this... we... go, agi?" Jae said. He rubbed his cheek against my temple, much like his cat did when she wanted me to do something for her. "I have my mother and my sisters I have to take care of. My brother, he sits back and lets people praise him for how my mother is taken care of, but he doesn't give her any money. I can't walk away from my family, Cole. I can't."

"No one's asking you to." I sounded confused, even more so than I usually am. "Money isn't a problem."

"Yes, it is. Money and family are always problems. She will not accept me if I tell her I love men, and then what will happen to her?"

"This is bullshit, Jae. If you don't want me sniffing after you, then that's all you have to say. You don't need to pretend to be interested in me to stay here. I'm not that guy." I stiffened as his hands cupped my face and his mouth found mine.

"I'm not pretending," he murmured.

Our tongues fought, and I wanted to swallow him whole, needing him inside of me. I breathed him into my lungs, not wanting to come up for air. His back arched when I slid my hands under his shirt, holding him closer still. The moistness of Jae's mouth made me weep, and I was thankful for not drinking a beer. The taste of him was heady enough to make me dizzy.

He came up for air before I did, pulling away for a brief second, and stared into my face. Then I was falling again, when he leaned in, and I pushed him back against the couch to cover him with my body. I stripped his shirt off and closed my teeth over a small bruise on his throat, marking him with a sharp bite before moving down his collarbone.

Hissing, Jae parted his legs, nesting me into the V of his thighs. I tore at his reserves, wanting to strip away every layer of ice he'd thrown up between us. I wanted to see the Jae Scarlet knew and loved, the wild one that I knew lurked inside of him. My fingers flicked over his nipples, and I pinched at one, watching his face when he panted with need, responding to my touch.

The press of his sex jutted against me through his clothes. I rubbed slowly up and down over his body, creating a slow friction between us. When his lips opened for mine again, the heat of his mouth seared me clean through, and I groaned, shifting my hips up, hoping the spare distance between us would cool things off before I lost all control and embarrassed myself.

Moving proved to be a mistake. There was now room for his hand to brush my belly, tracing the smatter of hair around my navel. Dipping a rake of fingernails under the button of my jeans, Jae bit his lip and played dangerous games with my equilibrium when his touch brushed against the crest of hair under the waistband of my boxers.

"Open your mouth for me, baby," I urged, coaxing another kiss from his mouth. I wanted more than his body, and that scared me. I was willing to take anything he'd give me, set on fire by his mouth and the fierceness he had inside of him. "Let me make love to you."

He molded into me, fitting into my belly and arms. I bit into the softness of his lower lip, making him moan and twist me into another kiss. I needed to hear that moan again, drawing it out when I suckled on his tongue. Our teeth hit, and he laughed, a deep throaty sound that went straight to my gut.

"Want you." Murmuring, he pressed his hands on the back of my thighs, frustrated by my jeans. Small pecks at my throat and then a bite, closing in on the pulse that beat wildly under my skin. "Wait, hyung, this is bad. You're hurt...."

"I like agi better," I growled, not letting him get away. Pulling up, I lay on him, gasping for air. "Look at me and tell me you want to leave, and I'll get off of you."

It was a struggle for him to look at me, even harder for me when he said, "You should."

"No," I refused, grabbing at his wrists and holding his hands above his head. "You make me crazy and you piss me off, and fucking damn it if I don't want you. Are you telling me you don't want this? You don't want to try this?"

"Cole." The heat of him under me burned, and he licked at the corner of his mouth. "When I'm with you... being with you... pulls everything out from under me. I shouldn't want you, but I do. There's nothing right with you, your mind, and you go around wishing you were dead. I can't do that. I have to take care of my family. I can't take care of you too. I can't."

"Yeah, so I'm a mess, but you are too, baby," I said, pulling him up until he sat against the arm of the couch. Crowding him in, I sat with my knees on either side of his legs. He wavered. I could see it in his tawny, brown eyes, and I pursued that flicker. "You run away from me and then let me catch you. You want this as much as I do. Just admit it."

He slid away from me, easing out from under my legs. It hurt to watch him stand there, his back to me as he trembled with emotion. No, I didn't understand what he was going through. I'd made my choices a long time ago and watched my parents turn their back on me, but I didn't have the familial needs that he did. I didn't have that cultural pull that demanded I live my life a certain way. Just guilt and a longing to have my father back, but it was a choice I made willingly.

"I'm not asking you to walk away from your family, Jae. Just walk toward me," I said softly. "We can make this work, babe. We can."

Bobby might believe gay men have sex first and then work on relationships, but I disagreed, especially staring at the sliver of skin peeking out from under Jae's shirt. I didn't want sex as much as I wanted... Jae. Even with everything that he'd put me through, I wanted him close to me. Sex is always great. I wasn't a fool, much less a celibate fool. God made Jae an erotic, gorgeous, and complicated chaos—one I wanted to drown in—but I definitely wanted more.

Leaning forward, I kissed him there at the small of his back, a gentle brush of my mouth on his body, and felt my touch ripple through him.

"Take me upstairs, agi," he whispered, turning around to take my hand without looking into my eyes. "Please."

HE TASTED of mint and laughter. Kissing Jae's mouth was like taking a sip from his soul. I held nothing back, kissing him hard and stealing the breath from his lips. He left wet kisses on my shoulder and moaned when I moved my mouth to capture his in a hungry kiss. I fought with his shirt, catching the sleeve on his elbow.

"Stop," he laughed, pushing me away. "Let me do this before you break my arm. Get your own clothes off."

I never tired of watching him get naked. Artlessly smooth, Jae shed his clothes slowly, revealing his tightly muscled torso and long limbs. A light purple line threatened to leave a scar over his right collarbone, a memento of the explosion. Tossing my clothes on the floor, I reached for him, pulling him close.

"God, you're gorgeous." I licked at the maybe-scar, leaving it wet. Tracing the column of his neck with the tip of my tongue, I found the line of his jaw and bit, making him gasp and arch against me. My fingers found his nipple, and I played with it, drawing it to a peak with a pinch.

"Need you," Jae moaned, tilting his head back when I moved to kiss his throat. His hands dug into my shoulders, and the tip of his cock left a trail of moisture on my bare thigh. I fumbled for one of the foil packets on the nightstand, tearing it open with my teeth.

I was so hard it hurt, so I rolled the condom over my cock before I lost my head and buried myself in him. The throb along my shaft pumped a rhythm, echoing the pulse pounding in my ears, but I wanted to take my time. At some point, Jae was going to leave, and I'd miss having him within reach at all times. Shaking away the melancholy, I pushed Jae down onto the bed, covering him with my naked body. He writhed under me.

Tearing my eyes away from Jae's mouth, I roamed, flicking a nipple with my tongue. I played with the other nub, tweaking it roughly, grinning when Jae groaned and twisted his hips. Unable to wait, Jae blindly searched for the small bottle of lubricant I'd tossed on the bed. Nearly desperate to have me buried in the hot snugness of his ass, Jae flicked open the top and held it up so I could coat my fingers. I laughed and licked at Jae's belly button, tracking the shiver of goose bumps across his hip bone with a swipe of my tongue.

"Spread your legs, baby." I listened to my lover's moan and nudged Jae's leg with my shoulder so he moved aside. "Let me see you."

"Cole...." Jae turned his head, his dark eyes hooded and hot. "It's...."

"You're mine, yes?" I nudged again and teased Jae's cock with a nip of my teeth, licking at the damp slit until I coaxed out a drop of Jae's salty heat. "Let me see what is mine, baby."

I buried my face in his thighs. Nestled between Jae's legs was a mingling of masculinity and crispness that I couldn't seem to get enough of. Parting the soft skin around Jae's head, I teased and licked at the sensitive spot until he twisted and cried out. Unable to pull away from my tonguing, Jae raised his knees, anything to stop the delicious torture of his sex.

"Ah, much better, baby." I chuckled and dipped my hand down, the warmed lubricant spilling down the crease of my lover's body. Spreading the aromatic oil around, I flicked my fingertip around Jae's opening, stroking the velvet crimping.

"Agi." Jae crawled slightly back into the bed, pushing his shoulders into the soft pillows. Splayed apart, he looked vulnerable, and I saw a shyness creep into his eyes. Keeping my gaze on his beautiful face, I swallowed the length of his hard sex, fitting it into the cradle of my mouth. Closing his eyes to ride the sensation, he gasped and crooned, running his hands over my shoulders.

Hot was the only way to describe Jae's entrance on my fingertip. It was a wicked, sinful feeling, and I pulled back from sucking on his cock to leave a flickering touch of my tongue around his hole. Fully exposed, Jae let go of his control, falling easily into the rhythm of my mouth and tongue moving over his crotch. My fingers played with his sac. I suckled first one orb, then the other, pulling them out before letting them drop back with a wet slurp. I moved back to his cock, licking up and down Jae's shaft, following the ridges along the top and across the shiny, slick skin.

The vein on his cock throbbed, pulsing with each butterfly kiss I left along its length. A deep kiss left his head puckering on my tongue, and a ripple of need rocked Jae. Catching his breath, he was ill-prepared for the thrust of my finger into his depths. Rocking Jae in my mouth, I plunged in deep, stroking at the tender heat inside until I found the spot I was looking for.

A flick of my fingertip against the burl in Jae's channel drove him up onto his toes, his hips rising with the shock of my touch. His panting breaths became cries, loud, mewling, begging noises. The sounds rose and fell, peaking, then numbing to a whimper when I pulled away. The splash of seed on the back of my throat warned me that my lover was close but I wanted to feel Jae's tremble around me when I came.

Clutching the sheets, Jae gasped and moaned, "Why did you stop? Driving me crazy."

"Because I'm going to be inside of you when you come," I whispered, rising up to my knees. Leaning over to give Jae a fierce kiss, I slid another finger into my lover's warmth, stretching him out with a twisting motion. My cock was wide, nearly too much for Jae to take comfortably without a lot of play. He hissed as I toyed with him, panting and biting down on his lip as his cock bobbed in time with my fingers.

"Want you inside of me," Jae murmured into my mouth.

"You have no patience, Jae-Min," I teased. I fluttered my fingers around Jae's entrance, and he exhaled hard and rubbed his thighs against my legs. "Silly boy."

"Silly?" Jae growled and lifted his head, biting into my earlobe. He pulled hard, and I was forced down as he twisted his head to the side.

I laughed, sliding my fingers along my hard length to cover my shaft with lubricant. "Let go."

"Get in me," Jae said, releasing me and kissing the spot before I pulled away. "Now."

"Anything you want, baby," I murmured. "Turn over."

I guided him as he lay on his stomach, pulling down a pillow to put under his hips. Angling my cock, I thrust in gently, rocking my hips as Jae's entrance sucked at my head. Pushing on the tight entrance to his body made me crawl into Jae, my cock dripping in anticipation for the stretching of his flesh. There was a trembling along his body, and I knew from experience the shivers could only be satisfied by my length on the center of his nerves. As I eased further in, he rolled his hips up, hitting the spot he craved to be touched.

"There, Cole," Jae panted, gritting his teeth. "Right… there."

The pillow already bore the print of his teeth, its linens soaking up his spit. Stifling his need to scream, Jae bit down into its feather plumpness, then lifted his head as I drew out slowly. His breath came in short little bursts, and he ground his hips back, telling me I was taking too long to fill him.

I liked hearing him moan, so I pulled back out, my fully engorged cock dipping and bowing as I slid from Jae's pout. His body heaved with the effort to remain still enough for me to find his entrance again, his fingers scrambling to clutch the pillows resting against the headboard.

Looking down, I watched the head of my cock slide past Jae's tight ring. Flexing my fingers into the meaty globes, I spread them apart, trying to get a better view of his entrance. Jae licked his mouth with the tip of his tongue, thrusting up and spreading his knees further apart for me. The sight of my tip being swallowed up by Jae's heat was nearly too much to bear. It became doubly erotic when he moaned in frustrated pleasure and bucked his hips back, pushing down on my cock in an attempt to plunge me deeper in.

"I want to take my time, baby," I cautioned, grinning at the Korean pouring from his sweet lips. "Ah, that mouth on you."

"I need you in me," Jae growled, dipping his rear down, pressing the tip of my sex up against the moist walls inside of him. "I need you. I need this."

I marveled at Jae's prone body, his long form twisting under me. My shadow fell across Jae's shoulders, and I slid back, then pushed forward, feeling the tight whorl around me open up. The ridge of my cock's head rubbed and slid, then entered fully, my shaft easing past the ring.

The soft skin on my cock twitched when it struck Jae's moist heat. I paused, letting the feeling of satiation roll over him. Trembling, Jae fought for some control, and I held back from plunging down into the welcoming body.

"Now," Jae spat, his voice low and rough.

I knew better than to argue with him when he'd reached that point of frustration. Fingernails dug into my legs as Jae reached behind to clutch me closer. Curls of skin peeled back under his onslaught, small stinging reminders that I was too far away for his liking.

I started with leisurely motions, a dip of my hips to plunge my shaft deep into Jae's guts. He grunted, then let go of a long, strident mewl, his head cast back in ecstasy. Drawing nearly all the way free of my lover's body, I forced back in, gripping Jae's hips to hold him still.

Jae writhed against my hands, wanting to have some control over the driving shaft piercing his ass. Slightly frustrated at his lack of movement, Jae growled and ground his hips in a small circle around my cock, squeezing down as I pressed in.

We worked against one another, loud groans working up from Jae's chest, mewling cries that quickly became arching pleas for me to go deeper or faster. I rocked against his ass, pressing deeper until I heard my thighs hit his body with a loud slap. I couldn't get any further in, but my body needed more, wanted so much more of the beautiful young man offering everything of himself for me to take.

The scant moans from Jae's mouth soon dried up under my continuous thrusts, and I lifted up with each long stroke, my cock driving the moisture past the ring and into Jae's body. His pants became tortured, and my climax nearly reached its peak under the mingled pleasure-pain of his tightness. A slight burn began along my balls. The push and pull of my shaft rubbing at him set off a ripple of spasms in his inner muscles as I hit the sweet spot in his ass over and over again.

Gripping at the bed, Jae bent his head down, resting his forehead on the pulled-back sheets. Surrendering himself to my thrusts, I watched him ride the sensations of being pulled apart and his ass being taken by my cock. When my strokes hit his core, he trembled under the sensations overwhelming him, and I wasn't sure how much more he could take. Jae was gorgeous under me, his body fully open and accepting my width. With his ass stretched open, my shaft now rode in easily, rocking back and forth in a steady rhythm broken only when I reached under Jae to grab his cock.

He was so close that the touch of my fingers on his tip brought him to his peak. Jae stiffened and moaned, falling forward, and his limbs twitched with the power of his climax. I felt my own balls tighten in the hollow of my thighs. Then a prickling sensation started in my face, a familiar near-blush warning me I was close to coming.

My blood thundered in my ears when Jae clenched, folding his body over until he was firmly locked over my dick. I let the sensations of my release wash over me, and submerged deep into his own passions, Jae rasped out my name as his seed gushed from his cock and over my fingers.

I let go. Bending my shoulders back, I thrust hard once, then again, burying myself deep into Jae's body. A lightning storm worked over my nerves, shocking me into release. When Jae's muscled ass closed over me again, the spasms carried me over the edge, and a hot rush of cum exploded from my body. Another thrust pushed me deep enough inside of Jae's body that I felt his clench on the base of my cock.

I rocked gently, carrying my climax along its course, slowing my body. It seemed as if Jae had spent his entire spill. Bending over Jae's heat-flushed back, I kissed at his shoulder, rubbing at his strong neck with trembling fingers as he fought for breath. I was about to pull free of his body when he reached back and put his hand on my leg.

"Stay, just for a little bit. Please," Jae finally gasped, his voice harsh and rough. His breath staggered in his chest, unable to fall back into a steady rhythm. Weak-boned, he lay under my heavier weight, obviously enjoying being pressed into the mattress. The feel of him under me was a comfort, and I relaxed into the feeling before pulling him over onto his side.

"I'm too heavy for you," I groaned, leaving another kiss on his back. "Here, let me get a towel."

He complained softly when I reluctantly pulled away, but I assured Jae I'd be right back. I disposed of the condom, flushing it down the toilet, and came back with a damp cloth to clean off Jae's trembling body. He lay on his side, letting me bathe him, and smirked when I hooked the balled-up cloth over my head like a basketball, landing it in the laundry basket by the door. Crawling onto the bed, I fit against him. Neither of us wanted to let go, and the bed creaked with the movements of our tired bodies. My heart pounded when I turned his face toward mine, and I kissed him, lingering in the taste of his mouth.

"I like this too much. It scares me," Jae whispered. "You scare me sometimes because I want you so much."

"This is a scary thing," I agreed, curling up against my lover's long, warm body. Stroking at my back, Jae leaned in and gave me a gentle, sweet kiss that left us both breathless. He rested his cheek on my chest and wrapped his arms around my waist. "If it makes you feel better, you scare me too."

CHAPTER FOURTEEN

I WOKE up with the taste of Jae-Min in my mouth. Sadly, I seemed to be lacking the feel of him on my body. Moving was an excruciating lesson that taught me that even my tongue appeared to have bruises on it and my hair could hurt. I blinked my eyes open and then promptly closed them again when the light set my corneas on fire.

"What time?" My voice sounded distant, lost under the white noise captured in my ears. Neko sat on the windowsill, chittering at the birds, a low clicking noise that fought with the buzz in my head. The light began to hurt, stabbing triangles of pain digging into my brain. Blinking brought tears, and the world swam, blurring back into thick swaths of color. Jae turned into a splotch of black and golden pale, a stark wave against the red ocean of sheets and dark wood.

His vowels were rounder again, stretched from speaking Korean. I decided I liked the sound of it, a burble, like tea being poured into a cup. Swallowing the melt, I nearly choked on the sliver of ice, saved only by Jae's fingers working on my throat.

"Sorry," I repeated. There was a fuzzy memory of hot kisses and then Jae's sinful mouth on my nipple. After that, everything went black. I had a feeling there was a lot I had to apologize for. I risked opening my eyes and found Jae sitting on the bed next to me.

One of my old shirts swallowed his slender frame, and the marbled purple spots on his throat were turning yellow around the edges. I tried lifting my hand up to trace one of the bites, but my arm refused to obey me. His face turned to a watery gold as my eyes went wonky, and blinking only seemed to make things worse.

"Kiss," I demanded, using my apparent uselessness to secure some affection.

"No, not until you brush your teeth." He laughed, refusing me. "Come on, I'll help you up. You probably need to pee, too. Scarlet's coming to get me. I need clothes, and she wants to shop. Are you going to be all right if I leave you?"

I am not susceptible to the power of suggestion. My dick had had other things on its mind until that moment, and suddenly the bathroom looked like heaven. Shakily, I got to my feet. Jae's height hindered me a bit, his long legs tangling in mine as I slid off the bed when my knees gave out.

"I'm okay. Have fun shopping," I said reassuringly, and Jae rolled his eyes at me. He waited until I waved him off before closing the door behind him. My arm ached after I was done brushing my teeth, but a shower was a necessity.

Splatters of purple and red covered my temple and worked down one cheek. Mike teased me about being pretty, but I'd not take home any dog show prizes in the condition I was in. A trail of dried blood, smeared from a thin slice over my right eyebrow, matted the hair at my temple. My mouth was slightly puffy, and I rubbed at my lower lip, feeling the bite of Jae's teeth on it.

Turning the showerhead on to full, I didn't wait until the water turned hot before stepping in. The icy shock bit into the cuts on my back, growing warmer until steam covered my body and pushed the pain on my skin into my frazzled nerve endings. After drying off, I pulled on a pair of jeans and picked at the scab on my forehead. My house had a cat in it, and one of my favorite T-shirts was gone, but it made me smile. I'd never thought missing clothes from my dresser could bring a flicker of something bright to my heart. I finished dressing and headed downstairs.

I was working on getting information when the house's peaceful silence was shattered by Claudia coming through the front door.

"You finally dragged your sorry ass out of bed," she greeted me warmly, almost as if I were one of her sons. "'Bout time. You've got some things to sign."

"Love you too." Mumbling, I sipped at the cup of coffee I'd made myself, grateful for the jolt. Its black bitterness mingled with the mint of my toothpaste, and I swallowed, watching Claudia over the cup. I signed off on the papers she put in front of me, drinking half of my coffee as I read the contracts. The paper on the bottom caught my eye, and I waved it under Claudia's nose. "What's this?"

"Insurance payout for your car. They were quick. I'm surprised they're still going to cover you." She sniffed, pulling herself up to get herself a cup. Back in less than a minute, she stood over me, placing a hand on her wide hip. The bright red flowers of her dress were as vivid as the bruises on my face, and I turned my head before my eyes were burnt out from the color. "They sure gave you a lot of money for pieces of scrap metal."

"It was a good car." The amount was ridiculous, but then, the insurance company hadn't seen the car before it had become tinsel all over the road and the front of my building. "Did the rental company drop off a car for me?"

"One of those blocky SUV things that rich people drive with no sense." Claudia sat down, the couch creaking under her. "It's in the carport. I put a big sign on it that says, 'This is *not* Cole McGinnis's car. Please do not blow up'."

"Well, you said please. That'll make all the difference." I nodded. "Thanks, Claudia. For helping Jae and, well, for everything."

"Boy's easy to take care of. Very pleasant and polite. You could learn something from him."

"That's what you think." I snorted. "He's about as easy to take care of as a hedgehog with a toothache. Did they give you the keys? Or is it like an Easter egg hunt?"

"Giving you keys to that car is possibly the stupidest thing I could do in my life." She dug them out of her purse, slinging them across the table in a skittering glide. "You going to do something equally stupid?"

"I'll leave Jae a note for when he comes home so he doesn't worry." I grabbed the keys from the table and leaned over to kiss Claudia on the cheek. "Don't wait up for me, Ma. I'm going to go see a man about a dead Korean hooker."

"You taking Bobby?" she yelled at me before I could close the door behind me. "You'll need someone with you when you do this stupid thing you want to do."

"Nope." I grinned at the scowl wrinkling her round face. "He can go find his own dead hooker."

THE laptop and some digging gave me Brian Park's address and a few personal tidbits. Park graduated from USC and was the third son of a prominent Korean family, mostly doctors and engineers, but a lawyer wasn't anything to sneeze at. He had a juvenile record, sealed against my prying. No amount of finagling proper channels would get around the seal, but there were ways to get to the information if I really wanted it.

Bobby was taking care of that for me. Cops still liked him. Some even admired him for his silence during his years on the force. I didn't have that kind of popularity. Hell, I was pretty sure a few of Ben's friends used my face for target practice.

Ben.

I pulled the SUV into a shady parking lot and sighed, wanting to force my mind from wandering around the memory of my partner. The steering wheel dimpled my forehead, gouging into the bruises on the side of my face, and I laughed, remembering Ben teasing me when I would rest my head in the unmarked we shared.

"Can't steer with your nose, McGinnis," he'd say, flicking a fingertip across his own nose. "You need one like this."

His Italian father's blood gave him hawkish features, dark eyebrows, and a strong profile as well as a booming laugh. He'd known I was gay before he met me. I'd never hidden it, and no one gossips like a cop. Ben crowed over my cockiness, poking at my arrogant confidence when he told me I should just keep my mouth shut.

"No one needs to know your business, Cole," Ben once told me over a beer after a hard night's work. "If you're different, no one wants to hear it. They can ignore anything if it's not in front of their faces. You're better off just keeping your mouth shut."

I disagreed with him, sure in my rights as a person that I should be able to love anyone I wanted. Ben must have thought otherwise. I'd never know. His reasons for trying to kill me had died with him.

"Fuck that." I shoved Ben back into the closet where he belonged. Wiping at my face, I jumped when my cell phone chirped at me, then danced across the passenger seat as I chased it with clumsy fingers. Flicking it open, I answered, hoping Bobby would have something for me.

"Hey, Princess," he drawled, and I heard Claudia in the background admonishing someone for not wiping their feet. "Funny thing. I'm at your house, and you're not here. I thought we agreed that you weren't going to go gallivanting off without me."

"You agreed to it," I responded, flipping open my case notebook and finding a pen in the backpack I'd slung on the seat. "Do you have anything else on Park that I need to know? I'm heading to his place right now."

"Anything I can say to get your ass back here?" More commotion crept around the edges of his voice. Then a riot of laughter prevented me from hearing anything else he said.

"What the hell's going on over there?" I asked, pointedly ignoring his question. "Sounds like you're having a party. If you are, don't break the good china."

"It's like a bad joke over here: a black woman, a Filipino transvestite, and a Korean ex-stripper walk into a gay man's house. All that's missing is a priest and a talking dog." The noise grew softer, and I heard the screen door close, its peculiar snick as the door latch caught. "I'm serious, Cole. You shouldn't be out there wandering around alone."

"I'm fine. My eyesight's clear, and I've stopped hallucinating, except for the little pink lizards, but I hear that's normal. Bobby, for the last damned time, what the hell did you get?"

"Tell anyone you heard it from me, and I'll kill you." The threat was meaningless. He tried to kill me every time we got into a boxing ring together. Luckily I'd grown up with Mike, so my dodging skills were extraordinary. I grunted a yes to get him talking and nearly choked on my own spit when he ran down Brian Park's rap sheet.

"You're kidding me. Did you talk to Jae about what you found?" My mind alternated between blown away and gearing up to be pissed off at Jae-Min. It wouldn't be unlike him to have known about Park's past and not said anything. I was beginning to think honesty had a very different definition in his dictionary than it did in mine.

"Yeah, I asked him. He gave me a look, then shrugged. I'm not sure if that meant he knew and it wasn't important or that he just didn't care. Want to talk to him?"

"No," I muttered into the phone. The last thing I wanted was another fight about Jae keeping secrets. "I'll ask him when I get home."

"Want me to tell him that you love and miss him?" Bobby made kissy noises into the phone.

I hung up on him without answering and called Papa Kim's office. With any luck, Park would still be there and I could swing by to talk him up. The receptionist answered, speaking in a fluent babble of Korean that I had no chance in hell of understanding. Unless she called me baby, idiot, or any other endearment, I was pretty much lost.

"Um, I'm sorry," I replied. "I'm looking for Brian Park. Is he in?"

"Hold on, please. May I ask who's calling?" She sounded hesitant to put me through, then switched me over.

I listened to the phone on the other end ring, and then Park picked up. "Hello, Brian. How are you doing?"

"I'm fine." He sounded confused. I could imagine he was wondering why the private investigator in his friend's death was calling him in the middle of the afternoon. If he'd gotten word that I'd suffered injuries from a few badly placed pipe bombs, he certainly didn't offer up any sympathy. "What do you want, McGinnis? I don't have a lot of time."

"I need to ask about a couple of things," I replied, watching a pert-assed man throw a wobbly Frisbee at his golden retriever. The dog bounded after it, glad for the game. The man caught me looking and smiled, an easy invitation if I wanted it. I smiled back but dropped my eyes, keeping focused on the notes I'd written down.

"I don't think we have anything to talk about," he said, trying to shove me off. "Unless something new has come up about Henry. In which case, you probably should talk to Mr. Kim."

"Actually, I was thinking we could talk about the first time you met Hyun-Shik." The Frisbee spun again, and the dog drew closer, bounding after the plastic disc with an unabashed joy. "Or maybe the first time you got arrested."

There was a long silence on the other end, and if I hadn't heard him breathing, I would have thought Brian Park hung up on me. There was a long sigh, and then he responded in a whisper. "Not here. Not at work."

"Where, then?" I admit I felt a cheap thrill of elation. For the first time since Jae had gotten hurt, I felt like I'd made it out from behind the eightball. The hard part was going to be staying there.

He gave me directions to a place near his work. Someplace quiet we could talk, or rather, I could ask questions, and he could talk. Casting one final look at the dog's long-legged owner, I started the rental car and drove off.

Park was there before me, sitting in a far-off corner of an old-fashioned coffee shop. The place had a diner feel to it, brightly lit and running to black and white with dots of red here and there, a far cry from the trendy brown on darker brown corporate shops seemed to favor. The smell of burnt coffee lingered in the air, and a selection of flaky pastries withered slowly inside of a glass display case. I ordered a large coffee and a bear claw, then was pointed to a table sporting a meager variety of condiments when I asked for cream and sugar. Brian shifted nervously as I fixed my coffee, becoming visibly uncomfortable when I sat down and smiled at him.

"Hi. How are you and Victoria doing?" I was aiming for friendly, but he wasn't going to play along.

"Let's just get this over with. What do you want? Money?" Leaning forward across the table, he hissed under his breath, drawing the attention of the woman behind the counter. If you want someone to notice you, whisper loudly in public. It's better than wearing plaid with polka dots and clown shoes. "Is that what I need to do to make you go away?"

"Actually, if you could tell me who killed Hyun-Shik, that would be great," I said, sipping the coffee. Despite the darkness of the brew, or maybe because of it, it was surprisingly good. "And stop whispering. People are going to start looking at you like you're crazy."

"I keep telling you, I don't know who killed him." He played with his cup, turning it around in his hands. "I'm not lying to you. I don't know. Hyun-Shik was a friend. We were close."

"Does Mr. Kim know you used to work at Dorthi Ki Seu?" I leaned back in the chair, watching his face carefully. "Is that how you first met Hyun-Shik? Was he one of your customers?"

Saying something out loud gave it weight, and my words hit Park like a ton of bricks. He visibly deflated, folding in on himself. Looking at his blocky form, I couldn't imagine him working the upper rooms, but then, I'd been wrong about Jae-Min too. Assuming I believed he was only a dancer. I was still working on that.

Brian let out a shuddering breath and covered his face with his hands, rubbing at the worry lines forming on his forehead. He mumbled from behind his fingers, barely loud enough for me to hear him. "I'll pay you anything to keep quiet. I can't have that come out. I just can't."

"I'm not here to extort you," I said. I probably didn't sound very reassuring since he gave me a dirty look as he dropped his hands. "No, really. I'm not looking for anything but Hyun-Shik's killer. Jin-Sang died because he knew the suicide note Hyun-Shik supposedly wrote wasn't real. I haven't figured out why Jae's important in this, but he's been targeted, and now someone's trying to kill me too. So I'm more than a little bit invested in this."

"Did you ever think that maybe if you left things alone, it would all go away?" he asked. His voice rose, desperate and shrill. "Why can't you leave things alone?"

"Because, despite what people think, I finish what I start." I took a sip of my coffee. "How close of a friend were you to Hyun-Shik? As close as Jin-Sang?"

For a moment I thought he was going to get up and run, leaving me with unanswered questions and a very good cup of coffee, but the resignation on his face deepened when he realized I wasn't going to walk away from this mess. There's always that moment when someone surrenders to the inevitable, and Park was definitely at that line.

"You have to promise me that Mr. Kim won't find out." He shook his head, rubbing at his eyes. "I'll lose my job. Hell, I'll lose my career."

"I'm not interested in destroying you. I couldn't care less about what you did. Shit, you could be doing it now, and I wouldn't care," I admitted over the lip of my coffee cup. "I just want the truth for a change, all of it. Nothing watered down and nothing left out."

"I met Hyun-Shik there. He was one of the guys I saw. Look, it was a shitty time. I was messed up." Park's eyes glazed over, and for a moment, I was sorry I'd made him remember things he'd probably thought he'd left behind in the past, but thinking about the bruises on Jae's neck and shoulders cured me of any remorse I might have nursed. "He'd just gotten a membership, and he'd come by. We hooked up a lot until Jae-Min showed up and my parents shoved me into college. When I graduated from school, Hyun-Shik got me an intern job at the law firm. Probably because he felt bad about tossing me over for his cousin."

"Did you know Jae-Min when he worked there?" I was fishing. I knew it. Park didn't, and he nodded, making my guts lurch.

"I knew him, but I wasn't working there, and he didn't work the rooms. Not like we did. Most of the younger guys just dance." Park shrugged. "He could have made a lot more money than what he got from tips. A couple of the older guys would have paid a lot for a piece of his ass, even if he was illegal."

It never is a good thing to punch the shit out of the person who is telling the truth, but my fists itched pretty badly. I tightened my mouth to keep my tongue under control, smiling widely when the counter lady came by to refill our cups and sling a pot of cream and packets of sugar on the table.

"Tell me about Hyun-Shik and Jin-Sang," I prodded.

Park laughed, a short, bitter snort that left me in no doubt as to how he felt about his boss's ex-lover. "Jin-Sang was a user. I knew what I was there for. I needed the money, just like everyone else, but Jin-Sang always had to push it further. He'd beg for things: more money or clothes. Hyun-Shik would give him what he could, but he didn't have a lot of disposable income. That came later, after he married Victoria. Mr. Kim gave him a promotion and a bigger salary. That's when I got hired to work for him."

"He'd stopped seeing Jin-Sang by then." I thought back to the note. "He'd broken it off before he married Victoria, and after his son was born, Hyun-Shik decided he was going to go back to him?"

"No," Park said, shaking his head. "We didn't talk about Jin-Sang, but I know Hyun-Shik was done with him. If he was going to Dorthi Ki Seu, it wasn't going to be for Jin-Sang."

"Did you know he was going to the club that night?" That was the big question. I still didn't have a good answer for why Hyun-Shik Kim had gone to Dorthi Ki Seu that night. If it wasn't to see Jin-Sang, then who?

"I knew he was going, but it wasn't for sex. He said he was meeting someone." Park added a packet of sugar to his coffee, rattling a spoon around the edges of the cup. "Hyun-Shik told me that he'd be home later. I was going to drop off some contracts, and he'd meet up with me around midnight. By the time I got to his house, the cops were already there, and I found out he was dead. They're the ones who told me it was a suicide."

"Were you surprised when the cops told you he killed himself?" The picture I had gotten of Hyun-Shik didn't seem like the type of person to kill himself. He was too self-centered and, from the looks of things, had the world handed to him on a silver platter.

"Yeah, I thought, why would he do that?" Park nodded. "Hyun-Shik got everything he ever wanted. The only time someone said no to him was when his mother insisted Jae-Min move out. It's hard to pretend your son's not gay when he's fucking his cousin under your roof."

I shouldn't have been surprised. Eventually, Jae's idea of the truth would dawn on me, and I'd learn to accept the hidden mines that seemed to litter the landscape of his past. But surprise was definitely right up there on the list of emotions I was running through, a close second to pissed off.

"Wait a second." I stopped Park for a moment. "How old was Jae when he got kicked out?"

"I don't know. Fourteen? Fifteen? There were a lot of guys that age working there." He made a face, trying to think back. "I didn't pay much attention then. I was busy with school, and I didn't care."

"Hyun-Shik was an adult by then." I exhaled hard, wondering why the Kims' son hadn't been murdered before someone got him in Dorthi Ki Seu. "Did he expect Jae to work the rooms like Jin-Sang?"

"Like I said, I didn't care," Park replied. "One of the trannies downstairs took Jae in after one of the customers roughed him up a bit. He wasn't anyone I worried about. Look, I've got to get back to work soon. Mr. Kim's going to be looking for me."

"Almost done," I said, scribbling down notes. "Are you sure your girlfriend Vicki didn't know Hyun-Shik was gay?"

"No, it was a shock to her. I'm pretty sure of it." Brian fidgeted, and I saw him glance away. By now, I was beginning to get an idea that he wasn't confessing everything he knew, especially when he shifted nervously when I cleared my throat.

"What aren't you telling me?" I pried. He was an oyster of information. The right pressure and a sharp prod and pearls spilled out. I just had to string them together and make some sense of it all.

"She's not really my girlfriend," he admitted, dropping his eyes again. "Mr. Kim suggested I keep her company so she wouldn't head back east. That's what Hyun-Shik was planning on doing before he died. Victoria's from Connecticut and keeps talking about going back."

"Why is that a problem?" I asked.

"The Kims want her to stay here. She's got their grandson." Park looked at me like I was insane for asking. "Family's everything. They won't let her take Will from them. He's all Mrs. Kim has left of Hyun-Shik."

Things suddenly made a bit more sense. Hyun-Shik could solve a lot of his own problems by leaving California. He'd be out from under his family's watchful eye and could easily return to the lifestyle he preferred. His wife would be busy and out of his hair, so she wouldn't be a problem anymore. No, it would be a fantastic opportunity for Hyun-Shik, and one that someone else didn't want him to take.

"Got it." I stood, tucking the notepad into my pocket. Tossing a few dollars on the table for a tip, I folded a napkin around the bear claw to take with me. From the look on the counter lady's face, I didn't have high hopes of begging a bag from her. The refill of our coffee was more from curiosity than good service.

"So we're done, yes?" He stood as well, brushing the wrinkles out of his suit pants. "You're not going to go to Mr. Kim about... well, that?"

"Brian, think about it," I said with a smile. "You've gone from selling yourself to Hyun-Shik to whoring yourself to his wife. Considering Mr. Kim is the one who put you up to it, I'm pretty sure he doesn't need me to tell him a damned thing. And you might want to think about lining yourself up another job soon. I'm pretty sure that once it looks like Victoria's staying, he's going to make you wish you were working back at Dorthi Ki Seu."

CHAPTER FIFTEEN

AFTER I got into the car and watched Brian Park drive off, I called Scarlet. I needed to find someone at Dorthi Ki Seu who'd seen Hyun-Shik with the person he'd met, even if it was a short glimpse, and she seemed like my best bet to find someone willing to talk.

"Hello?" Jae's silken voice grabbed me and threw me down. I hated that he could drive me to wanting him with a single word. Actually, I hated that we'd not done anything that morning beyond a few kisses, but that was mostly my fault in my rush to get out the door.

"Hey." It wasn't the time to bring up the relationship he'd had with Hyun-Shik, not over the phone, and I needed time to think about what life had been like for a fourteen-year-old Jae living in the poisonous atmosphere of the Kim household. "Where are you?"

"At the club. Nuna wanted to leave some clothes she picked up from the dry cleaners." He sounded happy, or at least less worried than I'd heard him in days. "You were gone when we came by to drop off groceries. Bobby told me you were meeting Brian."

"Yeah," I replied. "He told me he knew Hyun-Shik was meeting someone at the club that night. Do you think Scarlet can help me out? I need her to see if anyone saw him and who he met with."

"Why didn't you do that the first time you talked to her?" He made that throaty hissing sound I'd heard him do in the past, usually when he was exasperated with me. It had been a constant sound during the three days I'd spent on my back in bed. "You sure you've done this before?"

I'd be insulted, but he was right. I should have spent more time talking to the staff and less time mooning over Jae's picture the first time I'd been at Dorthi Ki Seu. Still, I wasn't going to give Jae the satisfaction of knowing he'd dug in a good one. "Just put Scarlet on the phone, okay?"

"Hello, honey," she bubbled at me through the phone. "How are you? Passed out on the side of the road yet?"

"I'm doing fine. Thanks for asking," I said, gritting my teeth. "Didn't you tell me Hyun-Shik was there to see Jin-Sang the night he was killed?"

"Yes," Scarlet replied. "Why?"

"Who told you that? Hyun-Shik?"

"No." There was a tapping noise, and I imagined it was Scarlet's long fingernails hitting a table as she thought. "It was Jin-Sang. I saw Hyun-Shik come in, and he said the boy was there to see him. I didn't think anything about it. A man usually comes back to sniff around something easy when he's been gone for a while. His ego needs it."

"Are you two going to be there for a bit?" I started up the car. With traffic, it would take me about half an hour to get to the club, more if the freeway was feeling particularly puckish. "I need to find someone who saw Hyun-Shik that night. He met someone, and it wasn't Jin-Sang Yi."

"I can ask one of the boys in the front. They're usually working," she said. I nearly lost her as I pulled onto the street, a blare of horns erupting around me. "One of them might have seen Hyun-Shik with someone, but I can't promise anything."

"I'll take anything right now, Scarlet."

The freeway gods were kind to me, clean open lanes with only a few rough spots to negotiate. When I pulled up to the club, the sun was settling against the horizon, leaving long trails of lemony light and deep shadows behind. Dorthi Ki Seu was beginning to get ready for the evening when I walked in.

Under the bright florescent lights, the club appeared worn around the edges, its floor-length curtains faded around the hems. A couple of white-shirted waiters, their ties either undone or left completely off, set about taking down chairs, arranging the seats carefully around round tables. Another stood on a ladder, replacing the blackened bulb of a stage light. Below him, the stage glinted in spots, cast-off sequins from dresses caught in the cracks of the painted wood.

"I'm looking for Scarlet," I said quickly when one of the bouncers detached himself from the long bar and approached me, his glowering frown deep enough to carve his face into deep crevices.

"Honey!" Scarlet swept out from the back, shoving aside the curtains with one elegant push of her hand and stalking into the main room. "It's good to finally see you on your feet."

"That sounds particularly dirty," I said, kissing her cheek. "You look nice."

"Thank you." She wore her femininity well, her long hair in a smooth, complicated up-do that defied my reasoning. A line of small diamonds winked at me from a barrette nestled amid the loops, as bright as her wide-toothed smile. Jae followed, his hands tucked into his jeans pockets, a pretty shadow attached to a beautiful woman.

"Hey, baby." I reached for Jae, intending to kiss his mouth, but he pulled back, his eyes sliding around the room.

Our worlds were different. For me, to kiss him was natural, a normal thing. He shied away. Even though the people around us knew he preferred men, Jae kept up the pretense. He was used to hiding who he wanted without even a second thought, and it hurt me in ways I didn't think possible. Not for the first time, I was angry at the world for doing this to him, taking away the simplest pleasure of a kiss from a young man.

He leaned into a semi-hug, and I felt the smallest brush of his mouth against my jaw. It was all I was going to get, but it was enough to make me hard.

"Cole, come here." Scarlet dragged me away from my temptation into sin, her ringed hand motioning one of the larger mounds of meat toward us. "This is Johnny. He was working that night."

He lumbered closer, and I involuntarily took a step back. The Korean looked like he'd been hewn directly from a granite slab, his face pitted with pockmarks and a dark red scar sliced down one cheek, an angry, vivid line on his pale skin. His uniform shirt had long since given up its battle with his arms, the hems stretched out with popped stitches. If I were the management, I might briefly consider having a talk with my bouncers about adhering to a more proper dress code, but only if I wanted my face rearranged with their fists.

"Hi." I debated shaking his hand but decided I wanted to keep my fingers.

"Miss Scarlet said you wanted to ask some questions." His voice matched his girth, full bodied and dangerous.

"If you don't mind," I said. Scarlet and Jae abandoned me, heading to the bar for something cold to drink. The air conditioning hadn't yet kicked in, and the club was stuffy, the air stagnant and still. I sat down, hoping he would join me and relax. His paw swallowed the back of the chair, and it made a loud noise as he pulled it out to sit down. "Did you know Kim Hyun-Shik?"

"Yeah, I knew him." Crossing his arms over his chest, Johnny stared at me from across the table. I was guessing verbal skills weren't high on his priority list. A good bouncer knew when to keep his mouth shut, and that usually was always.

"Were you working the night he died?"

"Yeah, or I wouldn't be sitting here talking to you." He glanced over his shoulder to where Scarlet stood. I wasn't sure if he was checking to see if she was watching him cooperate or if he was assigned to keep her safe. I didn't think she'd come to any harm by the bar, except for the real risk of choking on the lime pith in her gin and tonic. "He sat over there."

I looked over to where he pointed. It was a smaller table, nearly hidden by a froth of palms and overgrown ferns. The spot was secretive, the perfect place to have a talk away from the rest of the action in the club.

"Why don't you tell me what you saw?" I said.

"He shows up and sits down. I hadn't seen him in a long time, but I knew who he was." He nodded toward the young man changing the light bulb. "Took him about four minutes before he was talking to Kwang-Sun, trying to get him upstairs."

"Not something he should be doing?" I asked, cocking my head to look at the young man. He was young, a lot younger than I like, but some men prefer that. Thinking back on how old Jae had been when Hyun-Shik had probably seduced him, it wasn't much of a stretch to believe Kwang-Sun had caught Hyun-Shik's eye.

"No," Johnny said, tapping at the table to get my attention. "The upstairs boys work there because that's what they do. Kwang-Sun's not going to do that. Not if I can help it."

"Is he your lover?" I ducked to avoid the spit flying from Johnny's pursed snort.

"My baby brother," he answered with a smile. "He's going to go to medical school. I'm not going to let some asshole like Kim Hyun-Shik fuck him up like he did his cousin or Jin-Sang."

"Fair enough," I agreed. "So you scared him off Kwang-Sun, then what?"

"Some blonde woman came in. I didn't see her face, but she was pretty fine. Long legs, and dressed nice. Expensive-looking. I remember thinking she had to be white because her hair was very blonde and natural-looking." Johnny's eyes were distant, trying to call up the details of that evening. "I thought she looked out of place. Most of the women who come in here aren't... really women. Or if they are, they're hookers. She didn't look like one."

"You didn't see her face?"

"No, she was too far away, but she made it straight to Hyun-Shik," he replied thoughtfully. "I guess he called her or she called him, but she went right over there. I didn't pay him too much attention after that. He kept away from Kwang-Sun, and my shift started."

"Anything else you can remember?" It wasn't much to go on, but I had a sneaking suspicion I knew who had met Hyun-Shik that night.

"Nope, that's it. Just some white girl." Johnny headed back to work, which to me looked mostly like standing around watching the waiters get the club in shape for opening. Scarlet had disappeared while I was talking to the bouncer, but Jae remained behind, leaning against the bar. He headed over when the other man left the table, carrying the sodas he'd gotten from the cold case.

"Do they know you stole those?" I asked, taking one of the chilled bottles from him.

"You're welcome." He sat down in the chair Johnny had vacated. "Did he help?"

"Yeah." I wiggled the bottle at him. "I'm going to head out, and I'm taking this with me. You going to be okay?"

"I'm with nuna. She has a driver that makes that guy look like he's a twig." Jae pointed at Johnny. "I'll be fine. Where are you going?"

"I think Victoria came here and, with Jin-Sang's help, killed her own husband." I told him about the blonde talking with Hyun-Shik, adding the part about Kwang-Sun at the end, and Jae nodded, as if his cousin hitting on a young man was no surprise.

"Do you really think she killed Hyun-Shik?" Jae asked after digesting the information. "She's a bitch, but a killer? I don't know, Cole."

"I didn't think so at the time, but now, yeah, it looks like it," I said. "To be fair, Hyun-Shik didn't seem like a very nice guy."

"Nice and Hyun-Shik were rarely in the same sentence together," Jae agreed. "He once told me the only reason I made tips as a dancer was because I had a pretty face, not because I actually could dance."

"He sounds like an asshole," I commented. He nodded, sipping at his soda with a delicious pout of his mouth, and I cursed Hyun-Shik for getting himself killed. I thought I'd have enjoyed beating him to death for putting those shadows in Jae's eyes. "Jae, why do you want to know who killed him? If he was such an asshole, why do you care?"

"Because he's family," Jae said, shrugging his shoulders under the shirt he'd stolen from my dresser. "Because he helped me when I didn't have anywhere else to go. I owe him that at least."

"He brought you here." I looked around the room with its worn drapery and the smell of sex lingering in the air. "This wasn't much of a help."

"It was something," he replied. "I thought I was in love with him. Maybe I was then, but Hyun-Shik didn't love anyone but himself. He was honest about that. Hyung told me from the start that he didn't love me but he'd help me at least get on my feet. So yes, he was an asshole and a cheat, but considering the rest of the family, how was he going to be any different?"

I had to give Jae that. For all of Hyun-Shik's faults, he had at least seemed to do what he could to help, first with Jae and then with Brian Park. I found my keys in my pocket and picked up the soda bottle.

"I'll see you at home," I said, catching myself before I kissed him goodbye.

Standing, Jae leaned his head back, leaving me a touch of his mouth on mine. Murmuring against my lips, Jae breathed into me, a soft laugh escaping him when I sighed.

"Don't get shot at or blown up again," he said, pushing me toward the door. "I've got plans for you, hyung. And they don't include you lying in bed unconscious."

PERSONALLY, I would have loved to go home with Jae-Min, kick everyone out of my house and see how much my bed could withstand. Or at least how much my bruised-up body could take. It would be a sacrifice, but one I would be willing to make. Instead, I fought my way back down through the canyons and into the depths of Los Angeles's heat. Despite the sun being down, the inner valleys retained their mugginess, a sweltering stew instead of air that clogged the pores. As the amber lights of the cities flickered on, it caught on the low brown haze, turning the night sky to a deep sienna.

Smog sometimes made for lovely sunsets, but it was hell on the lungs. I was about to take the toll road when my phone buzzed me. Clicking on the headset, I frowned when my brother's voice bellowed at me from the speaker.

"Where the hell are you?" Mike had never been subtle or one for hellos.

"Hi, Mike," I chirped back. "How are you?"

"I need you to get your ass back here." From the sound of my brother's strained voice, he wasn't in the mood for any of my usual crap. "Did you talk to Brian Park this afternoon?"

"Yeah. Why?" I took the off-ramp and circled around to get back on the westbound lanes. Avoiding a long-trailer semi, the SUV bounced a bit on the uneven cement freeway, its new tires catching on the grooves ground down to leech rain from the surface. "Did he call you or something?"

"Cops were called out to his apartment about an hour ago, Cole. He was shot in the back of the head." Mike's words chilled the warmth Jae had left in my stomach, and I swallowed the sourness rising up my throat. "His secretary told them he canceled his afternoon appointments to meet with you. They want you to come in."

"Hey, he was alive when we finished," I protested. "We met at a coffee shop, and then I headed straight down to Dorthi Ki Seu. I couldn't have killed him."

"Just get over there. I'll meet you there."

"That'll look good, me bringing my brother with me." I snorted. "I'll be fine."

"Cole, as soon as you open your mouth, you stop being fine," he replied sharply. "And I'm not going as your brother. Until I get another attorney in, you're going to have to deal with me. I don't want you talking to anyone about Brian or what you discussed with him. Not unless I'm in the room."

"Are they charging me?" I knew better than that, but it was good to poke at my brother's doomsday predictions. The detectives on the case were following the first thread they hit, regardless of who was on the other end. There was silence on the other end of the phone, and I nodded triumphantly, even though I knew Mike couldn't see me. "No, they're not. Mike, you know how this works. I'm going to go in and let them ask their questions. I'll call you if I run into any problems."

The dial tone in a headset is a very loud thing, especially when the person on the other end doesn't have the satisfaction of slamming the receiver down. I anticipated another call from my brother after he paced around his office for a few minutes, so I turned my phone off and headed back into the mess I'd inadvertently left behind me.

Most cop houses have an atmosphere to them. To the general public, it probably looks like everyone is working or scurrying about with something important to do. Things are usually very different if you know what to look for. There's a sense of desperation and frustration that comes with being a cop. Most of the people a police officer meets on a day-to-day basis really don't want to see him and will in fact, at times, either run away or possibly even take a shot at him. Murders happen, and robberies seem to come like tidal waves, hitting every few seconds without fail. It's a good day when someone confesses to killing someone else, and it's a banner day when there's a drug bust that takes a serious crimp out of what's on the street, but for the most part, being a cop means getting used to being a speed bump for a bullet train.

I smelled the frustration first. It rolled off the female detective I was escorted to, her frenetic tapping of a pencil against the side of her desk a strong barometer of which way the storm was blowing. She gave me a quick glance, rifling through a sheaf of papers, and then pointed to a battered metal chair next to her desk.

Detective Dell O'Byrne looked more Latino than Irish. Her long brown hair hung straight down her back, pulled into a queue with a no-nonsense black hair band. Tanned and lean, she had a strong face, high cheekbones, and sharp eyes, nearly as dark as her hair, which took in every detail of my face. I would lay money down that she could describe me to a sketch artist, down to the small scar on my chin. Leaning back, I drank in the chaos around me, watching uniformed officers maneuver handcuffed suspects down a corridor to a detention area.

The detective hung up the phone and turned in her chair, staring at me down her long nose. She was younger than I had initially thought, only a year or so older than I was, but she wore her badge on her skin. If I'd seen Detective O'Byrne on the street, I'd have known she was a cop without even a second glance.

"Cole McGinnis?" Standing, she was nearly my height and had a strong grip. Grabbing a manila folder from her desk, she waved me toward an open door. "Let's go in there and talk. It's more private."

The rectangular room was painted in latter-day drab, the station's budget running toward faded puke instead of the warm beige that covered most of the walls. A long mirror separated the room from the observation alcove. The light was on behind the glass, and I could see past the one-way mirror into the empty side room. If O'Byrne had suspicions, that light would have been off and the small room would have boasted one or two other cops, each watching me and taking notes.

"Have a seat." She sat without waiting for me and opened the folder, flipping over the top sheet. I pulled back the heavy chair, sitting down across from her. "Nice bruises you got there on your face, Cole. Did you run into someone who didn't like you? Maybe Park?"

"Nope." I tried a grin when she looked up from her papers, but O'Byrne didn't look impressed. "Someone tried to blow me up. I ended up face first into my front lawn."

"So I guess that someone doesn't like you." Her smile did nothing to make her beautiful, but warmed her face. "Tell me about your meeting with Brian Park."

I had nothing to gain by hiding anything, not with Park being dead and my one lead on who killed Hyun-Shik resting on the memory of a pissed-off bouncer. Leaning back in the chair, I sketched out my steps, starting with the Kims hiring me to investigate the death of their son and ending with my conversation with Brian at the coffee shop.

"You've got a Glock registered to you," O'Byrne said slowly. "Fire it recently?"

She lifted the folder so I wasn't able to see anything other than the back fold, its surface doodled over with blue stars and leaves. A few words stood out, part of a grocery list. From what was written, I gathered the detective had a cat and a fondness for hot dogs, but beyond that, I couldn't read anything from her expression.

"A few times at the range," I admitted. "Just to keep in practice."

"People seem to have a difficult time staying alive around you, Mr. McGinnis." The glint in her eye gave me an uneasy feeling that she was looking for a way to pin something on me, if only to keep me out of the way. "I've asked around about you when I found out you're an ex-cop."

"I can imagine." I met her gaze with a steady stare, keeping eye contact until she glanced down at her notes. I didn't fool myself into thinking I'd intimidated her. I wasn't sure if she was talking about Jin-Sang Yi and Brian Park or Rick and Ben. Either way, she was right. I didn't seem to be a good luck charm for the people around me.

"Did you go to that coffee shop with the intention to blackmail Brian Park? Maybe to kill him?" I couldn't have been more surprised unless O'Byrne had punched me in the face. She waited until I finished choking on my own spit, leaning back in her chair. "It's not an unreasonable question, McGinnis."

"Money isn't a problem for me," I reminded her. "If you asked around about me, you'd know that. I went to talk to him about Hyun-Shik Kim. I told you that already. There's no reason for me to want Brian Park dead."

"Park was killed up close with something pretty powerful." She slid a photograph over toward me, and my eyes caught on the splash of red on the bright white of Brian's shirt. "You own a Glock 23. That kind of gun can do this to a man, especially up close."

There was not much left of Brian's face except for the ridge of his nose and parts of his jaw. The exit wounds took off most of his cheekbone and blood pooled around the shredded edges of his torn skin. He lay on a short blue carpet, speckles of spit dried on what was left of his lower lip. It looked like someone had emptied the entire clip into his head, and I forced myself to look away, closing my eyes against the memories I knew would soon overwhelm me.

"Do you need a minute, Mr. McGinnis?" I barely heard O'Byrne over my breathing, a patent concern laid thinly over the steel in her voice.

"No." I shook my head, concentrating on keeping my mind in the present. Unexpectedly, the scar on my chest ached, tendrils of pain spiraling outward as my skin began to itch. Brian's death was different than Rick's. There was rage there. Someone angry killed Park. I didn't know what emotion had driven Ben to kill Rick. "I can give you my gun for testing. It's at my house. I don't carry it with me."

"You've got a license for concealed." She looked at me curiously. "Why isn't it with you?"

"I don't normally carry it with me," I repeated calmly, opening my eyes and blinking against the glare of the light. "I brought it out with me a couple of days ago, but it went back into its case. I was meeting Park for coffee. I didn't think I'd need it."

"You admitted you had knowledge of his arrest for solicitation. Something like that would make Park nervous." O'Byrne eased back and angled her body, hooking one arm over the back of her chair. "Could he have called someone to talk to? Maybe someone else who could be threatened by you?"

"I don't know. I'd only spoken to him twice." O'Byrne wasn't going to let me off easy. There was no clock in the room, but the seconds drew out, ticking off in the back of my head.

I took another look at the photo the detective had left on the table. Something nagged me about the picture, and I risked staring at the image, fighting to keep my rebellious stomach in check. Rounds of light shone through the carpet, the dark grey fibers nearly melted around the edges of the holes.

"Where was he shot?" I stared at the photo, trying to make sense of the close-up. She'd chosen that particular picture to shock me, hoping the vivid starkness of Park's death would shake something loose in me. If I'd actually killed him, I might have thrown up seeing my own handiwork, but other than the lingering revulsion of seeing another man's brains splattered out of his skull, I had nothing to feel guilty about. "This looks like a car."

"It's funny that you'd ask that." O'Byrne drew out another photo, a long shot that showed Park's legs sticking out of the open doors of a Ford E-150. "Park was shot in the back of his van, one that matches the description of one that ran you off the road a few days ago."

The exterior of the van looked like it had been through a battle, its sides and back battered in. Its white paint was smeared with long streaks of paint, the exact same color as my Range Rover. As casual as she sat, I knew O'Byrne was moving in for the kill.

"So, Mr. McGinnis, do you want to tell me again how you didn't want him dead? I'd say a man trying to murder you with his car is a good enough reason as any."

CHAPTER SIXTEEN

MIKE took his damned sweet time getting down to the station after I closed my mouth and lawyered up. It seemed like a good idea, considering the tone of the questions was getting serious. After I asked for my big brother, Detective O'Byrne led me into an even smaller room, this one with a one-way mirror that I was pretty certain had people peering at me every once in a while. Or at least I'd like to think so. It's always a blow to a man's ego when no one pays attention to him, especially when he's waiting for his older brother to come rescue him.

As always, Mike didn't disappoint me. He arrived looking very stern. My mother's Japanese genes were good for stern. There were times when I wished I looked less like my father. There were times when I could have used a bit more intimidation and less charm.

His hair was sticking straight up, more from his hand running around the back of his head than any product he used. The ugly red tie his wife had bought him for his last birthday was masterfully knotted at his throat, and the expensive suit cut for his square body hung nicely from his shoulders. Madeline probably thought he looked hot. I thought he looked like a yakuza thug from a movie.

O'Byrne got word the bullet came from a Browning and not a Glock, but she still forcefully requested I get tested for gunpowder residue, something Mike fought but I agreed to. I had nothing to hide, and if I balked, it would have meant a longer stay at Chateau O'Byrne. I was tired and sore. I wasn't staying a minute longer in a cold room on a metal chair than I had to. When they were done, he retrieved me from the interrogation room they'd dumped me in.

"Get your shit and let's go," he barked through the open door.

Sometimes when I see my brother, his left eyelid twitches a little bit. It's a small tic, and I'm pretty sure I put it there, right along with the small scar below his lower lip, but that matches the one he gave me on my shoulder. When Mike spotted me sitting there, his left eye began to telegraph landing instructions to aliens circling the Earth.

"I don't have any shit," I said, leaning back in my chair until it rocked. The tic started to move into full-blown spasms, a sure sign my brother was either about to walk away or come toward me with fists flying at my head. "No, really. Just my cell phone and my wallet. Maybe some lint. I could use some gum."

If Mike's lid moved any faster, it would burn his eyeball. I did the intelligent thing and got up off the chair.

"Swear to God, I didn't kill that guy," I said to the back of Mike's head. "It was just questions, then she got pissy."

"Shut up, Cole." My brother cut through the bullpen, swerving around the desks with as long a stride as his legs could make. He growled at me over his shoulder. "Keep your mouth shut until we get outside."

"I wasn't arrested," I pointed out. O'Byrne was nowhere to be seen, and the desk clerk barely looked up as we walked past. "She was pushing for information, that's all."

"Here's some gum. Don't choke on it because I'm not going to resuscitate you." Mike patted at his jacket pocket, pulling out a pack of gum. He unwrapped a stick and offered me one before putting the pack away. "Well, now Detective O'Byrne considers you a person of interest."

"Did you tell her I don't swing that way?" The gum was fruity. I was expecting mint, but I chewed at it anyway, clearing the stale taste out of my mouth. "I'm flattered, but Jae's more than enough."

"I don't want to hear that."

"Sorry," I said, shrugging but not really feeling apologetic. "It's the truth."

"You should have called me before she got you in that room." Mike stopped at his car, turning to poke me in the chest with a stiff finger. "Your smart mouth makes her suspicious. I can't talk everyone out of looking at you sideways, Cole. Especially when there's a trail of dead bodies leading straight to you."

"I'll say it slower. I didn't kill Brian Park."

"I know that, but she doesn't." My brother puffed out his cheeks, and the tic slowed as he caught his calm. "Cole, you've got Jae staying with you. He was present when Jin-Sang Yi was murdered and had his apartment blown up. She likes Park for both of those things. Then they found three incendiary devices under your car after someone tried to run you off the road, and possibly that someone was Brian Park."

"Okay, so it looks a little bad." In retrospect, the detective had just cause to think that I'd want Park dead. "But then why would Brian do all those things? Because he was pissed off at the guy who gave him a job, even knowing he was going down on old Korean men in a sex club?"

"Maybe Hyun-Shik was blackmailing Park." Mike's idea had some legs, but it was a weak runner. "Maybe it wasn't for money. Maybe Hyun-Shik had Park doing sexual things with him."

"I've seen what Hyun-Shik likes," I said, making a face at my brother. "Park couldn't compete. Not even on his best day. Besides, he was too old. Hyun-Shik preferred young, sometimes a bit too young."

"More stuff that I don't want to hear," he replied, holding his hand up to stop me from continuing.

"You've got to work on that tolerance thing, Mike. You're younger than Mad Dog," I pointed out. "Do you want to hear what I found out at the club?"

"Fine. Tell me what you found out." He unknotted his tie and tugged it free from his collar, undoing the top few buttons on his shirt. Flinging the jacket into the back seat of his car, Mike listened as I recounted Brian's words in the coffee shop and then what the bouncer said to me at Dorthi Ki Seu. He processed the information, chewing on his fingernail as he thought things through. "Did he see her face?"

"No, but he said the blonde was either natural or really well done." I rested my hip against his sedan, watching a squad car roll by. "It's got to be Victoria. She's the only one in this that has a reason to want Hyun-Shik dead. Hell, I'd want him dead."

"It could be someone else," Mike commented, his eyes distant. "But yeah, she seems like your best lead."

"I'm going to go see her. That's where I was headed when you called me about Park."

"You think that's smart? Suppose she's the one who killed him?"

"It's not like I was going to accuse her straight out." I shook my head at him. "What? You want me to take you or Bobby with me?"

"Yeah, I do. Wait until tomorrow so one of us can go with you."

"I'm not a child, Mike." Arguing with him wasn't going to do any good. My brother was possibly more stubborn that I was.

"That is why I wanted you to stop investigating the Kim case," Mike said. "If she did kill Park, then she's not going to think twice about killing you too. You should leave it to the cops."

"We've already had this talk, Mike." I looked around for the rental, pretty certain I'd parked in the front lot. "I made a promise to Jae-Min, and the cops don't give a shit. Hyun-Shik might have been an asshole, but he shouldn't have died for it. Where the hell did I put my car?"

"I had it towed," he replied sweetly. "Get in the car. I'll take you home."

"You had my rental towed?" I counted to three and breathed out. "Where? Why?"

"Because you would have left here and headed off on some other stupid stunt that would get you into trouble. This way, I know you're home for at least one night. And I'm not telling you where. You'll get it back tomorrow morning."

"You've got some serious control issues, Mike." I gritted my teeth and got into the car, slamming the door shut.

"Yeah, I do," he admitted. "I like knowing my brother's alive. Call me crazy, but that's important to me. And if you get killed, Madeline's going to be pissed. She's counting on you to show up at that dinner for Mom and Dad."

"Great," I muttered as my brother turned the key in the ignition. "Just what I needed. A reason to want to die."

I WAS tired, and the bruises over my body were complaining about not being soaked in a hot bubble bath. I've been bruised enough times in my life to speak pain fluently. I knew what my body was saying. It was time to get off my feet, but I wasn't giving my brother any fuel for his satisfaction. My stomach was also complaining about the lack of food, but it was going to have to wait until I dragged myself into the house.

Mike dropped me off, then drove away. We'd spent most of the car ride in silence, he in a smugness that only an older brother can manage while I was grumpy at being handled. The cement sidewalk seemed to stretch on into eternity as I plodded to the front door. Jae was safe in the living room, engrossed in looking at photos on a laptop screen. He glanced up when I came in, smiling widely before returning to his work. My stomach's grumbling stepped aside, leaving room for my libido to take over.

He smelled good. The scent of my soap clung to his skin, and I leaned over, licking at the softness along his throat. Jae pulled away, laughing while he pushed me away. I liked coming home to find him wearing one of my shirts and smelling like he belonged to me. The cat mewed at me from her perch on the sill, her ears twitching as she intently watched a brown-headed sparrow pecking at the lawn. Alcohol was still off my to-do list, and I mournfully waved a hello to the lager at the back of the fridge, choosing a cold bottle of water. A pot bubbled on the stove, as fragrant and exotic as the Korean sitting in my living room.

"What are you working on?" I sipped at the water, wincing at the cold plastic on my abused mouth. Sitting sideways on the couch, I slid one leg behind Jae, resting my hurt knee against his back. He leaned forward to make room for me, absently rubbing at the inside of my thigh with his fingers.

"I shot a wedding before the accident," he murmured, his attention more on the splashes of color displayed on the screen than me. I didn't mind his distraction. It gave me time to relax against the couch and watch him. "I keep all of my work on a server, so I don't lose anything. I don't have my equipment, but I have my shots."

Jae's long fingers flew over the keyboard, renaming files after he inspected his photos down to the pixel. The bride wore a long robe, its red vivid against her pale skin. Its sleeves were shortened rainbows, flowing over to hide her hands. Pink and white flowers floated down the front of the robe, and her smile was mysterious, promising to keep her secrets from the moon-faced young man standing beside her.

"We can get you new equipment," I said, stroking his leg.

"Sit over there and look pretty. I'm almost done." I'd been around him long enough to know that almost done in Jae time meant an hour or so. It was a pleasant enough view, one that could keep me occupied, so I settled down into the couch cushions and waited.

After ten minutes, I offered what I supposed would be an ultimatum, hoping he'd see the error in his thinking. "If I don't get a taste of you soon, I won't be held responsible for what I'll do."

His dark lashes brushed his cheekbones, and he slanted a curious look at me. I was left to wonder what was going on behind his unreadable eyes. He stretched up over me and placed his hands on either side of my shoulders, dimpling the couch arm with his weight. I moved my legs together, giving him room to place his knees on either side of my thighs, and moaned when he bent his head down to kiss me, opening my mouth to take his tongue when it slithered over my lower lip.

"So that was a good threat?" I murmured into his mouth.

"You do some very stupid things, agi. I couldn't risk it." His hand moved under my shirt, finding the edges of the scar along my ribcage. I twitched under his touch, tender from my unexpected flight into my front lawn's bushes. "I don't think you're up to doing much."

"Baby, I can honestly tell you that I'm up enough," I said. The itch Jae caused by looking at me now grew along the length of me, and I reached down to tug at my jeans, hoping to give myself some room. His fingers followed mine, his thumb rubbing against the swell, and I heard him literally purr, his mouth closing down on mine in a long kiss.

"Hey, wait." I pushed at his shoulders, forcing Jae to look up at me. "I need to have something on me. I can't risk you."

"Do you have something down here?" His teeth were dangerous, and I wanted to bury deep inside of him, stretching him apart until I could grab onto his soul, never letting it go. "Or do I have to go upstairs?"

"Um." When faced with the hard questions, my mind tended to scatter, picking up tendrils of thoughts I'd left behind hours ago. The only thing I could think of was that we needed wet cat food, a piece of information that would do me little good at the moment. "Shit, in that box over there, the blue one on the bookshelf. Bobby gave me some gag stuff for my birthday a couple of months ago. I think there's some condoms in there."

Jae slithered off me, a long curve of grace I could watch forever. I laughed when he opened the box, his eyes widening appreciatively as he dug through its contents. Pulling out a streamer of gold coin condoms, he tossed one at me, tucking the others back in. Straddling my knees, Jae settled back down, kissing at my bared belly as I struggled with the foil.

"Bobby gave you some strange things," Jae mumbled, nudging my shirt further up my body until his tongue lapped at my nipple. I nearly choked on a piece of the condom wrapper, my teeth snapping off a corner and flicking it back into my throat. Gagging it out, I spat it into my hand, wiping the foil on my shirt, and ordered Jae to behave.

"You're going to kill me before I get this thing open," I warned. He ignored me, much like his cat did when I needed to open the front door and she lay in the way. Jae rounded my nipple again, leaving a hot, wet trail of spit behind, then went back to blow it cold, leaving me with a shiver down my chest. The foil ripped open and the condom plopped out, unceremoniously landing on my belly with a splat. Grinning, Jae gave me a kiss and bit my chin.

"Let me do this," he said through his teeth. "Don't go anywhere. I just want to do this."

Apparently a few hours was too long for my body to go without Jae's touch. My dick agreed. It twitched and throbbed under Jae's light touch, hurting with every stroke. The button at my waistband popped open when Jae's thumb worked it loose, and his teeth snagged at the tab of my zipper, pulling it down slowly. I reached for him, cupping the back of his head in my palm, and leaned my head against the cushions, breathing in deeply. My control was shaky at best, a razor-thin thread holding myself in.

He fit the tip of the rubber sleeve over me, stroking down to my root and back up over my head. The muskiness of my body mingled with his, a rich loam of masculine lust that excited me. His fingers rolled the condom down slowly, stretching out the membrane over my heft. Strange things popped up in my head, worrisome, stupid thoughts that I couldn't shake loose.

"You didn't choose one that was lubricated, right?" I yelped when Jae's sharp teeth bit down on the tender inside of my thigh. "What? Hey, let go."

"You let go," he said softly, looking up at me through his lashes. "Stop thinking, Cole. Just feel."

He was too beautiful for me. I wanted to drag him upstairs and fill his world with anything he needed, as long as it included me in it. I wanted the living room to be the only place in the world, a sanctuary where I didn't have to share Jae with his culture or the close-mindedness of his family.

I fell hard and fast into the promise of pleasure he offered. I wasn't going to think anymore... not of anything beyond the man stretched over me and the small bit of heaven he was giving me. When he enveloped me, I lost reason, closing my eyes to the sweet velvet darkness of his mouth. The air was tight, sharp-edged stabs in my chest, and I struggled to breathe, unable to hold on to the width of his shoulders with my palms. I explored the jut of his shoulder blades and the line of his back, wanting to remember Jae on my hands before I had to let him go.

"Jae," I said before lightning rode my body. He nuzzled and licked, drawing out every ounce of strength I had in me. Reaching for him, I tried to pull him up, wanting to be inside of him, but his teeth closed down on the ridge of my sex, dipping dangerously into the soft skin. "Baby, I need you."

"Lie down." Growling playfully, he nipped and tugged at me, his hands spread over my stomach. With a groan, I lay back, willing the spasms on my ribs to subside. An ache had begun to crawl up my skin, the tenderized flesh beneath a sea of bruises twisting as I moved. "Don't move."

I couldn't breathe anymore. There wasn't space in my lungs for my cries and air both, and I gave up, wanting to die from the pleasure Jae was giving me or the pain that was beginning to curl my belly into a tight knot. Every dip of Jae's tongue made me clench, and the damage from the bombing began to hurt anew, throbbing nearly in time with the ache along my shaft.

The storm in me broke, and I cried out, spilling into Jae's warmth. The condom stopped me from filling his mouth, splashing back onto my head and puffing out the receptacle at the end. I was pretty sure I screamed his name, pushing up into the tightness of his throat, needing to bury myself into any part of his body.

He lay gasping against my stomach, laughing softly into the nest of hair below my belly button. I fought to speak, lost in the waves of white noise flowing over me. Languid, I reached for him, nudging him up to lie on me, wanting the curve of his body tucked against mine.

"Wait," Jae whispered. "Let me clean you up."

I tried to protest, too weak to do anything more than mumble nonsensically when he stripped off the condom and wiped at me with a water-damp napkin.

"Aish you for complaining." His words were rounded, that soft burr of Korean that made me smile. It felt like he was sharing the deepest part of himself when he grew English-lazy. We'd spoken of it, lying against one another in the darkness when he slurred a few words, and his embarrassment made me laugh harder, cuddling him closer. Inspecting his handiwork, he cocked his head to one side and nodded. "There. All better."

"Come here," I said, patting my stomach. He lay down carefully, watching my face intently as I tried to hide the wince jerking at my face when my ribs twisted painfully.

"I am here." He sighed, stretching out with his body half on me. I was going to have to send a thank-you note to whoever made my couch wide enough for us to spoon on. It was a good, firm piece of furniture, comfortable enough to cuddle on. I tried remembering if it was one I liked or one Madeline had picked out, but Jae's fingers on my lips drew my attention back.

"Stop thinking." He sighed. "You're always thinking."

"I'm thinking about you."

"Now you're just lying." Jae snorted when I grimaced. "You're a horrible liar. How were you a cop?"

"I was a decent cop." I defended myself. "Most of my work was about talking to people. That's most of the job, really. Getting people to trust you. Sometimes that's hard."

"I trust you," he said, resting against my shoulder. "Mostly."

"Mostly?" I debated feeling hurt but forgave him, considering the laziness creeping through my body. "Did you know Brian Park worked at the club?"

"I'm beginning to think everyone Hyun-Shik knew worked there." Jae sighed.

"Someone killed Park," I said softly, stroking his hair. "There are too many people Hyun-Shik knew that are dying. I'm afraid you're going to be one of them."

"You wouldn't let that happen to me." He shifted, and my cock stirred, hardening when he rubbed at my stomach. "I am sorry about Park. I wish I knew something that could help you."

"Knowing you're safe helps me," I teased, then frowned as he sat up.

"Make sure the door is locked, and we can continue this discussion upstairs." He slid from the couch and gave me a sultry look. "Too much death around us. Maybe we should concentrate on living?"

CHAPTER SEVENTEEN

WHEN I woke, the morning sky was grey, and thin watery streams of light were coming through the bedroom curtains. Nudging the cat from my ankle, I let myself have the luxury of snuggling against Jae's long, warm body. He smelled of sex and spice. Between the bruising from being blown up and a long night spent deep in Jae's body, I ached in places, but it was worth it. My dick stirred half-heartedly as I rubbed against Jae's hip, but I told it no. If I was going to pay a visit to Victoria Kim and catch her unawares, I needed to start moving.

I lingered long enough to brush the back of my hand against his smooth cheek. I'd teased him about not growing facial hair, wondering aloud if he was old enough to be in my bed. He'd shoved me down and shown me how wicked his mouth could be when he put his mind to it, and I moved slowly, feeling a slight bruising along the inside of my thighs left by his teeth. Kissing the back of his neck, I let him sleep, sliding from the bed and shushing Neko when she mewed at me.

My bed was empty when I got out of the bathroom, and the smell of coffee came from downstairs. I thanked God for Jae's domesticity as I dressed quickly, then grabbed my Glock from its lock box. Jae was right. There were too many people dying around us, and while I wasn't planning on a shootout at the OK Corral, I'd feel more comfortable with my gun under my jacket. The Widow Kim probably killed Park when he became unnecessary. I didn't have any illusions that she'd find any use for me.

I was greeted with a full mug. Then Jae-Min kicked me in the balls before I'd even had a sip of coffee. Or at least it felt like he did, then punched my teeth out for good measure. I set my mug down on the kitchen counter hard, almost burning my hand when hot coffee sloshed out.

"What did you say?" It seemed like an innocent question, certainly not controversial enough to earn me Jae's wary gaze as we moved around the kitchen. "I wasn't sure I heard you?"

"They're releasing my SUV today," he mumbled around his mouthful of tea. "So I'm going to go looking for a place to live."

"I'm not good enough to live with now?" It was petty of me, but I was fighting a bellyful of pissed off, and Jae's resigned sigh didn't help matters. I knew he wasn't going to live with me. In the back of my head, I'd known he'd be leaving, but I wasn't ready for it. Certainly not when it looked like someone seemed to be killing off everyone Hyun-Shik knew.

"You knew I can't...." He took a breath and turned, resting against the kitchen counter. His mug joined mine, steaming, squat towers on grey granite. Jae rubbed at his face, running his fingers through his hair and pulling at the ends before answering me. "I can't live with you. It's too... hard... too soon... just too everything. Being here is complicated."

"For you," I said. "It's only complicated for you in your head. For me, it's fine."

"I'm not going to leave until you feel I'm safe," he said softly, tucking his fingers into his jeans pockets. "But I have to get my life going again, Cole."

"And what about us?" I moved in to straddle his legs, placing my hands on either side of his hips to lean into him. "Where does that put us?"

"Us?" He licked his upper lip and stared at me. "What us is there? Do you know? Can you tell me? Neither one of us said anything about forever. We don't even talk about right now."

"Then let's talk about the right now." I clenched my mouth shut and forced my anger down. He was back to cold, a glacial front to my heat, and if I didn't turn down my temper, he'd close me out. Jae put his hand on my stomach and tried to push me back, but I refused to budge. His body tightened, angling hard as he tilted his jaw up. "No, I'm not going to let you run away from this."

The cant of his head was defiant, and if I'd gained any common sense where Jae was concerned, I'd have backed off, but I wasn't willing to give in. "Fuck you. I'm not running away from anything."

I hissed, fighting not to spit angry words back into Jae's face. Growling, I took a breath and closed my arms tighter around his waist, cupping the small of his back. He was rigid, standing on the balls of his feet as if prepared to take me in the ring. Forcing myself to look at him, I swallowed hard, and his breathing hitched.

"Talk to me about this." My nerves were shaken, and I wanted to touch Jae's face, but there was a good chance he'd bite my fingers. "You can't go back to that area. It's a shithole."

"I'm going to look for something around here, if you want me to," he replied, exhaling hard. "Someplace cheap where I can have Neko."

"Around here would be good," I said, somewhat relieved, but the pissed still rankled my gut. "And I don't know what you mean by complicated."

Jae bit his lower lip. "I don't know. It's confusing sometimes. I think I need some time to figure out what we are doing with each other."

"I thought I've been pretty clear on what I've been doing to you."

"No jokes, hyung," He cautioned with narrowed eyes. "I'm serious. Being with you makes me forget who I am and what I should be doing. I don't like this confusion. It would be easier for me to walk away from you and pretend I never was here."

"Then why don't you?" I asked softly and held him tighter when he tried to break free from my arms. "I'm not looking for an argument. I'm serious. You know there's something between us. What's wrong with seeing where we go? Suppose it's something solid? Do you want to give up on that?"

"You don't know what you're saying," Jae replied calmly. "You're asking me to give up my family."

"I'm not doing that…."

"You are," he insisted. "If my mother finds out I'm gay, then she'll turn me out of the family. I'll be nothing to them, and no one from the rest of my family will acknowledge me. I'd be dead to them."

I remembered Joshua Yi saying that about his cousin, and I struggled to comprehend. "Other people get cut out of their families' lives and they do fine. If they don't accept you as you are, then they don't know the real you."

"Who I am isn't important to me, Cole. Not like it is to you." He looked frustrated. "I can't hurt my mother that way. Without me, she has to scrape by. Jae-Su doesn't give her any money, and my sisters are teenagers. They need things. I can't be selfish like that."

"So your mother will turn her back on you even if you're the one sending her money to live?" It seemed too stupid to be true. "She'd be cutting her nose off to spite herself."

"It wouldn't matter. She's very traditional. In her world, I couldn't be acknowledged as family," Jae replied slowly. "Auntie holds it over my head all the time. Every time they need something, I'm there. I have to be. I owe her for her silence."

"Your aunt's a hypocrite. Her son was found dead in a private club that caters to gay men. Did she think he went there to watch the show?"

"Hyun-Shik was her only son. She can forgive him for that because he kept it from her sight, or she blamed others. If I lived here with you, what would we do when my mother calls or comes down from the Bay Area? You could stand it for maybe a few months, and then you'd hate me for shoving you into the closet. It's not fair to you."

"It's not fair to you either. That's a lie, baby."

"You don't understand, and I don't expect you to. You're too white. You think that everything should be how you want it to be and damn everyone else. I can't be like that. I don't think that way. That's what you're asking me. You want me to think and be like you, and I can't. I need... time."

"Yeah, I get that." I tried to wrap my head around being tied to people so unwilling to bend their hearts for me. Even in the silent battle with my father, I knew he asked Mike about me, hoping I'd come to my senses and fall in love with a girl. I had friends whose families threw them out, but they found others to call brother or cousin. Jae talked as if he was falling into an abyss. "So that's it? We're too different?"

"I don't know." At least he was upfront with me. I hated it, but he was honest. "I need to figure out what I'm going to do. I don't know."

"What is there to know?"

"Are you with me because you're getting over Rick?" Jae cocked his head, and I took half a step back. "You can't talk about what he was like, and it's been years since that guy killed him. I don't know if you are with me because I am like him or because I'm nothing like him."

"I never...." I stopped myself. I didn't know what to say without sounding like I compared the two of them in my head. They were contrasts, but wasn't that how it should be? "Shouldn't I move on with someone that's different?"

"I don't know," he admitted. "Rick's always there with you... somewhere. I don't think you've let go because you haven't had to. Now you might have to, and I don't want you to hate me for it later. If I give up my family for you, is it going to bite me in the ass later because you resent me? Then where would I be?"

"Okay." Sighing, I stepped back away from the counter. A part of me hurt. I couldn't tell if it was my gut or my chest, but the ache throbbed and pulsed. "Time I can give you. Space? I don't know. I don't want you to walk out that door and not come back."

"I can't promise that I won't one day." More of Jae's honesty dug spikes into my guts, leaving me helpless. "But it won't be now. I want to be happy for a little bit. Even if it's not real."

"This is *very* real, Jae." I stood in front of him. When he reached out to touch my stomach with his fingertips, I nearly lost all sense of control. My cock wanted him wrapped around me, and my heart wanted him to take up residence. I was turning into a girl, and if I wasn't careful, I'd be picking out china patterns and curtains. "This feels good. We feel good. You know? It feels right. Tell me it's not good between us."

"It is," he agreed softly. "It would be better if it was just sex and I could walk away from you, but I can't. So please, let me take a step back. I'm not going away, Cole. I promise I'm not. Not now."

"That's all I can ask, then," I grunted. I wasn't willing to let him go, but I could give him some room. "Just keep talking to me. Don't just walk away. No matter what, promise me that, okay?"

"Okay." Jae nodded. "But if things get bad, you have to swear to me you'll stop looking for Hyun-Shik's murderer. I don't want you to die because of me."

"How much worse can it get?" I bent over to steal a kiss, and his mouth tasted like chai tea, hot, with cloves and cinnamon. "I'm like a roach. Whoever it is has thrown everything at me, and I keep coming back."

"Just be careful," he warned me, shoving me aside with a hard poke. "Even roaches die when someone hits them hard enough."

FIRING up the rental, I stared at the ruin of my front lawn, the bushes blackened as if God had visited to drop off a bunch of stone tablets. The scorched grass was clear of any debris, and someone, probably one of Claudia's horde, had made a halfhearted attempt to cut away the damage but gave up after a few clips. The lawn was a lost cause.

"Everything's going to have to be replaced." I stared at the battered front of my business and home. I'd purchased the beaten-down building to give myself something to work on as I tried to get over Rick's death. The scar on my chest itched, and I rubbed at it, thinking.

My sweat covered nearly every square inch of the building. I'd bled and cursed over every piece of wood and nail, and the plaster probably had my spit in it too. God knew I'd eaten enough of the damned stuff. The porch tilted slightly where I'd not gotten a beam in perfectly straight, but for all of its flaws, it was mine.

Only mine.

It was time I embraced that.

Tears stung my eyes, and I blinked, trying to get both the memory and the wet from my lashes. No matter what I did, the two men I'd loved in the past were forever going to be bound together in death. I couldn't think of one without mourning the other as well.

Jae was right. I was fucked in the head.

I let the engine idle, listening to the soft slush of traffic from the streets around me. A misting drizzle coated the windshield, not enough to turn on the wipers but thick enough to leave tiny droplets on the glass. It was the perfect kind of morning to sit and drink coffee, cuddled up under a blanket or on the couch. Instead, I was going to visit a woman who I suspected killed her husband, all for the man I'd left sleeping in my bed.

Scrubbing at my lashes with my hand, I forced myself to relax. I missed Rick. My heart missed him, but the gut-wrenching ache in my body was gone. I'd built the building to please a dead man, painting the walls in Rick's favorite colors as if he were going to come through the door and gasp in delight at what he saw.

"I'm sorry, baby." Murmuring up to the sky, I hoped he could hear me, not knowing where God put murdered gay men. "I wanted this life for you—for us—and we never got it. I wished you were here. I did. I still do, but you're not and Jae is. I just don't want to hate myself for...."

I stopped before I admitted how I felt about Jae. Once I dug up Hyun-Shik's murderer, he'd be gone, leaving the relative safety of my house. There was never any talk about love or forever between us. Sure, there were arguments and laughter. He was as stubborn and willful as he was beautiful, but never once had he told me he loved me.

"But then, neither have you," I reminded myself, putting the car into gear. "Let's see what Vicky's up to this morning."

I DIDN'T tell Jae I was going to see Victoria Kim. I didn't think he'd call and warn her, but in case he spoke to one of the Kims, I didn't want anyone to let her know I was coming. Catching someone unaware was often the best way to get them to talk, and with both her husband and Park dead, I wanted to see if I could prod her into spilling some of her secrets. There was more than a good chance that she was the blonde at Dorthi Ki Seu that night and might have had a hand in offing Hyun-Shik. I didn't know if finding out her husband was gay would be enough to want him dead, but given her display of unremorseful disgust when I'd first met her, anything was possible.

Of course that was before I'd discovered Papa Kim, who hired me, also put Park up to seducing Victoria. The light on the on-ramp went green, and two more cars merged into the morning traffic. I glanced at the clock and did some mental calisthenics. Mike would be settling in behind his desk and sipping his first cup of coffee, probably plotting for some way to complicate my day. I thought I would beat him to it and dialed his direct line.

"McGinnis," he barked at the speakerphone, sounding so much like our father I nearly hung up.

"Nice." I laughed. "Like you're the only one."

"What the hell do you want?" He slurped into the phone, rattling my eardrum. "It's before noon. I'm surprised you're out of bed."

"I've got work to do. The Kim case, remember. I was wondering if you could hook me up to meet Papa Kim."

"He's in Seoul right now," Mike shot back. "And I thought I told you to drop the case?"

"I'm doing it on my own time." I merged onto the freeway and set myself into the stop-and-go motion of midmorning Los Angeles. "For Jae."

"Cole, I know you feel like—"

"Don't tell me what I feel, Mike," I cut him off. "If the cops won't play connect the dots with three murders, then who the hell is going to?"

"The case's been assigned to Detective O'Byrne. She took it away from Branson. I'm pretty sure she's going to connect any dots that look like they need connecting."

"O'Byrne's scary," I said. "She could definitely bust Branson's balls. I don't know if I should be happy or terrified."

"Be terrified because she still likes you for Park's murder. Get off the case, Cole."

"Sorry, no can do. I promised Jae."

"You've never been good with promises. Something shiny always comes along and distracts you."

"This time's different, Mike. Really." I couldn't explain the grip Jae had on my guts and heart. "I think I'm falling for him."

"Wait for the medication to wear off. I'm sure it'll go away once you're sober."

"Hah," I mock laughed. "Did I give you this kind of crap about Mad Dog?"

"You've only known him for, what? A couple of weeks, Cole? That's lust talking. Not love."

"Maybe lust is the only thing I've got going for me right now," I replied. "I've got to go. I've got some people to see this morning. I'll let you know if I find something out."

I cut Mike off before he could respond. Traffic was getting heavy, and so was my head. The sense of dread in my belly was increasing, the closer I got to the Kim house. Once the case was solved, Jae would be out on his own again.

"Gotta give Jae time, Cole," I growled to myself. "If it's meant to be, it'll be."

The neighborhood was eerily quiet when I pulled up. Having grown up in the rough-and-tumble of military housing, the silence gave the Spanish-style houses and manicured lawns a fake feeling, like I'd stumbled upon a movie set waiting for the cast and crew to arrive. A bit of movement broke the stillness when a house sparrow flew past, but the street quickly settled back into its dead calm.

I started to get out of the rental, and my legs groaned with the effort. My skin shifted around the bruises, rubbing sore when I took a step, and my back complained, creaking and twisting as I turned to shut the car door. Suddenly, it seemed like a good idea to have spent the day in bed, preferably doped up on something that would have turned my aching muscles into pudding.

"Having rock-star sex with Jae probably didn't help things," I reminded myself as cramping twinges moved up my thighs. Remembering the heat of his body on mine, I grinned. "But fuck if it wasn't fun."

The street was empty of people, but several cars sat along the curb and in driveways. An Escalade took up most of the space in front of the house, and my rental looked puny beside its bulk. The Kim lawn was clear of toys, but a pair of tiny mud-caked sneakers by the front door warned visitors of a child living there.

In this neighborhood, I'd expect triple dead bolts and a security system armed with tasers. What I found was the door to be cracked open an inch. The mud on the kid's shoes was fresh, dark, crumbling, and smelling of fertilizer, a distinct aroma that hit my nose as I approached the front door. Pushing the door further open with my foot, I pressed against the frame and listened for any movement inside the house. When I heard nothing but more silence, I cautiously peered around the corner, and my heart stopped cold.

The snot-voiced woman who'd let me in the first time lay sprawled on the tiled foyer floor, her eyes open and blankly staring at the now-open front door. A pair of rough holes shattered her face, and the blood from her wounds ran thick in the floor's grout lines, breaking the pool into grids.

"Shit." I pulled the Glock out and listened for any sign of life from inside the house, but I heard nothing but sprinklers and a few birds. Fumbling for my cell phone, I dialed 911.

"You've reached the 911 Emergency Hotline, all circuits are busy right now...." A woman's voice droned in my ear.

"Oh fuck me," I swore, disconnecting the call. Trying again got me the recording again, and after the third try, I dialed the next best thing to 911, cutting Mike off before he started speaking. "Just shut up and listen to me. I'm at Victoria Kim's house. The front door is wide open, and the nanny... or I think it's the nanny... is lying in the entrance. She looks dead. Emergency put me on hold, so do me a favor and call up O'Byrne and see if you can't get someone down here. Now."

"Don't go in that house, Cole. Wait for the cops." Mike shouted at me through the speaker. "I'm serious. Do not go into that fucking—"

"I've got to see if there's anyone else alive in there. There's a kid in here." I was in no mood to argue. "Make the call and tell them I've gone in so no one shoots me by accident."

"Damn it," I heard Mike say before I ended the call. I hoped he had better luck with 911 than me, and I headed in.

CHAPTER EIGHTEEN

HOLDING the Glock down, I stepped into the house, keeping my head down, and skirted around the woman's body. I didn't need to check her for a pulse. Even from the door I could see she was dead. There wasn't anything I could do for her.

The smell of human blood was overwhelming. She'd been cleaning when she was shot, and a bottle of lemon-scented cleaner curdled the blood near her right hand. Expended shells were scattered around her like stars in the sky. The kill was an ugly one, brutal and messy. The walls were punctured with holes, signs of an inexperienced shooter. How much experience didn't really matter to the woman lying on the floor. A bullet to the head killed whether or not it was an aimed shot.

From my position in the foyer, I peered into the parlor. There was blood on the walls, long smears ruining the room's blush interior. Vivid and glistening on the pink paint, the smears looked like they were recent. Aiming at the floor, I kept my back against the wall and rounded the foyer, stepping sideways into the room.

The room looked like a battlefield. One chair was upended, and the coffee table was smashed. The carpet was soaked where a vase had fallen and broken. A scatter of yellow roses lay around its remains, half of them stomped on. A portrait of Hyun-shik and Victoria at their wedding lay face up, its frame cracked and pulled apart. A large shard of glass was nearby, its tip coated with drying blood. Something sparkling on the cream carpet turned out to be broken-off fingernails painted a glittering pink.

A moaning caught me before I left the room, so I stepped in, trying not to disturb anything. The cops were going to have my ass for just stepping into the house. I was going to make things worse by taking a tour, but I was already in.

I spotted two bare feet in the corner of the room and carefully started forward. Surprise choked me, and I stared at Victoria lying still on the carpet behind the loveseat. Her blonde hair was in a tangled mess around her shoulders, and a crescent bruise was forming on her cheek. I stepped forward, avoiding a broken teacup, and bent down to see if she was alive.

She was, but barely. The carpet under her soaked up as much of her blood as it could, and it squished under my weight, wetting the sides of my shoes.

Victoria lay on her stomach, and her eyes were unfocused, blinking slowly as I came into the room. Her legs were motionless, and the black, flowing skirt she wore was torn and pushed up to expose most of her thighs. Victoria's once-cream shirt was speckled with bullet holes, and bloody circles had expanded out from the wounds until they touched. Her gaze fixed on me for a long blink, and she murmured something, a broken tumble of words, clawing at the carpet with her fingers.

"Don't move," I said, coming to her. Laying the Glock on the carpet, I kept it in arm's reach in case I needed it. Sliding my hand on her neck, I tried finding a pulse, but it was too weak to feel, and she gurgled, her throat spasms jerking the skin under my palm.

It seemed wrong to me that the sprinklers outside were louder than the woman struggling to breathe under my hand. Victoria fought to draw her breath, and I shushed her, telling her to hold on. The phone in my pocket buzzed, and I flicked it open after seeing Mike's number scrawl on the screen.

"Mike, I need an ambulance here. Victoria Kim's been shot." I eased her shoulders up with one arm, trying to help her keep her lungs free of blood. Her breathing grew easier but was still ragged.

"I called 911. They'll be there soon," Mike said in my ear. "O'Byrne should be right behind them. I'll be there as soon as I can."

"Thanks." I wasn't going to tell him not to come. O'Byrne would lay this on me if I wasn't careful, and for all I knew, the shooter was still in the house. I hung up and put the phone down, leaning over Victoria. "Hey, you've got to hang on for a bit. The ambulance is going to be here soon. They'll fix you up."

I knew it was a lie. There was nothing a medical team would be able to do. My hand brushed on an exit wound on her chest. It gaped, and her right breast was gone, leaving nothing behind but a flat, wet mess. There were at least four more holes on her back, and if the others were like the one I was trying to put pressure on, her insides were an organ smoothie.

I didn't know how she was still alive, much less conscious, but she was going to tell me something... even if it killed her to do it.

"Will...." She grabbed at my leg, pulling at my jeans. Too guttered to get a proper voice, Victoria stuttered around the word.

"Will I what?" I was torn between telling her to save her energy and letting her speak. Victoria's breathing hitched, and her chest shuddered in my hands. "Victoria, stop talking. It's not good...."

"Upstairs." Her face grew rigid as she strained to look up. The herculean effort to lift her chin strained Victoria's chest muscles, and the wound I held pressure on gushed blood around my fingers. "Will...."

Shit, her son was Will. Hyun-Shik's son. Will, soon to be the only one left alive in his family, was upstairs.

"Don't move, okay?" Victoria was getting anxious, her limbs shifting and flopping. Gasping, she tried turning over, and I held her in place. "Hold on, I'm going to get a pillow to hold you up, and then I'll go upstairs. Okay? Don't talk. Really, don't."

Victoria's nod was small, but her body relaxed in my arms. Reaching over the loveseat, I grabbed a small pillow from the couch and placed it carefully under Victoria's sternum. I wiped my bloody hands on my jeans and picked up my gun. I wasn't sure if she would still be alive by the time I came back downstairs, but right now, all that mattered to her was finding her son.

With Victoria probably dying in the parlor, that left me with no one else to blame for the murders.

"Gun down, walk softly," I murmured to myself. "Don't know who's going to be up there."

I stepped around the dead woman in the foyer, careful not to track through the blood. I'd already compromised the scene by going to Victoria, but only an asshole would have left her to die there, even if I did think she'd had a hand in killing her husband.

"Who the hell else is there left?" I paused at the foot of the stairs.

The staircase was a stream of black-speckled white marble, trimmed in an elaborate black, wrought-iron banister. A carpet runner cut the curve in half, a golden ribbon stretching across the center of each step. Small drops of blood marred the pile. They were evenly spaced, and tiny. Victoria probably had gotten a hit in with something, but the shooter wasn't worried or panicked.

Worst of all, he'd known Will was upstairs and had headed straight for the kid. He'd either come to take the kid or kill him. Either choice would be disastrous for the Kim family.

The house was big, and the upper level split off into two directions at the top of the marble staircase. I took a chance that the smaller jog in the hallway would lead to the master suite. Lady Luck was either with me or against me because the bullet aimed for my head missed me but hit the mirror hanging on the wall behind me. I flinched and ducked as the glass exploded, cutting through my T-shirt and digging into my already torn skin.

Rolling, I tried to find cover, but there was nothing to hide behind. The hallway was clear of anything useful except for a portable kiddie gate the shooter must have moved from the top of the stairs. Grabbing the plastic gate, I flung it out in front of me, hoping to at least drive the shooter back into the room so I could get to the corner and to some cover. The gate flung wide and hit an open door, rattling as it split in two, falling onto the floor.

Grace Kim emerged from the end of the hallway, holding a crying Will in one arm. She shakily held a Browning in her hand, the muzzle pointing at me in a vague, uncertain tremble. Her face was white and set into a firm grimace. She was in shock, but determined, and her eyes were wild as she stared me down.

"Does Daddy know you've got his gun?" I stood slowly, keeping the Glock to the side. I took a step forward, and the muzzle of her gun steadied, aiming for my chest.

"Don't m-m-move," Grace stuttered, and the gun trembled again. I held my hands up, letting the Glock dangle off my index finger. "And this isn't Daddy's gun. It's mine. I bought… it."

"Okay, good." I kept my voice steady. There wasn't any way to know how much ammo she had left, if any, and the kid was starting to wail. Grace shushed the toddler, bouncing him against her leg. She could have reloaded after she did Victoria and the other woman. I had absolutely no way of knowing.

"Shhh, it's okay. We'll get you to Grandma's. She'll take care of you, baby boy," Grace murmured and kissed the side of Will's head. For a moment her face was lost against the boy's sweat-dampened hair, but she pulled back too quickly for me to make a grab at her. The gun was still on me as she stalked forward. "I don't want to shoot you. I don't. I know you were just doing your job. I know that."

"That woman lying by the front door was just doing her job, and you killed her," I pointed out, then winced. My common sense had once again deserted me.

"She tried to stop me." Her shriek echoed in the open space above the foyer. "I had to kill her. I didn't have a choice. No one ever gave me a choice."

"Park? Did he give you a choice?"

"He was going to tell Daddy I'd killed Hyun-Shik. I couldn't have that. I wasn't done yet. We weren't done yet." She paced back a step, trying to comfort her nephew and hold a bead on me. I took a step toward her when her back was turned, edging closer. "If he'd kept his mouth shut just a few more days, it would have been over."

"And Jae? Your cousin?" I pressed in. The gun waved erratically, falling off me more than staying on. I edged another step, hoping she'd be rattled enough to drop either the gun or the kid. Either way, I'd make a grab for her.

"Jae-Min doesn't matter. He's... disgusting. A pervert. Look what he did to Hyun-Shik! My brother would have been normal if it weren't for him coming on to him, making Hyun-Shik want him." Grace hiccupped, and she quickly wiped her eyes with the back of her gun hand. "I told Brian he should have made sure Jae-Min was dead when he killed that whore, but he didn't. See? I couldn't trust him! He never did what he was supposed to do!"

"Why'd you kill your brother?" I had too many questions, and keeping Grace talking seemed to be working. Will was calming down, although he didn't look comfortable dangling from his aunt's arm.

"He was going to take Will away from my mother, and he was sick. He caught his perversion from Jae-Min, and it made him sick in the head. What kind of man wants other men?" She explained slowly as if I were a child. "After he was dead, that bitch downstairs was supposed to stay, but she changed her mind. Everything would have been okay if she just left things alone and stayed."

"Maybe she wanted—"

"Our family is all she has. We give her everything, but it wasn't good enough. She wanted to take away the only thing... the only person Umma loves."

"Your brother didn't need to die because you thought he was... sick," I said quietly. "He just...."

"No! You don't know how it is! Hyun-Shik was.... What he was doing was wrong. He shamed us... fucking men. How can we look anyone in the face knowing that he did that? With Will, everything is different. Umma can have another son... a good son this time." She held Will close, and I took another half step, hoping her attention was focused more on the kid than me.

I must have moved in too close because she fired rapidly. The booms of the gun going off scared Will, and he howled, shrieking at the top of his lungs. I hit the floor, tasting the carpet in my mouth. I rolled over onto my back, tucking against the wall, and aimed for Grace's thigh.

A quick pop of the Glock and she went down, yowling in pain. Will fell forward, pitched from his aunt's arms, and I made a grab for him as Grace's scream peaked. The Browning skipped and bounced on the carpet, and I kicked out, hoping to keep it out of her reach. It flew further, hitting the marble at the top of the stairs, and its weight carried it over the edge. The gun hit stone a few times. Then I lost the sound under the kid's crying.

Cradling Will against my chest, I inhaled hard and gasped when a stinging pain radiated out from my collarbone. Looking down, I stared in slight amazement at the hole in my shoulder. It bled in a trickle, running down my shirt and arm. Will's hand touched a wet spot, and I soon had toddler prints on my face as he flailed to get free.

I heard noises coming from the street outside. They grew louder, and the ringing in my ears from the gunshots was soon battling with the high-pitched whoo-whoop sound of police sirens. Hard footsteps hit the foyer, and the shouting began, announcing the arrival of the local law enforcement. Drawn by the screaming and crying, several armed uniforms arrived on the landing with their guns drawn, and I dropped the Glock to the floor.

A cop grabbed Will while another crossed over to Grace, and I whimpered when a pair of plainclothes dragged me to my feet and slammed me into the wall. This time, Lady Luck was there to save me from making any cocky, smart-ass remarks to the cops.

I passed out before they could get their cuffs on me.

EPILOGUE

AFTER three days, Mike took me home from the hospital. I'd been tormented and poked at by a cute but sadistic doctor who didn't look old enough to date, much less treat a gunshot wound. One look at the bruises on my body from the bombing and he'd pegged me for someone with a brain injury and kept me hostage.

My brother helped me into the house, lecturing me to rest and eat. I told him to go home to his wife and collapsed on the couch. I didn't want to see the emptiness in my house. It was early afternoon, and the neighborhood was alive with activity, but my place was dead silent.

Jae was gone.

And he'd taken the damned cat with him.

I knew before I came home that he'd found a place about a mile away. A friend of a friend called him about a large open space with lots of light and didn't care if there was a cat. Jae was gone from my home before the hospital served me my first plate of watery green Jell-O.

When I'd come home, there was a large arrangement of Mylar balloons floating in my living room, colorful and hopeful messages for my recovery, and an envelope with my name on it. It held a Kwikset key, identical to the one I'd cut for Jae so he'd have a key for my front door. Very identical.

I passed on taking the painkillers the cute sadist had sent home with me and instead took care of my pain with an ice-cold beer. I made it through half of the bottle and passed out.

The living room was pitch black when I woke up and smelled like green curry.

Really good curry.

"Mike called." Jae walked into my living room. He held a bowl of steaming food, and I almost cried with relief. "I told him you were asleep."

Reaching for him, I pulled Jae down, grabbing the bowl and putting it on the coffee table, burning my fingers in the process. His weight on my legs hurt, but the pain felt good. More than good, because it meant he was real.

I took a small taste of his mouth, savoring the sweet of his tongue and the spice of curry lingering there. He must have tasted the stew as he cooked. His mouth moved over mine, his lips parting when I pressed in. I loved him surrendering to me. Jae moaned and slithered on my lap, parting his knees until he straddled my hips. They hurt too, but in a different way. My dick wanted into his heat, longed and begged for it.

Shifting, I tried to give my erection some room, but the sweatpants I wore had other ideas, cinching tighter as Jae writhed. Swearing, I lifted him up, straining even with his slight weight as my shoulders protested the strenuous movement.

"You're here." I was the king of obvious, and my cock further announced Jae's presence with a steady throbbing as he settled against my chest. I held his face in my hands, staring up into his beautiful, dark eyes and at the sinful, full mouth I wanted to have wrapped around my dick.

"Yeah." He leaned back, perplexed. "Where else would I be? You came home. I'm here to make sure you stay here."

"I thought... fuck." I grabbed at the envelope with the key still inside of it and held it up for Jae to see. "I thought you'd walked."

"No, I found a place and moved my stuff in," he said slowly, shifting until he was sitting on my belly. "That key is to my place. It's yours if you want it."

"Yeah, I want it." My stomach was warm from his body heat, and my cheeks were flushed with embarrassment. "Trust. I need to work on that."

"Okay," he said with a smile. "Me too."

"I'll... miss you." I could be honest about it. I'd grown used to having him nearby, and even the lack of cat was troublesome, but mostly I would hate not waking up next to him in the morning and hearing him murmur for me to turn off the sun.

"I'm not dead," he shot back, pushing lightly at my shoulders. "I am just down the street. Mostly. Around a few blocks at least."

"Yeah, I get that." I grunted, placing my hands on his thighs. I worked my fingers up to the V of his body, stroking at the soft skin exposed from the gap between his shirt and his jeans. "Not staying here… it's about your family too, huh?"

"Some," Jae murmured and looked down, confusion and fear clouding his pretty face. "I'm not ready to have them kick me out. I can't."

"No, I get that too. You didn't see your cousin's face when she was talking about her brother. You could have squeezed her skin out and gotten about a cup of pure liquid hatred from it. Kind of made me sick."

I did understand now. I didn't like it, but I understood. It was hard to grasp Jae's self-image being tied up into a larger mass. It wasn't just about being a part of a family. His whole mindset revolved around not living for himself. *That* was going to take some getting used to.

"It's hard to be Korean—being Asian—and loving a man." He sighed. Closing his eyes tightly, he hung his head, almost turning away from me. I hated seeing the pain in his face and reached up to cup his cheek, wishing I could take the anguish away.

"I didn't understand it, not really. I can lie here and talk to you about walking away from it all… about telling them to fuck off because you don't deserve to be treated like that, but I can't. I know that it's something… inside, like you're all stitched together into this mass. If someone gets cut out, they bleed to death, but the rest of it is okay." I started to wipe the tears falling from his eyes, wishing I wasn't the one putting his pain into words.

"I know you think it's stupid." He sniffed, but he leaned into my touch, a subtle sign of trust that made my heart soar.

"It's not. It's just that I didn't get it before. I think I get it now. It's like you… you're not just Jae Min… you're your mother… and sisters… and that fucking worthless brother… and it doesn't matter to them if they cut you out because they think you're rot, but it would make you die inside. I can't have that. I can't ask you to take that much pain for me. I know you deserve better than that, baby. I do."

"Grace didn't. Aunty… doesn't." His words were bitter, nearly acidic with pain. "I think they'd both rather I be dead instead of hyung.

Aunty told me not to come around anymore. That I'm not welcome because of what I brought the family to... like I was the one who killed Hyun-Shik. Me."

"Yeah, well, I think that family's got some shit for brains," I murmured, pulling him down on top of me. I kissed his eyelashes, licking away the bitter salt I found there.

"What happens now? To Grace?" he whispered, slipping his arms around my torso. I grunted as the pain flared through my body, but I held him tight as he tried to move away. "I know she's in lock-up. Uncle thinks he can get her out, but how? She killed so many people... Victoria...."

"With Victoria, she's killed five people." I shrugged, hating the hitch in Jae's shoulders as he tensed in my arms. Rubbing at the small of his back, I soothed him as best I could. "They could get her off for crazy. I don't know. But she is getting what she wanted. Will goes to your aunt, and everyone she wanted dead is dead. He doesn't have any other relatives."

"They have money," Jae mused. "Lots of money, and Uncle knows people. From what he said, it didn't sound like she would be too hard to defend."

"Yeah, sad to say, that's probably how it's going to work out." I sighed as I thought of my brother's diatribe as he drove me home from the hospital. "Mike thinks your uncle's going to fire him because I nailed Grace for the murders."

"So you think he knew? About Grace being the killer."

"Mike?" I glanced down at Jae, who gave me a sour face. "Oh, your uncle? Maybe. I don't know. Does anyone really know what their kids are doing? My dad was shocked when he found out I was gay, but Mike said he knew I liked guys before I hit junior high. Maybe parents are just blind to what their kids are doing because they don't want to know."

"I'm pretty sure my mother knows. About me." He rested his chin on my chest. His eyes were dark in the shadows, but the minute amber flecks in their depths shone when he kissed me. "Sometimes I wish she'd just say something. We keep circling around and pretending. I keep hoping she'll end all of this, but she never does."

"She might never say anything." It was too much to hope that she would. Even with what little understanding I had of the situation, Jae seemed to be stuck between the life he wanted to lead and the obligations he had to his family. "Maybe it won't matter one day? I don't know, baby. This is all new to me."

He shivered in my arms, and I lay my cheek on his hair, inhaling the sweet vanilla scent he used. There was a tiny mew from the top of the stairs, and I glanced up when his cat jumped onto the back of the couch. She settled into a puffball and began to purr, probably more from plotting to suck out my eyeballs than from actual pleasure at being back at my house.

"What are you going to do now?" I asked, kissing Jae's mouth when he lifted his face to me.

"I thought I would feed you, then maybe get you to bed." He shot a sour look at my now-warm beer. "Maybe get some of those drugs into you so you can sleep."

"Sounds very romantic," I murmured. "Will you spend the night? Here with me?"

"Do you promise not to start anything?" He eyed me when I nodded innocently.

"Promise," I swore, holding up my hand. "Maybe. Yes."

He slid off my body to retrieve the curry, leaving a cold spot on my torso where his heat had been. I wanted to reach for him, to pull him close and not let him go, but for now, I had to be satisfied with what he gave me. I let Jae pull me up, even allowing him to spoon some of the spicy stew into my mouth, demanding a kiss for every two mouthfuls of food.

"You're supposed to be resting," he murmured when I finally let him come up for air. Raking his hands through my hair, he held me steady and rested his forehead against mine, staring into my eyes. "Saranghae, agi."

"This using another language thing on me is very unfair." I splayed my hands on the small of his back, savoring the feel of him on my body. For the first time in years, I felt like my own skin fit, and despite the twinges reminding me to take it easy, I'd never been more comfortable… and horny. "What does that mean?"

Jae's beautiful face stilled, and he smiled gently. Kissing me on the lips, he whispered into my open mouth, "Learn Korean."

RHYS FORD was born and raised in Hawai'i then wandered off to see the world. After chewing through a pile of books, a lot of odd food, and a stray boyfriend or two, Rhys eventually landed in San Diego, which is a very nice place but seriously needs more rain.

Rhys currently has a day job herding graphics pixels at an asset management company with a fantastic view of the seashore from many floors up and admits to sharing the house with three cats, a black Pomeranian puffball, a bonsai wolfhound, and a ginger cairn terrorist. Rhys is also enslaved to the upkeep a 1979 Pontiac Firebird, a Qosmio laptop, and a red Hamilton Beach coffeemaker.

Visit Rhys's blog at http://rhysford.wordpress.com/ or e-mail Rhys at rhys_ford@vitaenoir.com.

Suspense Romance from DREAMSPINNER PRESS

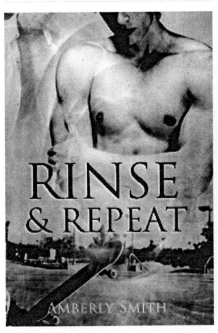

http://www.dreamspinnerpress.com

CPSIA information can be obtained at www.ICGtesting.com
Printed in the USA
LVOW10s1124060414

380224LV00011BA/165/P